Welcome to Ludens Bend. Good luck.

Down from the Dog Star

A NOVEL

DANIEL GLOVER

Black Belt Press
Montgomery

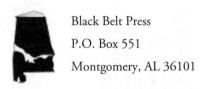

Black Belt Press
P.O. Box 551
Montgomery, AL 36101

ISBN 1-57966-023-1

Design by Randall Williams
Printed in the United States of America
First Edition

*The Black Belt, defined by its dark, rich soil, stretches across
central Alabama. It was the heart of the cotton belt. It was and
is a place of great beauty, of extreme wealth and grinding
poverty, of pain and joy. Here we take our stand, listening to the
past, looking to the future.*

To Honey,
who came down from the Dog Star, stayed a
little while, and then returned.

Contents

Down from the Dog Star

Prologue

(Some Time Later)

Tony O'Brien
4610 19th Ave N.
Phoenix, Az.

Dear Tony,

It is very late and sleep seems far away. This April night is so still. Quite cool outside. We have all the windows open and the A/C turned off. The smell of honeysuckle on the fences, the smell of magnolia blossoms, the aura of Mom's perfume, and always the scent of pine underlies every other fragrance. The wonderful old smells of our home, Quarter Pine. Two hundred years' worth of bees wax and lemon-oil furniture polish. We still make the polish from the recipe Great Grandmother Luden brought from Ireland.

Pine trees smell differently in each season. They're especially nice in hot summer. In the winter Honey would run into the house to find me, and with my nose buried in the fur on her neck I could smell winter outside. Her fur held the cold, held the cold smells of pine and cedar.

When I was so terribly sick and could not get out of bed all that winter and most of the spring, Honey brought the world in to me.

This is why I can't sleep. This is why the fat I picked up in Phoenix is dropping away. Mother and Helen think that it's just sensible eating. The truth is, I don't eat much at all, and the food usually comes right back up again.

You see, Tony, what I can't understand, simply can't believe, is how it's possible for the night to be so still and fragrant, how Mother can sleep so peacefully, how Helen can cook, and even how I can walk about during the day and smile and say yes and no and maybe, and breathe in and breathe out, when all this time my little dog is down in the front yard, underground, giving her sweet eyes and her big ears and her beautiful fur back to the Earth. That's not where she really is. Her spirit is free and waiting for me, but it hurts.

The brightest and most beautiful memory I hold, since Honey was poisoned, is the look on that little bastard's face as he slid down, down the side of the sinkhole. He scrambled back up the crumbling slope and might have gotten out except that I was waiting at the top. As he slid down a second time, he screamed for help and begged to know why this was being done to him. I didn't give him the satisfaction of an answer. The last thing he said was, "If I weren't down in this hole, you'd be sorry!" Of course my response was irresistible. Although that little moron could have no idea from where the monologue was quoted, in a perfect Bette Davis (Bette Davis before the stroke) I answered, "But you are in that hole, Blanche. You are in that hole."

I remember watching his hair burst into a flawless dandelion of flame, listening to the rasp of his dying breath. Then he disappeared into the smoke and a new fragrance drifted out over Jefferson County.

His bike was right at the edge of the pit. I just grazed it lightly with my boot and it tumbled down after its owner. It stopped about fifteen feet down the incline, the front wheel turned a few times, slower and slower, its spokes twinkling in the sun above the smoke, and then stood still.

But you are in that hole Jimmy. You are in that hole.

I got back on Sarah, turned her towards home. She was glad to leave that area. Livestock seem to naturally fear the sinkhole.

The sun is coming up, the sky is lightening. The birds are starting to state their plans for the day. In her stall, Sarah dreams warm sorghum dreams, breathes in and breathes out, her breath the creation and destruction of countless dusty universes. Perhaps I will sleep for awhile.

Love,

Jackie

Down from the Dog Star

BOOK ONE

Jackie:

I will not regret the shattered glass
Nor the drying blood on the scarred pine floor.
I will not regret the soft brown earth
Nor the narrow nest into which she went.
I will only miss her warm golden eyes,
Her chipped-tooth smile
Which brought me to this slaughter.

PART ONE

QUARTER PINE

March 1

Stephanie Cost
6465 Tiverton Court
Louisville, Kentucky

Dearest Steffie,

In March, especially, I miss you and the Wet Weasel Gang badly.
You probably don't know how much it meant to me when you took me
into your home and life after that fiasco with my last "friend."

Yes, perhaps I jumped just a bit too quickly into that relationship. I
met John Bigbow on a street corner in Toronto around nine in the
morning, we were in bed by noon, and by eight that evening we had
moved in together, married.

Yes, perhaps it was a mistake for me to sign my car over to him and
to put him on my gold card. And it certainly showed a lack of healthy
boundaries on my part to allow myself to be separated from all my
friends.

The thing, Steffie, is that those changes happened so gradually, so
slowly, that I didn't realize I was giving my freedom away until I ended
up in a tent in the Canadian wilderness. I still believe I must have been
under some dark native mojo.

If you hadn't sent Bill to rescue me, I might still be there pounding
our blue jeans in that muddy, chilly stream.

I've always jumped into almost everything too quickly. All some cute
crunchy-mumble has to do is smile at me from across the room and in my
mind, we've married, moved to a house in the country, gotten a dog,
joined the grange, he's died, I've collected his insurance, and the dog and
I now live in Miami in deep mourning.

Down from the Dog Star

I've learned why I do this. My disease tells me that I'll always be cold, always be hungry. It tells me that there will never be enough of anything, that I had better hold on to whatever I have managed to catch, even if it hurts like the devil. I'm getting better with it. At least I'm aware of the behavior.

Went to Dr. Wulmothe last week. He found what he thought might be a little skin cancer. He had me shave my head so he could do a better examination. I actually became a vegetarian and quit smoking for a few days. The biopsies all came back negative and, of course, so did the beef, the cigarettes, and my hair.

But I'm living a slightly healthier life style. By the World Convention of NA, I hope to be a sleek, mean, recovery machine: some great, deadly, puma-like cat lurking through the rooms of Narcotics Anonymous giving huge loads of guilt to newcomers and old-timers alike.

Somebody once told me, jokingly of course, that in our program, if one managed to pull six months together, one was an old-timer. That's changing.

My sponsor told me that I've been getting a bit self-righteous lately. He's unhappy with my chip spiel. You know how we give out chips or key tags at our meetings to allow people to stand up and be recognized for their amount of clean time. Each key tag or chip is a different color and everybody has a different spiel to give them out. I say, "And here's an orange chip for thirty days clean, orange you glad you're here" and, "here's a blue chip for six months clean, it's a piece of the sky." Corny but sweet.

Well, nobody had really come up with anything that seemed to me to be effective for the gray chip, the eighteen-month chip. So I started saying, when giving out chips, that gray meant that there were no gray areas in recovery; we are either living in our disease or in recovery. I wanted to say, "Either YOU are living in YOUR disease or in recovery," but it seemed that might be going a little too far.

My sponsor is working on resentments now. He seems to want to pick a fight with me so that he can get a resentment going between us. This game is not acceptable. Today, I have resigned from the debate committee. This all bores me to tears, and I bet after fourteen years clean you've been there and seen it.

Speaking of the word "share," isn't it odd how we use that word? When I think of the word "share," I think of you giving me a slab of your chocolate cake or perhaps a bon bon, something pleasant.

What usually happens in meetings, however, is that I get shared upon by people who have lost their jobs, lost their families, lost their lives and blame everyone under the sun but themselves! Here! Share this!

I bought a neat word processor and, as you can see, am typing. I told my friend, LZ, I wanted to write a book, that if I only had a typewriter I could do it.

"Can you use a typewriter?" he asked. "Have you ever used a word processor?"

Noticing the vulpine look on his face, I should have been very careful at that point, but was too busy prattling on about my vast experience as a stenographer to remember his usual reaction to bullshit.

So he called me on my literary ability by telling me that his wife, Charlotte, had a word processor for sale, cheap.

Luckily, she had already sold it to her brother. I breathed a deep sigh of relief. No word processor, no need for me to prove to the world that there was no book in me. Logical, yes?

But then, the next day, the disease of addiction began to talk. It told me that I NEEDED a word processor, HAD to have a word processor. I went out and bought one.

Obsessive-compulsive thinking goes deeper than drugs with me. We say in the program that powerless means using drugs against our will. I can even be powerless over a word processor.

Hope to see you all in the fall. The World Convention of Narcotics Anonymous is calling.

Much Love,

Jackie

Down from the Dog Star

March 2

Becky Bright
61 Lamont Street
Phoenix, Az.

Hello Becky,

Yes, I am sure that you are furious at me for not writing you sooner and I know that you feel deserted and unloved. Don't give people that much power over your feelings. Nobody is worth a smidgen of your serenity.

I'm happy for you about your son. Finding your birth child after eighteen years is sort of like being given a fully grown, fully trained German Shepherd. No house breaking, no chewed slippers, no howling in the night. Write and tell me how that came about.

I had to shave my head for some biopsies. I looked just like Uncle Fester from the Adams Family. My friends used cute names. Junior Wulmothe called me his "Little Kiwi Head." But even I can't sink that deeply into denial.

Becky, I want to talk seriously to you about Honey. I know how she died.

You know, I got her when she was just a few weeks old, when I was trying to get clean. She slept in bed with me every night. She would put her little snout under my chin and just snooze and snooze.

Then she began to grow. And grow! By the time she was about a year old she was a great big seventy-five pound dog. She learned that if she waited until I was asleep, she could put all four of her feet into the small of my back and nudge me off my bed. That's when she got the upstairs guest room for her very own.

I tell people that my first year clean was a breeze. I don't know why I lie. It wasn't as hard for me as it is for some, because I took the suggestions. I made my ninety meetings in ninety days, got a sponsor, worked the steps, hung with winners. So it wasn't too bad for me. Once past the withdrawals from opiates, I started making friends and actually had some fun.

But I wasn't Alexis and it wasn't Dynasty. I cried into my dog's fur on several occasions. And now I think that she was poisoned. I hope not. I hope that if it's true, I never find out.

It's sunset now. In a little while Helen and Mother will start their rounds around the house, locking doors, closing windows and drapes. It's cool and damp.

I've set my writing table up in a bay window overlooking the horse barn. Beyond that, in the valley, the pines begin. They shade from bright distinct greens, just beyond the barn, into hazy blue-greens and deep purples far away where the mountains begin. Canecutter Creek wanders in and out of view.

Sunsets are incredible from this window, every shade of pink, blue, salmon and violet imaginable. And then the brief flash of green on the horizon when the sun finally falls into night.

"A green flash? Only on the ocean," you say. Well, where do you think this is? We live on the shore of an ocean of pine. It covers the state of Alabama like a carpet. Mile after mile, acre after acre of pine trees rising and falling like the waves of the sea. On the coast you find a tree called Slash Pine. It is unhappy here in central Alabama. There is a White Pine that's a Yankee tree. We sometimes buy them for Christmas trees but they never thrive when planted outside. The trees that make up the ocean surrounding Quarter Pine are Loblolly and Long Leaf. Loblolly are fairly nondescript, but oh the Long Leaf! As babies they stick up out of the ground like cheerleader's pompoms, pea green and courageous, stiff, and sure of their place in the scheme of the Alabama wilderness.

I have seen that green flash on our horizon. The legend says anybody

Down from the Dog Star

who sees it will have love and luck in his life. I know for a fact that luck and love are both manufactured items, like toasters or space shuttles. I don't trust to fate, my dear.

Life can take a man down unpleasant roads if left to its own devices.

I don't feel totally safe out here without a watch dog. We need one, but I don't see the point of learning to love another dog when she just might die.

The price I pay for love is sometimes tears.

Write me, love,

                        Jackie

March 2

Penny Warshack
22 Castlerock
Scottsdale, Arizona

Dearest Penny,

I'm so sorry about your dad. You've had a lot to deal with lately. I know your program is humming like a floppy disk in a thunderstorm. I heard somebody say in a meeting once that they didn't pray for lighter burdens, they prayed for broader shoulders . . . What I seem to be getting are broader hips and breasts.

Finally I am able to write. I'd gotten so depressed that I was starting to freeze the dishes again instead of trying to wash them. Helen became alarmed and snitched to Doctor Wulmothe. He put me on this wonderful, new experimental anti-depressant.

I like it better than the last med I was on. There is no nausea or sweating or anything like that. Just minor hallucinations, breast development in men, and I seem to be developing the ability to astral project. My physical body doesn't even have to leave the house any more to go to meetings. I just send my mind. The only problem is, I can't share or drink coffee or smoke when I get there. I must get some loose shirts. Some folks just don't understand the sacrifices one must make for medical advancement. Doctor Wulmothe, my M.D., has been taking care of us for three generations. He is really more of an old family friend than a doctor. Oh, how we used to love to eat at the Wulmothes'! Dear, funny Aunt Bessie and her homemade cheese! Imagine, eighty-four years old and still able to catch those goats. Those goats . . . They ran and frisked all over the grounds of Wulmothe Manor. There wasn't a blade of grass or a tree in sight. Those bastards ate everything but the '26 Packard that Wooley (what we always called Doctor Wulmothe) drove on his rounds. When the sinkhole finally opened up the old coal mines behind Wulmothe Manor, Junior Wulmothe (who absolutely HATED those goats) discovered that if he threw bales of hay down it, the goats would skip down the sides of the hole, burst into flame or be suffocated by the methane, and never be heard from again. I can't blame the dear boy. It really is a shame that he had to end up like he did.

My pawpaws are growing nicely. I hope to have a contract with Lilly someday to sell them pawpaw extract. It seems to have a lot of medicinal values. Grandpa Luden's old pharmacy is one of Mom's prized possessions. That's an odd thing for a recovering addict to have in the family! But it was Gramp Lude's old impotence formula that started our family fortune. No, it was not used to help men get erections. Gramp Lude sold it to women who would slip it to their men so that they COULDN'T get erections. Side effects, side effects.

I hear a car pulling in. Mom and Helen are back from grocery shopping. I'm gonna set this word processor on "print" and go help them unload the supplies for the week. We're really stocking up on groceries. Helen is leaving for Meridian, off on her yearly pilgrimage — her homage to integration.

Here's all my love, Hunny Bunny.

Write me,

Jackie

March 7

Becky Bright
610 Lamont Street
Phoenix, Az. 25601

Hello Becky,

Yes, I was very glad to get your nice note. You do indeed have more than a year clean, you certainly have worked decent fourth and fifth steps, and you do have a remarkable program. On your side of the fence, you can have a relationship. I wonder, however, why you would choose someone with only twelve days clean, on house arrest, with no job, and facing twenty-six years in the pen if he screws up one more time. No, I don't mind the tattoos. I have a tattoo. And there's no objection that he only has one tooth. At least it's a canine. If one is to have but one tooth it might as well be a fang, I always say. YOU'RE the one who has to kiss him. It might be a good plan to wait until his divorce is final, his wife moves out of his house (his mother's house, actually, but why split hairs?), or until their baby is born. I know your sponsor is jumping for joy.

Helen is back from Meridian. She spent three days there with her sister for some esoteric African-American holiday. She always comes back from Meridian full of fire and brimstone. If she shows me that picture of the Freedom Bus one more time I will self-destruct. This morning, when she served my waffles, she told me that I was the bastard child of George Wallace. Mother just grinned at me from across the table and tried to sneak some sugar for her coffee.

Helen and Mother were girls together here at Quarter Pine. Helen's mother cooked for Mother's mother. Helen's title *is* cook, and she *is* the

Down from the Dog Star

best cook in the county, and she does indeed cook for us, but mostly she and Mother sit in the den and watch soaps and torment each other. Helen protects Mother from food she shouldn't eat and Mother complains. Mom's diabetes is getting pretty bad. Mother protects Helen from faulty thinking and Helen complains. If anything happened to Helen we would all collapse.

As for the Freedom Bus: Helen claims to have been on it. She has a picture of the bus and it is autographed by someone whose name I cannot read. She has a face in the bus window circled and says it is she. I asked her where the Freedom Bus went and from where it came. She mumbled something about "having to work for an ignorant fool" and "even LOOKS like George Wallace" and something about "big-butt, pill-popping, fat, ugly sissy-boy." We were both well aware that she was talking to and about me, but since this was mumbled barely within range of my cat-like hearing, Helen had some leeway. Besides, as you well know, I look nothing like the Governor. I am classic Luden: blonde, with cobalt blue eyes, strong, cleft chin, and a perfect, straight nose.

I said, "Beg pardon?" Helen gave me the smile of an escaped serial killer and said,"Be sure and take your umbrella, Mr. Jackie, it dooo look like rain!" She has never forgiven me for stealing all her pain medicine when she had her surgery.

Oh, I heard some news. I hope nothing comes of this, but this morning I heard Mother and Helen talking about poison. This naturally aroused my curiosity. They were shelling beans on the back porch. I sneaked, very quietly, under cover of some camellia bushes, right up under said porch, and this is what I heard: Helen was at The Eternal Life Cafe and Souvenir Shop For Jesus (more about that place later) when she met her friend Estelle. Estelle was helping Louise Pierson with some spring housecleaning and she said that she heard Mr. and Mrs. Pierson talking about Honey's death. Mrs. Pierson was terrified that "he" (he being me) would find out little Jimmy Pierson's part in the matter. Jimmy is their nineteen-year-old lout of a son. I threw him off our land once. He was hunting and I don't let people shoot on our property.

Is it possible? Could this monster have poisoned my baby? I'm trying to let this go, but I feel the obsession moving in me. I'll have to get little Jimmy alone somewhere and have a talk with him.

Poor Junior Wulmothe is back in the sanitarium. He claims that some of Aunt Bessie's goats escaped the fire and methane gas in the sinkhole, entered the mines, and evolved into miniature, blind albinos. He says they come out of the mines at night and look for him. He also says that they search for automobiles and trucks with open windows so that they can eat the upholstery. Yes, this may sound a bit bizarre, but the old caverns run for miles under this part of Alabama. There are many entrances to the tunnels. And just last week the upholstery DID vanish mysteriously from a Blazer over in the village.

But I need Junior Wulmothe's support when he gets out. He and I have been working on a project: Cemetery Golf. I'll tell you more next letter.

Hugs and Kisses,

Jackie

March 8

Noland "Junior" Wulmothe
Building C, Room #238
Clarion Sanitarium
Tuscaloosa, Alabama

Dear Junior,

Well, to say the least, we MISS you! The county is just as boring as
can be with you away for a little rest. I hope they feed you better food than
they gave me while I was there. I'm pretty sure that Uncle Wooley is
looking after you.

Don't worry about your evil sister, Neva Jean, while you're away.
Judge Caps knows she's just a vicious little money-grubber with eyes on
your share of the estate. And her CLOTHES! My dear! The girl wears so
much polyester that she has actually been banned from the national
forest. Scientists are saying she's harmful to endangered species. I
specifically heard the word "toxic." You KNOW that I never exaggerate.
And that MAKE-UP! You also know that I have a kind and gentle nature
and I'd never say anything bad about Neva Jean unless it was for her own
good, but the only thing that comes to mind when I think of that makeup is something like, oh, maybe BABOON'S ASS? You know exactly the
kind of baboon's ass I'm talking about, don't you? Those great big blue
and red ones. Or is that a mandrill? Or a cock-a-something-or-other.

Tell me the whole truth now, Junior, is that big, rough, red-neck
orderly still abusing you? If he is I'm sure Uncle Wooley can get him a
substantial salary increase. Black rubber hoses and forced cold showers in
the night? Was that a big enemy or a big enema? Your penmanship leaves
a bit to be desired. When. oh when, will the nurses begin to trust you

with a nice, sharp pencil? It must be awful, trying to write your elegant letters with crayola.

But back to Neva Jean. It would seem that with all the money she's sucking out of YOUR trust fund, at the very least she could afford at least a cotton shift. I think we should get her a fashion makeover from one of those talk shows. But Oprah has been through enough!

Now don't be alarmed about your trust fund. I'm sure Judge Caps is watching it carefully. Although, I did hear Helen telling Mother that Helen's girlfriend, Estelle, saw Neva Jean and Judge Caps at The Eternal Life Cafe and Souvenir Shop for Jesus, and your sister was wrapped around the Judge like butter on corn. And can you believe that a Judge of all people would have his hand stuck all the way up . . . Oh, but forgive me. You know I love Neva Jean. You know I don't gossip. And I certainly don't want to upset you. Mother said that maybe the albino-midget-blind-goats will get Neva Jean some night while she's out roaming. I told her that Neva Jean was probably the only thing in Jefferson County to which the goats wouldn't put their dainty lips.

Junior, exactly where and when did you see those goats? It's been over fifteen years since you tricked Aunt Bessie's goats down into that sinkhole. I've seen that sinkhole. It's full of fire. It's full of black smoke. It belches methane gas. I really don't see how any living organism could survive down there. And if a few of the original goats did manage to survive, why would they stay under ground all these years? Why would they suddenly appear and why would they single out car upholstery for their favorite foods? Perhaps your theory on their diet could relate to this. If I remember correctly, you said once that the goats subsisted on fungus and moss growing in the dark. Perhaps their cravings for automotive fodder is the direct result of a vitamin deficiency.

I know you have your finger right on the pulse of the county, no matter where you're "resting," and I know that you remain interested, so I'm sure you heard about LZ and his son's collection of Scouts. You do know what a Scout is, don't you? You should, my dear, you've frightened enough of them! HA HA? Well, a Scout is sort of like a Jeep and sort of like a Blazer. Four-wheel-drivish and VERY butch. I'll stick to my

Down from the Dog Star

Seville, thank you, but I can see the advantage of a Scout.

Oh, Junior! Can't you just see us in our see-fairy gear? Can't you just feel the wind in your hair? Can't you just imagine the looks of wonder on the peasants' faces as we step down from our Scout, bringing bounty to the poor? Little baskets of scented soap. Tiny vials of Chanel. Pate. The rugged plowboy would weep, his worn mother wring her hands and shout: "Oh bless you, sirs!" And then we get lost, and then we have engine trouble, and we're rescued by the Dukes of Hazzard. You may have Daisy. It's MY fantasy and I'll control it till death.

But back to LZ and Shea's Scouts. Do you have a grasp as to what a Scout looks like now? My good friend and his son had collected eight of those things. They restored them. They became so obsessed with the restoration job that they worked for weeks, locked away in their garage. They would forget to eat. Charlotte would set pans of dog food out for the puppies and those two poor ravaged men would snatch it out of the dogs' mouths. They wouldn't bathe. They couldn't sleep. All they could do was sand and turn wrenches. I made the mistake of visiting them during this period. You know me, generous with my time and energy; codependent to a fault. No boundaries. And I was trapped down there in that garage for twelve hours. Every time I tried to creep away one of the dogs would growl and warn LZ of my attempted defection. So I sanded. And I sanded.

Those two fellows had installed a cobblestone floor in the garage. It was lucky that I had a fairly flat place on which to stand. Those two had not been so careful. Poor LZ now has a left leg three-quarters of an inch longer than his right leg. You know how white trash tries to pasture animals on steep hillsides, and how when the poor livestock finally finds a flat space to stand they tilt sharply to one side? I need say no more.

I finally got away by pretending to go in search of more sandpaper. I declare that those two looked just like the poor people you see in old newsreels about concentration camps. I warned them . . . I told them to keep those Scouts locked up in the garage at night. And, of course, they ignored me. After working for six years to perfect their eight vehicles they paid no attention to me at all. One thing I didn't tell you was that Scouts are built mostly of canvas and bamboo. A Scout is not even an hors d'oeuvre for a goat. And a flock of several hundred goats? Rumor has it that the albino goats have made up in number for what they've lost in size.

And so, last dark of the moon (when the goats are suppose to emerge) they left their Scouts out for the night. Next morning it was obvious that something had had a tete-a-tete with those Scouts. Nothing was left but a few crank cases and a drive shaft or two. I have been avoiding LZ for a while. He was last heard screeching something about "interior decorators" and "bamboo-rustlers."

Insanity is doing the same thing over and over exactly the same way and expecting the outcome to be different. I really don't expect them to do the Scout thing again. They'll do something. It WILL be esoteric. But not Scouts. And nothing involving canvas or bamboo.

I truly love my new anti-depressant. The Whackazoid-D has changed my entire life. Are you on it yet? Just a word to the wise, but I DID see Neva Jean and the director of Clarion creeping out of the I-65 Cut-off Holiday Inn at dawn last week. That girl is just a social butterfly. I would watch my meds.

Can't wait for you to come home; I have so many plans for our new project. I truly believe that when we perfect it, Cemetery Golf will catch on big time. I'm still not sure about "sudden death play-offs." Doesn't that have something to do with football, or basketball? But the idea to combine a golf course with a cemetery IS brilliant. And it was MY idea. I like your touches, though. It really will be nice to offer a free family plot to those who join the golf course. Should it be exclusive? Should we have a membership board like the Driving Club or just go for the bucks? I vote the latter.

No, I do NOT think Cemetery Trailer Park has a future. It lacks cachet, and besides it seems almost as though you were attempting to cash in on MY original idea. You should know that I've taken out a patent on the concept.

Not to be a bitch or anything, but I WOULD like to succeed at just one thing before I die. If I die. I don't ever plan to. I believe that when I'm

Down from the Dog Star

on my death bed somebody is gonna say, "No, Jackie. It's a mistake! Let's go to Dennys for coffee!" LZ says that's all very nice, but what if I can't HEAR them when they give that invitation. I've been thinking about sending him a tiny piece of canvas in the mail every few days. Should I?

I must run now. Neva Jean asked me to lunch. The Eternal Life Cafe and Souvenir Shop For Jesus has an exciting new menu. They discovered mushroom soup as a topping for almost everything. No stopping those Third Church of God Delivered Ladies!

Don't worry, Hunny Bunny. You know I always have your best interest at heart.

By the by, I went down to Mom's pharmacy to get my Whackazoid-D refilled and old Mr. Bell, the pharmacist, mentioned that he had sold some arsenic to the Pierson family three days before Honey died. I checked the OTC ethic log and there it was: Arsenic; for rats; Bob Pierson. I must cool off. Or perhaps I should get that little bumpkin to meet me at the sinkhole.

Hugs and Kisses,

Jackie

March 12

Penny Warshack
22 Castlerock
Scottsdale, Arizona

Hello Penny,

I'm so glad for you! Saturday night speaker at World Convention! I remember when I did that. Back in '93. I wasn't the least bit nervous. You'll do fine.

Are you enjoying your new condo? How sweet of your mother to buy it for you. Rewards, rewards, rewards.

Some news. A young man from the town has vanished. He's been gone for several days, now. The only clue to his whereabouts is his bicycle: it was found halfway down the sinkhole behind Wulmothe Manor. The tires, the handlebar grips, and the cute Auburn flag that rode on one of those six-foot white fiberglass rods were all missing. The police are trying to blame it on the heat of the sinkhole, but the bike is too clean for that. It is almost as though something has nibbled the missing parts away.

We will surely miss little Jimmy Pierson.

I promised that I'd tell you the true, unedited story of that psychic and the WD-40. I left out one important detail that will bring the story into focus for you. Here goes.

Remember Tim? Larry's good friend? Well, just before I left Phoenix, Tim asked me if I would like to go to Sedona and see some sights. I said yes. I had no idea, my dear.

He then said that he had to stop at a topless bar to visit a friend. You know I never go into bars. Hang out at a barber shop and you'll get a

Down from the Dog Star

haircut. But I got tired of sitting in his truck and wandered in. Well, here's a double whammy for Jackie! You know that the only way to stop a gay vampire is for a woman to expose either her breasts or a Wal-Mart label. There were naked women everywhere! They were writhing and pumping estrogen out into the atmosphere like that tacky cheap perfume NA newcomers usually drench themselves with. (I know I did!)

It was fairly dark in there but I finally located Tim. And much to my horror one of these creatures was actually DANCING IN HIS CROTCH!!! There's no more horrifying sight. She slithered away and I sat down. Now this is where the story really begins. Tim told me that this place had a nice luncheon special. A bean burrito, chips and a soft drink. I'm always up for food and he was buying so I agreed. We sat there in the dark. Tim's eyes were everywhere. I was busy trying to observe what effect these modern-day Salomes were having on the clientele. (I always make the best of a situation.)

Suddenly, out of the black-lighted dark, one of these girls spied an empty crotch! A crotch with no dancer! The crotch of a very attractive man with tasteful clothing, elegant jewelry, and the smell of money about him. MY CROTCH!!! And she approached the table. I swear that her breasts were twirling like propellers. It may just have been my meds kicking in. We'll never know. Just at that second my food arrived and I was saved. I just about always know how to handle any social situation, but how to tactfully tell a topless dancer to get out of my crotch was never covered at Miss Cathie's Sunday Afternoon Deportment Class for Genteel Gentile Children. (When integration kicked in, Miss Cathy folded.)

That bean burrito tasted odd but it was the only thing I had between me and fifty-six inches of chest. So I ate the burrito. It was huge and it was rank, but it was sort of like the shield of Sir Lancelot. My strength is the strength of ten and all that. Somehow Tim had managed to get some bean sauce on the thigh of HIS private dancer and was actually licking it off and stuffing money down her garter belt. I knew no good would come of all this.

We finally got out of that place and took off for Sedona. You know about Sedona. Three energy vortexes (or is it vortie?). Zillions of wanna-be yuppie-tourists traps and fantastic scenery. Tim wanted to show me a jewelry shop that he said had an actual resident psychic. We parked in this oh-so-cute parking lot full of iron Indians, wooden coyotes, and windchimes and entered the shop.

The first thing I saw was a salesgirl with a sort of retro-fit Cleopatra haircut and a ton of bad turquoise. I smiled at her and commented on all the wonderful stuff they had. She answered in a German accent reminiscent of Marlena Dietrich with a head cold and I immediately knew that she was actually Hitler in drag. Yes Hitler is alive and well in Sedona. In the back I saw the psychic. She weighed at least four hundred pounds and had on what looked like a necklace of chickens' feet. She had on a purple silk mu-mu (moo-moo?) and platform sandals. Trouble should have been apparent to me then and there, but right at that moment the bean burrito chose to take revenge for my cowardly treatment of the dancing girls. I needed a bathroom badly.

In the back of the shop I spotted a door saying "employees only" but I was desperate. I sneaked into the off-limits bathroom and did what had to be done. It was an odd little bathroom. There was a computer printer in there and some very sinister paintings of fruit. Then my worst nightmare came true. Somebody began to pound on the door. That bathroom had taken on the fragrance of a charnel house. I searched about desperately for a can of air freshener and thank God, found a bright blue and yellow can in the bottom of the vanity. I drenched the air, the toilet seat, the floor, the walls, the laser printer with this blessed substance. Lo and behold I discovered too late that it was WD-40!

I managed to get out of there gracefully and headed to the front of the shop. It was when I was looking at some handsome silver earrings that I heard what sounded like a slaughterhouse gone mad back in the powder room. Crashes, squeals, screams of rage. The psychic threw herself from the tiny abattoir and appeared almost instantaneously at my side. Only my classic good looks and obvious social position saved me from a severe thrashing. (Damned Smart of her not to mess with her betters!) She chose to pounce on Hitler/Cleo instead. She spoke in a low, icy voice about slippery floors, sliding off the toilet seat and landing on the laser printer, dangerous working conditions, and what in hell was all that grease all over the bathroom.

Cleo was having none of it. She smiled and said, "You're the psychic, darling. Can't you figure it out?" It was obvious to me that there was a massive power struggle here. Deciding to defuse the situation, I pointed at some earrings and asked if I could try them on. The psychic gave up, and returned to her nest. The salesgirl smiled wolfishly at me. Tim, as usual, was deeply involved with himself. With difficulty, I detached him from the tacky displays of windchimes, rainsticks, and semi-authentic "native" artifacts, and sailed grandly from the shop.

That's the real story. Ask Tim. As I said, he was there.

I'm so sorry about your latest boyfriend. I might have warned you not to date a known stalker, but a Tom Cruise look-alike can be pretty tempting. When is he getting out of the hospital? Let me see if I have this straight. What I think you said over the phone was that you were grocery shopping at that big price-cutter warehouse for a benefit food-and-fun fundraiser. You had the feeling that you were being followed and lo and behold there Nelson was, hiding behind a giant stack of canned green beans. Did you say you snapped and rammed the display with your shopping cart? You were crying so hysterically, I couldn't quite tell. If you two play it just right you could sue that store for a lot of money. Anybody with the faintest concept of grocery store management should know how dangerous a forty-foot stack of giant cans of green beans can be. I'm sorry Nelson lost an eye, but perhaps now he won't be able to see you well enough to do any effective stalking.

Gotta run. Mom just pulled in from an errand and Helen is too busy working on a sewing project to cook, so today, I'm the chef. Steamed veggies, tofu and fruit salad. YUMM! Bullshit. I've lost about a ton but there's a freezer full of beef in the basement and I hear it calling me. To be really honest, those two DESPISE tofu and steamed veggies, so one might almost think of this healthy feast as subtle revenge for desertion.

Hugs and kisses.

Jackie

Jackson K. Luden
Quarter Pine Farm
Ludens Bend, Alabama

March 12

Blue Cross Blue Shield
5678 Bluegill Parkway
Birmingham, Al

Dear Blue Cross,

We seem to be in a vicious, computer-loop kind of thing.

We have been getting a bill for $4,652.65 for five years now. This bill is addressed to my dad. My dad died five years ago.

Yes, he did owe this amount of money on his last (and I do mean last) illness, but would you hear this: THE MAN IS DEAD!

Now, perhaps you people have discovered a way to collect money from the dead. Perhaps you have a hot-line into Glory-Land. If indeed you have developed a method of communicating with the dearly departed, I would sincerely appreciate it if you would ask Father a few questions for us.

Ask him, first of all, where I can find Grandfather Luden's malachite cuff links. I always wanted them and Dad was the last person I saw handling them.

Ask him why he left such an incredibly screwed up will.

And ask him why, when company came, he was Mister Charm: "Come in! Take this chair! Drink some coffee! How the heck are you?" then, when the doors were closed, and we were all alone together in the house, he was a cold, silent, miserable, sour, son-of-a-bitch. No, he never abused us physically. His sins were those of omission, not of commission.

And do, for goodness sake, be sure and ask him, over your Glory-Land Hot-Line, if after he died and finally got to wherever he was going, if anybody said: "Come in! Take this chair! Drink some coffee! How the heck are you?"

It is easy to tell the truth to strangers. Lies seem to be necessary only for those we know.

Sincerely,

Jackson K. Luden

March 12

Becky Bright
610 Lamont Street
Phoenix, Arizona

Dearest Becky,

So nice to hear from you. No, I wasn't being snippy about your new boyfriend's tooth. I certainly understand genetic predispositions. I think it is interesting that for four generations his entire family has been born with only one right canine. Tell me, does it hang over the lip or is it neatly tucked away to surprise and astound people when he smiles? I can think of a lot of possibilities for having a fang.

But you demanded that I explain exactly what the Eternal Life Cafe and Souvenir Shop For Jesus was all about. It started about seven years ago. The Third Church of God Delivered Ladies had had a setback. Tara Wilcox came from Dothan, Alabama to visit her sister, Vernette.

Now Vernette has been the Keeper of the Snakes for as long as I can remember. You can imagine how this influenced her social position in the Church. Vernette had rattle snakes, copperheads, water moccasins, and even something she claimed to be a cobra. Her sister Tara, being from Dothan, had had exposure to the cultural life of a city that included a reptile farm. There had always been a lot of covert one-upmanship behavior in their relationship. Tara was livid that Vernette had achieved such fame from handling all those serpents and not once having been bitten. Tara, with her knowledge of snakes, and her extreme jealously, brought poor Vernette down to the level of hypocrite and backslider. Tara discovered, on her visit, that Vernette was actually handling chicken snakes, which she had stenciled into poisonous serpents with her

Down from the Dog Star

daughter Carla's paint-by-number set! This just about destroyed the credibility of the whole church. Attendance went down so far the doors were closing.

So a few of the true believers decided to have a big hot dog sale to make money to pay the light bill. This sale was so well received that the ladies decided to open a little hot dog/hamburger stand to continue to help support the church. It took off like wildfire. They named it The Eternal Life Hamburger Stand. Then they added a few religious icons such as praying hands and pictures of Jesus on the cross and Moses parting the water and such, and changed the name to The Eternal Life Hamburger Stand and Souvenir Shop For Jesus.

Then Sister Vernette (who had gone to the altar, confessed all her sins, danced the dance of redemption and thus was reabsorbed into the somewhat cheesy fabric of the Church) read an article in Good House-keeping about the joys of mushroom soup. The ladies revamped their menu and suddenly they were topping everything that didn't run away with soup, dehydrated onions, and cheese. Thus they became The Eternal Life CAFE and Souvenir Shop For Jesus. Tara Wilcox just about had a stroke. Vernette was back in the bosom of the Lord and once again the head hen of the barnyard. And the snakes? The church had them stuffed and they are now displayed behind glass in the church foyer with a typed card saying something about redemption. I know this all sounds slightly off the wall, but I was there.

Junior Wulmothe will be home soon. I can't wait to see him. He's been locked away a lot ever since the goat incident. Eight Scouts were destroyed over in the village last week. Nobody seems to take the goats seriously. But late at night I swear I can hear the hammering of itsy hooves deep in the earth. Must run, the doorbell is chiming. Mother bought a new doorbell that can be set to different tunes. She has "Dixie" on there now. I can't wait to hear what Helen has to say about that.

Much Love,

Jackie

March 13

Noland "Junior" Wulmothe
Building C, Room #238
Clarion Sanitarium
Tuscaloosa, Alabama

Dear Junior,

It's time for you to come home. That luncheon date I had with Neva
Jean was incredibly revealing. She actually tried to subvert ME, your best
friend, into covert operations involving your sanity and your trust fund.
I played craftily along but was totally noncommittal. I told her I would
give the matter my careful consideration. Here's my plan:

I whipped out Mom's trusty sewing machine and ran up a couple of
nun habits. I used those black satin sheets you gave me for Christmas and
a couple of nice percale pillow cases. Satin may not be really appropriate
but if questioned we'll just say we're a brand new order straight from
Rome. We'll use an Italian accent. Do you still do a decent Sophia Loren?
Perhaps I can carry a guitar and strum something holy. You'll have to
shave your beard. I hope you are still a petite 290.

I had Cleatus, down at the garage, weld us up a couple of *tres*-realistic
crucifixes. He used some old railroad spikes he had lying around and I cut
some rope off Daddy's anchor chain. (He certainly won't be doing any
fishing any time soon. I'm sure there's no water where HE is!) I can't
remember if those crucifixes are supposed to have a Jesus on them. I
thought about hot gluing a couple of my old Barbie dolls on there, but
as you often say, "Simplicity is the essence of good taste."

I'll be there to "visit" you this Sunday. I'll carry our costumes in a big
fruit basket (apropos?). We'll change and waltz right out. It'll be just like

Down from the Dog Star

when we were kids in Atlanta doing our Ethel Merman/Carol Channing act. Be prepared.

Major crisis! Uncle Wooley took me off of my Whackazoid-D. He said that new side effects — besides hallucinations, breast enlargement, and psychic abilities — have been discovered but he wouldn't tell me what they are. I think Neva Jean is behind it all. She knows in her heart that I would never betray you and is now out to get me. But it's ok. We have a ton of that stuff down at the pharmacy. I may feel a bit guilty taking something without a prescription but desperate times, etc., etc.

Here's something that may interest you. I was driving over to the Tender Tendrils Beauty Emporium to take Ronnie his lunch (while you've been away I've sort of been pinch-hitting for you, taking care of your special friend's nutritional needs), when I was High Jacked! Snatched from my appointed rounds by a thug! Yes, it's true. I was forced at knifepoint to take this monster all the way to Huntsville. I didn't actually see the knife, but by the way he was dressed, I'm sure he had one. When we got to Huntsville, he thanked me for the ride and got out. I almost used the front-wheel drive on the Seville to plow him into the roadside. When I finally got to the Tender Tendrils, Ronnie's lunch had become his dinner. I started to tell Ronnie and the other girls the story, and Sue-Lyn, the manicurist, popped off and told me that if I kept picking up rough-trade hitchhikers I'd come to a bitter end. Do you think I've lost credibility around here or something? I often hear people in meetings say that they really don't care what others think about them, that they're there for themselves. I care very much what other people think of me. We are each others' eyes and ears.

Must run. Ronnie's picking me for a movie and I need to get slung up.

See you Sunday.

Jackie

March 26

Lynda Verlance
6462 Marlette Lane
Glendale, Arizona

Dear Lynda,

Either you got my letter and are too busy to write, or you are a bit
perturbed at some of the things I wrote to you. I tend to be direct as far
as the program goes. I am especially blunt when somebody I care about
is headed for dangerous water.

No, I am not taking your inventory. I am making simple observa-
tions. You have the option of telling me to butt out.

When I first came into the program, I was willing to do anything that
they told me to do to get off dope.

Actually, now that I think about it, I didn't really want to get off
dope at first. The police wanted me either off dope or in jail. My family
. . . I don't know what they really wanted. We played so many games
within games within games. We played them automatically, without
even knowing we were playing them. As for friends, Junior was practically the only person in the county who would speak to me. Junior has a
special place in my heart.

I came to recovery in the usual way: life finally became so terrible that
there was no choice. I went to treatment, detoxed, and discovered
Narcotics Anonymous. I didn't like the meetings at first. I didn't think
they could work. But they did.

The miracle is, that after being with you folks for a few months, I
actually discovered that life without dope was simpler and a whole lot less
dangerous. For the first time in my life I had free choice over the things

Down from the Dog Star

I did. I discovered that not only could I use the program to stop the drugs, I could use the tools of the program in everyday life.

I am concerned about the new business you're considering opening. I'm sure there is a great need for that service, but just how spiritual is a phone line entitled 1-800-REVENGE? It sounds as though it could cause a few resentments. And do you think it wise to open this business using money from your home group treasury? Yes, I agree that the group should look at exactly how and why they have acquired and kept a seventeen thousand dollar prudent reserve. Usually, a prudent reserve is considered to be the amount of money it takes to run the group (coffee, rent, etc.) for one month. One might also wonder from where seventeen thousand dollars came. After all, the group rarely takes in more than forty dollars a night from donations, and according to Don, that last fundraiser actually LOST money.

Saying that you're taking it just because it's there is like me saying that because Helen baked six cheesecakes, that's why I'm going to eat them.

I've seen people take out these prudent reserve "loans" before, and it's always caused problems for both them and their groups.

It's none of my business. I'm just another addict. Our leaders are but twisted serpents, they do not give up.

Enough of that. Have you seen Becky's new boyfriend? Or should I say boyfiend? One tooth? I understand he is from some lost tribe of gypsies. The rumor is, instead of being stolen BY the gypsies, he was stolen FROM the gypsies. But you know that I never gossip. I follow that old Bible verse that goes something like: "And Mary kept all these things, and pondered them in her heart."

Helen is giving me grief about my meetings. She still can't understand that after being clean for five years, I still go to meetings. There's no way to explain. She says that I've been brainwashed.

Well good grief! Can you think of anybody on the planet who needs brainwashing more than me? I can't. It really is a matter of reprogramming. That's why it's called a program.

What you see here is an organic tape recorder. It is made of bone and flesh and nerve fiber and tiny electrical impulses. Over the years people put the wrong messages on my tapes. They put down words that said I was worthless and shameful. They gave me information of fear and hate.

I come to you guys to get those old tapes erased and new tapes laid down. The new knowledge is that I'm a pretty nice man.

Major controversy going on today. We three are all in different parts of the house attempting to ignore one another.

There are signals coming from these separate places, though.

Helen's in the kitchen banging pots and pans and muttering.

Mom's in the living room sitting on a sofa trying to look wounded.

I'm in my bedroom with Mozart blasting from my stereo and my word processor smoking.

We'll all maintain our separate orbits until we get bored or hungry and then innocently wander into the kitchen as though nothing were going on. There will come a gradual thawing. That's how it always happens.

This controversy revolves around what kind of new dog to get. Mother wants a small dog, some kind of hybrid poodle. She says I will probably "desert" her again and she needs a small dog so that she can take it to the vet. Mother considers it desertion if I so much as spend the night away from home, so you can imagine her opinion of my Canadian/ Kentucky/Arizona adventures!

Helen wants a puppy from her friend Estelle. She says it's a combination Chow/Afghan. She likes that name, Afghan. She told me that it was an African dog and the only way the freedom bus survived in Montgomery was they had a lot of killer, attack-trained Afghans with them. The Afghans routed the German Shepherds that police were using to attack people on the bus. That, according to Helen, is how integration came about.

I've seen those puppies at Estelle's. They are cute as bugs, tumbling around their exhausted mother, but they have nothing at all to do with Afghans or Chows. The mother is some sort of terrier and judging by the color of their fur, the father is Sister Amy Grant's old three-legged hound dog, Peanut.

I, naturally, want the best dog of all: a German Shepherd. This disturbs Helen, considering Montgomery and all, but Honey was a Shepherd and that's what I want.

It suddenly occurs to me that this farm is big enough for three dogs. I'll bring that up at our summit conference.

Dogs mean a lot to me. I lived with a tribe of Indians in Canada for about a year and among many other things, they taught me the concept of Dog Medicine.

Dogs bring healing. And they come from the Dog Star, which can be seen on a clear night in the constellation Canis Major. Sirius is the name of that star, from Greek, meaning "scorcher." It is the brightest star in the sky.

The spirits of puppies who are yet to be born are on the Dog Star. When a dog dies, its spirit returns there and shares what it has learned with the unborn puppies. Dog Medicine is based on love, service, loyalty, and fidelity.

Down from the Dog Star. Down to us.

I won't go into it right now, but Junior Wulmothe is coming home. That's good. Neva Jean is accumulating too much power around here. I need Junior's Ching to balance Neva Jeans Chang. Or is it Ying-Yang. Those Eastern religions are confusing.

But I don't have to be smart because I'M PRETTY!!!

Hell, yeah.

Love,

Jackie

ps: Poor Lynda! What a shock I know it was when you stepped out into your backyard, early one morning, to discover your dog, Zoe, being ravished by what you described as, "a big black dog from hell!"

Now you must know how your mom feels. It must be especially hard for a staunch, Southern woman, such as yourself, to face a mixed marriage. Did Zoe confirm the old myth about black men? I wouldn't know, my dear.

Jackie

April 8

Becky Bright
610 Lamont Street
Phoenix, Arizona

Hello Becky,

I am sure that "boyfiend" was a typographical error. You know I
don't gossip and you know I care far too much about you to say anything
that would wound your feelings. I am very new at word processing and
can barely get this thing turned on, much less be responsible for the
finished product. I am surprised that Lynda would show you my
personal letters to her. Ask Lynda if I've EVER said anything tacky about
anybody. Also ask her about her new business venture. I don't know a lot
about it but I think it is a phone line. Aren't you and Lynda members of
the same home group? If I'm not mistaken, you're alternate treasurer to
Lynda, aren't you? You might want to keep an eye on your books for a
while. This is just a bit of psychic forewarning I received from my spirit
guide.

You didn't know I had a spirit guide? Yes, indeed. Her name is Judy
Tallulah. She was the matron saint of blush before she was executed.
She's been coming to me ever since I got on this new anti-depressant. I
know some folks in the program say it's wrong to take meds in recovery,
but coming from a space of sweetness and caring, all I have to say about
those folks is that they are ignorant, self-righteous assholes, and need to
take their OWN inventories, not mine! I say that entirely in a spirit of
love and with only the desire to raise their consciousness.

It's been a good day, for the most part. We are thinking about a puppy or possibly puppies. Do you know anything about the history of Afghans?

Mom and Helen went poke salad picking today. Most people have never had this tasty dish, and it has lost popularity even here in the South. But the old-timers swear by it. Mom and Helen came in with a big basket of leaves. Preparing poke salad is one of the few things on which they agree completely, probably because if it isn't prepared just so it can kill you. The plants appear in mid-May, and by the time summer is here they are covered with clusters of dark-purple berries which contain a juice excellent for dyeing fabric, wood and bone. The leaves must be boiled three times, if they are old and tough but only once if they are young and tender.

After the greens are boiled and drained, they are mixed with sauteed onions, garlic, and beaten eggs. Some people add breadcrumbs. This mixture can be either baked or fried. Come to think about it, it is very much like a spinach souffle.

No, my book is not being written. I have too much on my hands right now. Junior Wulmothe, his "special friend Ronnie" (who would starve for food and other nourishment if it were not for me), keeping Neva Jean in check, dealing with my "special friend" on the next farm, meetings, sponsees . . . I barely have time to look after my program. Certainly no time to write a book.

And no, I am not working for a living. I know it says in the Basic Text to be "acceptable, responsible and productive" but I can assure you that I DON'T want to be acceptable to THIS society, I am responsible to myself, and as for being productive, I produce the most important commodity of all: light and love wherever I go. Somebody has to do it. It never made any sense for me to work or have a career. Why work when all I have to do to get whatever I want is just point and ask? It has been that way since I was first able to speak. I did manage to keep a job for about six months one time, but my friend Junior tells me if everybody were rich, nobody would work. I may be rationalizing here, and sometimes I get a vague feeling that there's a price to pay for being a pet, but I don't really understand it, yet.

It looks as though there's a police cruiser pulling up the drive. The town and countryside is all agog over a local youth's disappearance. Perhaps they would like our opinion on the matter

He was such a lively young man. I'm sure, wherever he is, he's having a really hot time.

Ta, and write soon,

Jackie

April 24

Tony O'Brien
4610 19th Avenue N.
Phoenix, Arizona

Hello Tony,

I've called several times and have never been able to get you. I hope that you are at the same address. I also hope that the deep confidence that I shared with you in my last letter was not upsetting. You have, after all, shared similar secrets with me, in the past. In fact, I feel singularly safe in giving you my "stuff" as I have even more of your "stuff." Understand? How lucky we are to have each other. Your fifth step is safe with me, and mine, with you.

Finally unstuck, I am able to write again. I was afraid that I was sinking into another depression. Back while I was in Phoenix I reached a point where I couldn't even write checks to pay my bills. I could just barely get out of bed to make meetings and stagger to work. One day I noticed that I had been putting my dirty dishes in the freezer so the bugs wouldn't get them. I finally ended up with a freezer so packed with dishes that I had no room for food. They were all frozen together in a mass. At this point I decided I needed help. A counselor told me that I needed anti-depressants. So my M.D. put me on a serotonin uptake inhibitor. After a few months I was functioning well again. This time it is different; Honey dying like that sort of pushed me over the edge. I get so angry when I hear ignorant assholes in the program say, "Just do it." If we could just do it, we would. I asked Nancy Reagan to speak at my fifth NA birthday and she just said "No." Poor Nancy.

Tell me about your house plans. Have you found a townhouse or condo yet? Please send me your address if you move.

I'm really enjoying this word processor. One feels so efficient, just like a professional. I've only had it for a month but I'm learning a lot about it. There are ten letters stacked on my desk that should have been answered months ago but just haven't been. Now they will be. I am grateful for these windows of activity. I like to get things done while I can. You know what I mean.

I hear chain saws close by. I always have to watch my land. There are sections of big trees that renegade lumber companies would steal in a heartbeat. And there is one special place, as only you know, Tony, I don't want anybody to go near.

Write and tell me what you're up to. I love you and miss you and I hope to come out this fall.

Bark bark bark!!!

Jackie

April 27

Stephanie Cost
6465 Tiverton Court,
Louisville, Kentucky

Hey Steffie!

So much to do and so little time! We're getting ready for our tenth anniversary at my home group. I wanted to do a big fancy sit-down dinner like we did in Phoenix for the Valentine's dance. Remember, we actually got a standing ovation for the food. But we don't have much money so we're having a poolside cookout and speaker meeting at a treatment center in town. Anyway, I would just be trying to repeat what we did in Phoenix. The same magic cannot be reproduced; only different magic can be made.

Sister Tara Wilcox is Back! No, not back from Dothan, back from South America. She had been missing for quite some time. The story is complicated, but bear with me.

Sister Ling-Ling Tarwater (her mother was absolutely obsessed with *The King and I*) was elected to head up foreign missions, a branch of the church that spreads religion and flip-flops to destitute savages of the third world. Well, Tara Wilcox had devastated not only her sister Vernette, but also the entire church, by her debunking of the snakes. (The "cobra" turned out to be a chicken snake with half of a rubber toilet plunger crazy-glued to its poor head). Then Tara Wilcox sinned the unpardonable sin. At the Easter-Service all-day-singing-and dinner-on-the-ground she said a terrible thing about Ling-Ling Tarwater's daughter Brunetta's Easter dress. She said, "It might look good on a twenty-seven-year-old stripper, but it's hardly appropriate for a child on Easter Sunday."

Well! Ling-Ling Tarwater and her mother had been sewing on that adorable outfit for months. Red velvet, huge flounces of cream lace, a hat and purse to match, a precious cape, and an irresistible finishing touch! My dear, you know about Alice Grant running away with that Latino boy don't you? He's the boy who had the Mercury with those thousands of blue velvet dice hanging all over the interior. Alice Grant's mother had a roll of that stuff. It's just like fringe balls but has dice instead of fringe or balls. Old Mrs. Grant owed Ling-Ling Tarwater money for an arrangement of artificial flowers for Mrs. Grant's husband's grave. Ling-Ling was famous all over the county for these roses which she made from bunched facial tissues that she would dip in melted paraffin. Ling-Ling saw the roll of velvet dice and was enchanted! She knew it was the final stroke of millinery genius for Brunetta's Easter service dress. So with some wrangling, they swapped.

Ling-Ling believes that there is no such thing as excess, so she used all fifty-four feet of dice on the dress. She put it on the hem, the sleeves, the sash, the bag, and around the brim of the smart bolero hat that she had made from a plastic ice-cream carton, Elmer's glue, and cardboard. She covered this hat in the same red velvet as the dress. Extra care was taken with the cape: row after row of the tiny blue dice were hand-stitched up and down the garment.

Tara Wilcox's comment was truly the final nail in her coffin.

Ling-Ling said nothing at the time. She was very patient. She was able to wait all the way into July when the Mission Fund Drive Week arrived. Not only is this week set aside to raise money for missions, it is also the time to appoint officers.

The greatest honor of all is to be appointed "Visiting Church Lady." This person is sent to a mission to check on its progress and to see to whatever needs it might have.

As head of missions, Sister Ling-Ling Tarwater had the power to make this appointment. And can you imagine the shock that rippled the surface of the church when she named Tara Wilcox "Visiting Church Lady"? They thought she was practicing divine forgiveness, but she had something else in mind. You see, Ling-Ling Tarwater was the only one who knew that the church treasury was busted and that there was only

Down from the Dog Star

enough money in missions funds for one helicopter ride *into* the jungle. Once there, Sister Tara Wilcox would stay for a long, long time.

The outreach is aimed at the Gungari Indians. The Gungaris are a little-known tribe of cannibals who live deep in the Amazon rain forest. It was only through great effort that they were contacted. They made tasty meals off the first two batches of missionaries sent them by the church, but the missionaries learned about the Gungaris' weakness for brightly colored flip-flops. By the time Tara Wilcox came along the Indians were fairly tame. As long as the flip-flops held out.

The copter pilot dropped Sister Tara off in the jungle clearing where she was met by the tribe, Jerimiah Flem, a smelly man who headed the mission, and a trained, giant spiny anteater for carrying the supplies that Tara had brought. A week passed and it was time for Sister Tara to be picked up by the helicopter. But it didn't come.

By the time the languid church ladies had pulled enough money together to rescue Sister Tara — and they were strangely slow about that — the Gungaris, who are a nomadic tribe, had moved deeper into the jungle and taken Sister Tara with them! She was forced to eat grubworms and roots and roast peccarries to survive, and said that the Gungaris had made her GREAT WHITE GODDESS or its equivalent. She lived with the Gungaris for a good while and only made it back to civilization by following a trail of beer bottles and broken flip-flops.

Sister Tara has not really changed all that much. She is now lecturing on her experiences in the jungle and illustrates it with night crawlers that she gets from the bait shop at the fishing camp on Canecutter Creek, an old dog skull she found on the side of the road that she claims to be an alligator's skull, and a ratty peacock feather fan she inherited from her grandmother.

She says that the authenticity of the objects themselves doesn't matter, only what they represent is important.

Sister Ling-Ling Tarwater listens quietly and smiles. This year she's head of prison outreach.

Terribly late, must sleep now.

Love, Jackie.

Jackson K. Luden
Quarter Pine Farm
Ludens Bend, Alabama

April 29

Dr. Richard Carlilse
University of Southern Kentucky
Department of Horticulture
Old Minway Road Level, KY.

Dear Dr. Carlilse,

I was so interested to read your article on Asimina Triloba in Farmers
Today Magazine.

My grandfather Luden grew pawpaws here at Quarter Pine and his
father grew them, too.

Enclosed you will find a picture of my mother and her father holding
one of our pawpaws. As you can see, they are rather large. This one
weighed-in at about seven pounds. These pawpaws would stay fresh for
weeks after they were harvested. In fact, once, Gramp Lude — as we call
him — sent one by parcel post all the way to Chicago to his brother,
Lucas. Travel time for the miraculous fruit was about three weeks, and
when it arrived in Chicago it was fresh and sweet.

According to Helen, our cook, her mother used to process the skins
and seeds of Asimina Triloba to make poultices of them. These poultices
were supposed to cure almost anything. It is said that they once cured the
shin splints on a prize mule that had snatched my great-aunt Lavinia
from a burning smokehouse.

There is still a grove of the original trees in an abandoned part of our
farm down near our creek. It is difficult to get to because of sinkholes that
have formed over the last few years.

When one does manage to reach the grove, one is surprised to find

Down from the Dog Star

no pawpaws on the ground under the trees, just lots of seeds and tiny hoof prints.

You are very welcome to come and see these trees. Write and let us know when it might be convenient for you to come.

Sincerely,

Jackson Luden

May 3

Becky Bright
610 Lamont Street
Phoenix, Arizona

Hey Becky,

It's cool and cloudy today. It looks like it wants to rain. I love rainy days. It's so peaceful . . . Nobody bothers me on rainy days. Nobody seems to expect anything of me on rainy days. Thomas Blaylock, our gardener, and his cousin Isabelle are burning brush down in the south pasture. We don't farm very much now, but scrub pine and blackberry brambles can take land back in less than five years. We have a few cows and a couple of geriatric horses, so we do bush hog and keep the best of the pastures open. I really don't want to use the lower pastures any more. Too close to the sinkhole.

I was saddened to hear about Fang going to prison. It concerns me, though, that you went with him on his high-speed flight to cross the border into Mexico, but I applaud your decision to throw yourself into the marshal's arms and say that you were being kidnapped. You certainly were clever to save your ass like that. No, don't worry. Kidnapping charges will add only about fifteen years to his original twenty-six year sentence. This way he will have time to work on his resentments. You could even take a meeting into the prison! But perhaps you should lie low for awhile. I know you were jealous of what was going on between Fang and Hematite. What a charming name his wife has.

I'm not sure how wise it was for you to turn him in for dealing crack from his mother's house, especially while he was under house arrest, but the miracle (always look for the miracle!) is the wonderful relationship that has developed between you and Hematite. It's so right that you two move in together to raise the new triplets, Lurleen, Earline, and Tourmaline! Those children would be right at home here in Alabama. Lurleen was the name of one of our greatest political leaders. Of course what brings me particular joy is that you two women have cast off the chains of masculine authority and discovered your true sexuality. Now none of that butch/fem nonsense. Be yourself. Although, if I remember your closet, the only thing you seemed to own was denim, leather, and biker boots. Funny, I never picked up on a thing.

Terrible crisis in my life. I went down to the pharmacy to get my Whackazoid-D refilled. I had a lifetime prescription for it, but Mr. Bell, our pharmacist, said it had been withdrawn from the market and federal agents had come and confiscated his stock of the drug. Just as well. These breasts I've grown are causing a lot of different reactions in the county. Some people think I'm having a sex change. Some people think I have been a woman all along. Some people still say I'm just some sort of freak. The ladies at The Eternal Life Cafe and Souvenir Shop For Jesus are very supportive, however. They say it is a miracle of God and that He is finally making me the way he meant me to be in the first place.

Of course I love these ladies best of all. They have been kind to me since I can first remember. If I had a choice between dinner at the Driving Club or dinner at Ling-Ling Tarwater's, I would choose Ling-Ling's table any time.

Ling-Ling is working hard on prison outreach for her church. It would be nice to get one of our NA meetings in the prison but they just don't seem to want us. I talked to the warden but he seemed confused by my breasts. Uncle Wooley says as the medication leaves my system the breasts will leave my chest. I feel rather ambivalent about this and I will miss my ability to astral project.

Beebus McCloud, our town sheriff, and his cute little hamster of a deputy came by the other day. They were asking me if I had seen the Pierson boy any time before his disappearance. I said the expected thing and they left. My relationship with Beebus is a story in itself, and I may give you the scoop on that sordid deal in the near future.

Gotta run, write soon,

Love, Jackie

Jackson K. Luden
Quarter Pine Farm
Ludens Bend, Alabama

May 3

Brother Jerimiah Flem
Gungari Indian Outreach in the Amazon
c/o: Third Church of God Delivered
2021 Montgomery Highway
Birmingham Al.

Dear Brother Jerimiah,

I am writing at the request of Sister Tara Wilcox.

Along with this letter, you will find a box containing two hundred hand-made, hand-painted flip-flops. These flip-flops are made from old radial tires and radiator hoses donated by Cleatus McCloud, owner and operator of our local garage. We all understand the importance of flip-flops in keeping the Gungaris close to the true cross (and keeping you from becoming brunch), and the church ladies say that these flip flops will not mold, dry rot, or wet rot. Goodrich has a warranty against such things. Please note the colorful religious paintings covering this footgear. I must give credit for this to sister Vernette. As you may have heard, she has had vast experience with stencils and paint-by-number sets. I especially like the picture of Jesus chasing backsliders out of Wal-Mart on Sunday. My friend LZ tells me that, at one time, one could be arrested for being open for business on Sunday, but that, of course, was long before my time. I must have been only a toddler then.

Sister Tara is unable to write. She lies on her bed of pain (according to the Ladies at the Eternal Life Cafe and Souvenir Shop for Jesus) with a case of near life-threatening Poison Oak. Eighty-seven percent of her body is covered with lesions and they have had to chemically restrain her to keep her from scratching away all her skin.

It all started like this: As you may know, Sister Tara has been lecturing all over the state about her experiences with the Gungaris. At first she only had a dog skull, an old peacock feather fan, and some dyspeptic night crawlers (a species of earthworm that can grow to up to four feet long) to illustrate her lectures, but as they grew in popularity, she added a few props.

She was invited to give her talk here at Ludens Bend, sort of as the climax (do forgive that word, Brother) to the Mission Fund Drive Week. Since she was heading into possibly dangerous territory, she wanted the lecture to be very special so she managed to hire Thomas Blaylock (a stunning Mandingo-like creature from the Hollow who is also our gardener) to appear in what she said was authentic Gungari gear. She had Cleetus McCloud fabricate a pair of size fifteen flip-flops (fluorescent blue) and, with a radiator hose clamp, she attached a big butcher knife to an old rake handle. She picked a lot of spring foliage and wove a loincloth of vines for Thomas. He was a touch leery of entering a white church in a vine loin cloth, but Sister Tara promised him half the love offering if he would appear.

Alas! The vines dear Sister Tara used to weave the loin cloth were of a particularly virulent strain of Alabama Poison Oak. Thomas, due to some probably genetic immunity to the shrub, was not affected. But oh our Sister Tara!

She'd had four deacons carry her on stage upon the fire rescue's hospital stretcher — as she claims to have been borne on a palanquin by the Gungaris for three years after being made Great White Goddess. Within minutes of beginning her lecture, she began to scratch! Scratching is right up there with burping and passing massive amounts of gas in the no-no list for Southern ladies, and it caused quite a stir. She began to roll about on the stage, clawing and shrieking. Sister Vernette, sucking as much drama out of this unexpected event as possible, ran forward with a large, economy-size bottle of olive oil and began to anoint her, crying out that Sister Tara had been possessed by a South American Demon. Thomas Blaylock fled the building taking with him the one good butcher knife that The Eternal Life Cafe and Souvenir Shop for Jesus owned. Sister Amy Grant, the church organist, tried to tackle him, but he got clean away.

After hours of relay prayer, and no relief for Sister Tara, she was put back on the stretcher and taken to the hospital. By this time she was so drenched in olive oil she could barely stay on the gurney. The emergency room doctor (who was a Baptist) said that it had nothing to do with demon possession, that she just had the most severe case of Poison Oak that he had ever seen.

Well, that's the news from Ludens Bend. I hope to someday visit you and your glorious ministry in the Amazon.

Sincerely, with the love of Sweet Jesus,

Jackson K. Luden

Jackson Kavorkian Luden
Quarter Pine Farm
Ludens Bend, Alabama

May 4

Mr. Ralph Nayder
Department of Health and Safety
Hart Building
Room 610-C
Washington D.C.

Dear Mr. Nayder,

A situation potentially devastating to the future of our country has come to my attention.

Recently, while visiting my dear friend Ronnie at his beauty emporium, The Tender Tendrils, I observed six women receiving various glamorizing treatments. Five of these women had their babies with them. The children were from eight months to two years of age and were all strapped into those infant car seat carriers. These children, to me, were all behaving in peculiar, bizarre ways.

You know those monkey experiments where they take the baby monkey and keep it away from its mother and the baby monkeys develop debilitating stereotypical behavior patterns? The same thing seemed to be true of these infants at the Tender Tendrils. They all had canisters of Kool-aid strapped to their faces and these children looked absolutely drugged. It could have been the vapors from the setting lotion, or perhaps mist from the hairspray.

All the babies were lined up on the floor next to their mothers, where residue was sure to gather, but I think this behavior stems directly from being strapped down for too long. This could lead to a generation of young Americans who have permanent bone damage from being restrained constantly into the shape of the letter L, people who are addicted to bucket seats, and people who are unable to communicate due to brain damage from the fumes of hair spray and setting lotion.

I suddenly see that we have two potential problems instead of one.

I will research the problem further and I will keep you informed.

Helen, our cook, often tells of how when she was a baby there were no infant carriers. Helen said when grownups wanted a baby to stay in one place they filled them up with Baby Soothing Syrup, an opium-based elixir, and placed the child on a blanket.

Sincerely,
Jackie Luden

May 4

Neva Jean,

I am sending you this note by Thomas Blaylock. I have instructed him to wait for a reply and to bring this note back with him. Also for him not to let this note leave his sight. Of course I trust you completely, but one must be careful in these delicate matters.

I would like to meet with you and chat about what you think you saw in back of Wulmothe Manor. I declare it's so smoky there, I hardly can understand how you could see anything at all.

As for me, I haven't been to that sinkhole in years. All that smoke can ruin the complexion and I have too much invested in Este Lauder to risk ruining mine.

But we need a place to talk privately. Meet me at the south pasture paddock tonight at midnight.

By the way, what's this silly gossip about you and Judge Caps? A birdie told me you two were planning a vacation in South America. You really must look up Brother Jerimiah Flem if you make it that far.

I had lunch with Jerry Ledbetter. I think you know him. He's the president of Planters Bank — the bank where Junior's trust fund has been for the last fifteen years.

So looking forward to seeing you, my dear.

By the way, rumor has it that you looked absolutely stunning at the Driving Club dance last night. A blue rayon frock that matched your eye shadow perfectly. And a blue fake fur stole to match! How do you do it? I swear you're the only one in the county that we can look to for fashion instruction!

See you tonight, Sweetie,
J.L.

May 4

Mr. Donald Johnstone
1717 Horsecollar Lane
Phoenix, Arizona

Dear Don,

It was wonderful to get your nice long letter. I am very happy Gran
is healthy, Ma landed that great job, and that they made you director of
Valley Investments. The first thing you should do is fire that savage little
wart hog who use to be your supervisor. I know he does a good job, but
he wanted the director's chair, and he'll get it if you don't get him first!
I am glad the video I took of the Christmas party was beneficial to your
advancement. I left the camera in Mr. Schaffer's bedroom strictly by
accident, under a pile of coats. I'm sure I have no idea how the thing
turned on just at such a critical moment.

By the way, I have a piece of tape of the wart hog and Mr. Schaffer
from the same source. If you need it, let me know. Just like slaughtering
hogs . . .

Do you still have that lovely diamond bracelet your brother gave
you? I admired it so.

Well, the ultimate horror has struck Quarter Pine. I have always had
the fear that I would some day see Mother and Helen on the side of the
road picking up aluminum cans. I could imagine Mother driving the big
riding mower slowly down the 78 Highway, while Helen walked along-
side throwing cans into the cart trailer. But this is worse.

It all started several years ago. A construction company bought the
range of hills directly across the road from Quarter Pine. They blasted the
top off the hills and built an eighteen-hole golf course.

Down from the Dog Star

Although it increased our land values tremendously, there was some inconvenience.

The problem came with golfers who really couldn't direct their golf balls. They would knock balls down onto Luden Drive, the road bordering our farm. The balls would roll down into the ditch and sometimes land in the wooded areas by the roadside.

For exercise, Mother and Helen usually walk two or three miles a day on that road. One evening, Helen saw her first golf ball, picked it up and put it in her apron pocket. Mother saw one, picked it up and put it in HER apron pocket. So a new, fierce competition began. They developed rules. Whoever saw a golf ball first would yell "GOLF" and leisurely pick up the ball. But when they spotted their first pink golf ball, all rules were abandoned. They would lunge for the colored golf balls and scrabble like hockey players. Helen is a bit more agile than Mother so her stash of golf balls began to outweigh Mom's. Mother kept her golf balls in a laundry basket in her office. Helen cleared out a kitchen cabinet and kept hers in a stack of plastic vegetable holders, sorted according to brand and color.

Things looked bad for Mother's collection until I went to Canada for a while and started dating that hockey player. I got very interested in his stick and decided to bring one home to Alabama. I picked out a nice white and black one. Mother fell in love with it the moment she saw it. She began using it for a snake stick on her evening walks. One devious tactic those two had developed was to yell "SNAKE" whenever a particularly lovely golf ball appeared. Southern women are not actually afraid of snakes. Southern women are not afraid of anything, but it just looks so pretty to faint at the sight of a drop of blood, or a small garter snake.

One day Mother used her hockey stick to rake a golf ball out of a deep ditch. She discovered how to scoop the golf balls up off the ground and flip them into her basket. It has been pretty downhill for Helen since that day. I am sure she will retaliate.

Anyway, that's how they got six laundry baskets of golf balls.

And here's the horror: This morning I saw them loading one of the farm trucks with a big folding table, the pool umbrella, two lawn chairs, a picnic hamper, and — God forbid — those golf balls. They were taking them to the Driving Club to sell! I could not reason with them.

Grandmother is positively clawing her way out of her grave right now. I remember her telling me wonderful stories about Mother bowing into society. They drove to Atlanta to have her gown made. Gramp Lude gave Mother a string of pearls that he had gone all the way to New York City to find. They used the old country club for the ball.

Of course, Mother was the most beautiful, accomplished, and sought-after girl there. Then why did she marry that *nouvo* money grubber of a yankee?

Signs and wonders.

Must run. Gotta cook some supper for Mother and Helen. They'll be tired and hungry after their day of keeping shop.

Love you, Buddy,

Jackie.

May 6

Penny Warshack
22 Castlerock
Scottsdale, Arizona

Dear Penny,

Yes, I know you are excited about speaking at the World Convention of NA. On Saturday night, no less! It's probably the greatest honor anyone could have offered to them. As I said, I did that once. I had thousands of addicts running up and down the aisles and shouting the glory of twelve step programs. It was just like a Pentecostal revival. I'm glad that I had Sister Vernette's snakes to handle. Imagine, fifty thousand addicts all speaking in tongues! What a spiritual awakening.

But of course some jealous and unevolved people had me taken before that new committee. You know, the Subcommittee To Keep Really Sick People Out Of The Program? They said I had made a travesty of the World Convention and had introduced some sort of religious element into the program. Luckily for me, Don, who headed the committee, was my sponsor at the time. Also luckily for me I had some very interesting video footage of a certain Christmas party that we had attended. I barely escaped being put into that trial sub-program: RSAA, Really Sick Addicts Anonymous. I'm glad World Service didn't pass that motion. I believe we'd all be moving. Layer upon layer.

What did you say you were going to wear? If I heard you correctly you said it really didn't matter. NO! NO! NO! It matters tremendously. What one wears at these events is even MORE important than what one says. When I spoke I wore mostly black: black Calvins, a *tres chic* white silk tank top and a long black silk shirt-jacket kind of thing. Very loose and free. Black velvet cowboy boots with four inch heels, big diamond stud earrings, and great big cheekbones with just a hint of eyeliner. Becky said I looked just like Elizabeth Taylor on a good day. Tony said I looked just like Maude. Well, Tony was going through a hard time then, and his being just a touch bitchy can be understood. Getting caught in that drill-press at his work must have been painful. But body-piercing is so popular now, he should have just been grateful and not whined so much about losing all his body fluids.

But back to World. What you need to do is have yourself helicop-tered onto the stage five minutes AFTER you are scheduled to speak. If you can't get a helicopter, you could use that old catapult we used at the Trusted Servants (savants?) Day. Remember? The-See-Phoenix-By-Air-Ride? It was great until Lynda did something to one of those huge rubber bands that powered the ride and Kevin overshot Mesa and ended up somewhere on top of Mount Lemon. Has he recovered? Miss Lynda is so protective of her sponsees, but that's really no way to keep them out of relationships. I have never understood why we pick a year as the magic number when we, in the program of NA, can start dating again. Yes, we certainly need a space of time in which to work on ourselves, and relationships can distract us, but, in my opinion, some people are sicker at five years clean than others are at six months.

Back to your big night. I visualize it like this: Five minutes after you are supposed to speak, from the back of the auditorium, Lynda and Becky catapult you onto the stage. You need to do an Ann Margaret look. What I see is white sequin toreador pants, a black lace bustier, and a white buckskin jacket with three feet of fringe on the sleeves. No, hold the fringe. If that fringe got caught in the catapult there could be a problem with your delivery to the stage. But of course the only footwear for this ensemble would be knee high, white, vinyl Go-Go Boots. VERY high heeled, white, vinyl Go-Go Boots. I have this outfit somewhere in a closet, but I think it would probably be a little large for you. In the background you could have the theme from "2001, a Space Odyssey." When I finished speaking I had Tony bring this big red velvet cape, with small, blue-velvet dice trim, out onto the stage and throw it around my shoulders. I exited stage left to the strains of Tina Turner's version of "Rolling on the River." That's when those Nazis caught me and dragged me before the Sub-Committee To Keep Really Sick People Out Of The Program.

Those are my suggestions. Just keep Lynda away from those giant rubber bands. Weren't you in charge of building that thing? I know you got that "sticky finger" problem of yours under control, but those rubber bands looked suspiciously like the new tires I had put on my Volvo. I never said anything, but I often wondered why your salad bowls were chromed, huge, and had the letter "V" pressed into the middle. But who am I to question? Just another addict.

Helen brought a puppy here yesterday. I tried not to fall in love with it, but you know how cute they can be. Why are puppies and kittens so precious? I think it has to do with their survival. If they weren't so cute nobody would put up with the havoc they bring. (Sort of like men, eh?) This puppy came from Helen's best girlfriend. Helen said it was half Chow and half Afghan. It certainly isn't, but who cares. When mother saw it, she forgot all about her hybrid Poodle. She's very happy with Killer, as Helen calls him. I still plan to get a nice German Shepherd. Junior Wulmothe told me that the Canine Cops department of the police has a big retirement home for police dogs. When a dog gets wounded or reaches retirement age, it is put on a pleasant farm somewhere in Wyoming. Perhaps I will drive to Wyoming and return with a Cadillac FULL OF GERMAN SHEPHERDS! I can just see it. A Shepherd sauteing veal in the kitchen, two shepherds dancing in the den, a shepherd napping in every bedroom . . .

The only problem is, no police that I know has heard of this place. Beebus McCloud, the town sheriff, told me, "Just click your heels three times, Dorothy. You'll find it!" I reminded him of a certain piece of tape that I recorded of him and me having a really deep and meaningful discourse in the back of his squad car — a squad car donated to the town by Quarter Pine, no less — and he got real quiet real fast. He tells me that he has his eye on a new deputy, Willie Gates. I've seen the boy. He's the cutest little thing. The child is right out of high school, built just like a half-flattened basketball, and is blonde as can be. Willie is terrified of Beebus and Beebus loves this dearly. Wouldn't it be interesting if that tape of Beebus and myself fell into Willie's hands? Food for thought. It is very possible that the Sheriff is trying to make me jealous by hiring this pretty, young man. He forgets where his loyalties should lie, and exactly who holds his leash.

I must run. Literally. For about a week now, Helen has been talking about how dull the den woodwork is looking and this morning I saw her getting out some of the lemon-beeswax furniture polish Mother so loves. Guess who will be up on a ladder scrubbing wax into wood? Not me. I'm hauling ass.

More love than you need,

Jackie

(undated)

Wulmothe Manor

Dear Junior,

I'm sending you this note by Thomas Blaylock. HANDS OFF!!! You people are always trying to steal our workers. Thomas is the best gardener we've ever had and I don't intend to lose him.

I'm glad you came home. I'm a hint disappointed that we didn't get to try out our nun costumes. Maybe we could put them on and head down to the Eternal Life Cafe and Souvenir Shop for Jesus. You don't have to worry about Neva Jean watching your every move. She and Judge Caps have vanished. They didn't abscond with your trust fund as we feared they might. It was simply a case of true love and Judge Cap's wife of forty-two years. That Neva Jean! Always into something!

No, I certainly have nothing "to say for myself" about Ronnie and my care of him while you were away. It was either me or that sleazy manicurist, and I KNEW in my heart you would rather have me than her looking after your special friend.

LZ was thumping me about my political unawareness again. I told him that all I needed to know about politics came from "Gone With the Wind." Southerners are Democrats and Northerners are Republicans. It's good enough for Scarlet and it's good enough for me.

He still holds me partly responsible for those Scouts. Charlotte was airing her collection of antique quilts on her clothesline yesterday but she took them in before nightfall. Charlotte pays attention. I asked Charlotte why and she just smiled. Charlotte says a great deal when she says nothing at all.

Will you get over your snit about Ronnie? As it says in Romans,

"And the great whore wipeth her mouth saying,'I have done no wrong!'" At least, I think it's Romans. But I never promised anybody accuracy, only heart.

Do come up to Quarter Pine. We're planning a welcome home party for you, and everybody will be there. Helen wanted a barbecue, mother wanted a nice buffet and cocktail party, I wanted a poolside, '70s costume party. What we came up with was a barbecue/buffet by the pool with a '70s theme. I've been looking for platform shoes. They're rare. Probably, I'll carve some heels from two-by-fours and use silicone glue to attach the heels to a pair of burnt orange and sky blue golf shoes of daddy's and we'll just disco the night away.

Don't disappoint us! I do have some news about Neva Jean; just too scrumptious to put on paper!

Hugs and kisses,
Jackieeeeeeeeee!

Down from the Dog Star

Jackson K. Luden
Quarter Pine Farm
Ludens Bend, Alabama

May 10

Louis Sullivan
Ahab Collection Agency (?)
P.O. Box 27495,
Phoenix, Az.

Mr. Sullivan,

I did indeed live in Phoenix for a short time, more of an extended vacation, actually, but I can't remember ever seeing a doctor named Mazzarella.

If you could send me a bill from Dr. Mazzarella or some sort of documentation verifying that I was there, I will take the matter up with my accountant.

This letter of yours seems a bit fictitious to me.

Mazzarella sounds like a cheese and I can hardly imagine anybody with the sense God gave a billy goat naming his (or her) agency "Ahab."

I remember a reference to Ahab in a naval picture, either "Moby Dick," or "Twenty Thousand Leagues Under The Sea."

At any rate, it would be wise, if you are an actual investigation agency, to find a better name than Ahab.

Truly, no offense is meant. Involved here is your best interest. Having been given the singular honor of becoming assistant to the director of the Gungari Indian Native Outreach, I leave shortly for South America. I have always dreamed of spreading The Word among the savages.

The Gungaris are cannibals and have made nutritious meals from the last two batches of missionaries that we sent, so write very soon.

Unless you contact me I will simply assume this letter you sent to me is either a practical joke from somebody with a nice word processor, or attempted fraud.

Really now, a doctor named after a cheese. If this person exists perhaps he and Ahab could get together and help one another think of more professional names.

Respectfully,

Jackson K. Luden

P.S. I must give you credit for a very nice, polite letter.
JKL

May 18

Stephanie Cost
6465 Tiverton Court,
Louisville, Kentucky

Greetings Precious,

I'm so sorry to hear about your snake. But you do have six more, don't you? I *have* had some experience with snakes, as you may remember from the World Convention. It was so unfortunate that it was your prize nineteen-foot rock python that was lost. I find it strangely sinister that both the snake and Brian disappeared at the same time. Brian was (I mean IS) cute as a pup. But to be realistic, he was also about the size of a pup. A pack of camels and his glasses, the only thing left in his truck . . . well, at least he went clean. Not that I am being fatalistic or anything, but after the narrow escape your dear mother had with that snake, and after it cleaned out your freezer, reasoning only points the way. We shall pray for Brian.

Steffie, what is this thing about the way country men like to pee in the back yard? And not just down South. Everywhere I've been, and you know I've been everywhere, country men will by-pass their nice warm bathrooms on a freezing sleeting night and sneak out into the back yard to mark territory. That may be it! It could just be the *eau-primatav* coming out in them.

Even I, star of the South that I am, have been known to indulge in this behavior. On very cold nights, way after midnight, Honey and I would go out into the yard and look up at the tiny, quiet stars. Honey would squat and pee against one of the twenty-five, ancient pine trees that gives my home its name. We would then walk about in the dark hoping for the aliens to come and get us.

They never came.

I've been thinking a lot about the God-shaped Hole. No, not the sinkhole, the God-shaped Hole in my chest. Before I started in recovery I tried to fill that hole with cars, with jewelry, with food, with lovers and it didn't work. What I discovered was, I can't park a Caddy next to my aortic artery. It takes God-shaped stuff to fill a God-shaped hole. I'm not waving my arms around saying that all these nice things are bad to have. I still have the Caddy, I still have the gold, and God knows I have more lovers and friends than I can talk to in a month. But only the friends mean a lot to me now. The gold is in the vault at the bank, and I don't get the kick I got from champagne.

Five years clean. Do you remember the first time we met? It was in the winter at Mount Cheaha. It was at Surrender in the Mountains. I couldn't understand why you and all your friends were so nice to me. I thought you all wanted something. A few years later I found out what you wanted: for me to find this way of life.

Helen's new puppy has sabotaged my heart. It is a nice brindle color, about the size of a small loaf of bread, and its bark sounds just like one of those rubber squeak toys that Logan plays with in his bath.

Blaire and Logan must be so big now. Is Bill still on his Harley? You know, he gave me a wonderful recovery book from our program. My new sponsor has us work steps from it. Do you remember when we were all sitting around and Blaire asked why Bill looked so old and I looked so young? And you said, "Oh honey, Jackie moisturizes!"

When you come down from Kentucky I'll take you to The Eternal Life Cafe and Souvenir Shop for Jesus. The ladies are getting very continental. Cleatus, from the garage, turned them on to an old acetylene torch and they're now flaming desserts at tableside!

No, Junior Wulmothe has not yet emerged from Wulmothe Manor. Ever since he got home from the sanitarium he's been in deep seclusion. Not that anybody cares a whole lot.

Now, Steffie, you know I never gossip, and I would never say anything negative about Junior unless it could in some way elevate his wounded mind, but ever since I sent Thomas, our gardener, over to Wulmothe Manor with a note for Junior, I have sensed a definite change in my magnificent Watusi's demeanor. And he's wearing Obsession. I know for a fact that Thomas wouldn't spend that kind of money on cologne. Not on what we pay him. And I gave Junior a bottle of Obsession for Christmas a couple of years ago. I remember that because Junior claimed that it broke him out in some sort of rash, closed his breathing passages, and made him late for the Tender Tendrils Christmas Fete. Junior thought that I had sabotaged him so that I could spend an evening with Ronnie. But he should be grateful that I watch so closely over Ronnie when he's away for his little "rests." There's this manicurist . . . Oh, but you don't want to hear all this boring gossip.

The state police have been interviewing everybody for miles around about the disappearance of a town boy. He just seems to have gone up in a puff of smoke. Of course I know nothing about it and told them so. But they seem slightly suspicious. They heard the rumor about this boy poisoning Honey. Some sort of fire department commando-like unit is coming from Atlanta to see what they can find in the old sinkhole.

Brother Jerimiah Flem, the visionary-missionary in charge of the Gungari Indian out reach, has invited me into the Amazon for a visit. He thinks I am a religious paragon. Where on Earth did he get THAT idea? His motives are probably pure.

I asked Thomas Blaylock if he'd like to accompany me and be my spear bearer. He tossed his head just like a pony in heat, giggled like a school girl, and said "Oh, Mr. Jackie, you do say the cutest things."

It is obvious to me, that my cousin, from Wulmothe Manor, has subverted and perverted Thomas Blaylock. As God is my witness, if it's the last thing I do, I'll see Junior Wulmothe's guts strung along the fence posts of Quarter Pine before Winter! Not that I would really hurt Junior. Or say anything tacky.

Love among the ruins,
Jackie

May 24

Mr. Donald Johnstone
1717 Horsecollar Lane
Phoenix, Arizona

HELLO, Daddy Don,

I am going on a little journey to the Amazon, visiting Brother Jerimiah Flem at his mission for the Gungari Indians. Good old Sister Ling-Ling Tarwater arranged it all for me. All I had to do was make a very generous donation to the church mission fund and give sister Ling-Ling my old Volvo. I will be traveling under the name of Cleetus McCloud. Cleetus is a church deacon and by using his name I won't have to bother with passports and such. Don't listen to any silly stories about the police and the sinkhole. You know how some people try to destroy the spiritually evolved.

That slut Neva Jean ran her big red flappy mouth once too often and did cause me a momentary lapse of serenity, but time in the rain forest will set me up just fine. I am packing my trunk carefully: insect repellent, Lomotil, jungle clothes, and helmets. Of course my portable word processor and a big supply of batteries is a must. I'm also taking along a solar-powered satellite relay dish so that I can beam my letters straight to Quarter Pine and I taught Helen to download them.

Mother is not as upset as I thought she would be. She just said that if I was going I'd better get going soon. Helen was very sweet. She gave me a lock of some strange looking beige fur. Said it was from one of the Afghans that was on the Freedom Bus with her.

You were saying something about my family's present security being built on the blood and tears of slaves. Not so. There has never been a slave at Quarter Pine. My great-grandfather Luden, his wife, their five sons, and great-grandfather's four brothers came to Alabama from Ireland in 1840. They had just enough money for this land and a couple of mules. They brought axes with them. We have one of those old axes on the wall in the den. They carved their shovels, eating utensils, and bowls from the poplar trees on the banks of Canecutter Creek, a stream that got its name from a type of water-hare that lives on its banks.

Quarter Pine was never a big plantation. It has always been a large, self-sufficient farm. They must have broken their backs and hearts to build the original cabin and clear the first fields. That same cabin is here, in the fabric of the house in which we live. It is now our kitchen. It has been remodeled a bit, but the walls are poplar logs. The fireplace is made up of fieldstone put together with burned clam shells and sand. That's how they made cement back then.

The family fortune was founded on pharmaceuticals. My Grandpa Luden invented an impotence formula called The Wife's Friend designed to MAKE men impotent. He went on to formulate a baldness cure made from the pawpaw plant.

So, as you can see, there were no slaves at Quarter Pine.

My Cemetery Golf project is getting off the ground. Mother gave me one hundred acres of land and a good-size loan to get it started. Junior has been little help at all. He is cloistered at Wulmothe Manor and does nothing but send me evil notes about my morals and hygiene. It's lucky I patented the concept. I have a terrible feeling that he and Neva Jean got together on something and I may be it!

That's OK. I have no opinions on outside issues. Anger and resentments are two things that I cannot afford today.

I only hope that Neva and Junior mend their evil ways. I love them dearly but you know how people can bring destruction on themselves.

Must close now. Dr. Wooley Wulmothe has some medical supplies for the Gungaris and I need to pick them up and pack them.

Write you from the Amazon,

Love

Jackie

May 26

Wulmothe Manor

Junior,

Got your note just as we were pulling out of the drive from home. I had a plane to catch so I couldn't stop at your house and talk. Tried calling you on the cellular but your phone was out. Is the insulation still disappearing from the phone wires at night? You might want to try some metal conduit pipe around the wires.

Yes, of course I accept your apology. You know I'm your biggest fan. I must say, however, that I was not the least bit surprised that Ronnie ran off with that manicurist . . . and your Gold Card.

And I knew Neva Jean would never separate us permanently. Her true colors came through, didn't they? I understand that the state troopers caught them just as they whizzed over the state line into Mississippi. Indecent exposure and driving under the influence—I don't know why Neva Jean removes her top so often.

In Neva Jean's case she would get a lot further with men if she gave them THAT nasty surprise AFTER she got them in bed. I think her unfortunate condition developed more from sinkhole pollution than the Wulmothe gene pool. I must admit that what with all the new miracle fibers and new engineering technology, one hardly notices.

I'm sending this note from the airport. Junior, old friend, don't get involved in this. It's possible the Luden Luck may have worn a trifle thin. I know I've done some pretty awful things to you, but you know I love you best of all. Will write you a nice report from the Amazon.

Keep your powder dry and your lip gloss wet,

Smooch Smooch!!

Jackie.

PART TWO

THE AMAZON

SOUTH AMERICAN ARCTIC

Once I saw that fabled bird
Whose diet is chocolate, cocaine,
And the curd of the milk of the jungle cow.
Blue lightning was its eyes!
And far below
On the forest floor
The jungle cow
With pancake feet
Goes flap flap flapping
Down the narrow path,
Pink udder a metronome
To the rhythm of her journey.
Black and white spotted,
The dalmation of that land!

June 1

Junior Wulmothe
Wulmothe Manor
Trimble Hill Road
Ludens Bend Alabama

Hello Junior,

Here we are in the Amazon. The first few days were difficult but things are leveling out.

I had packed very carefully, with medication, clothing and various little things to make jungle life pleasant. Thomas Blaylock, who has never been quite the same since his visit to you at the Manor, grabbed the wrong trunk and slid it into the Seville before I had a chance to inspect it. We were a touch rushed the day we left.

When I finally saw the trunk again, it was in the small clearing into which the helicopter had dropped us. It was not my Voitton, but an old old piece of luggage that had belonged to my grandmother. Imagine my feelings when I opened that trunk and found not the things that I had so carefully packed, but the costumes and wigs from the revival of "Mame" that we attempted at Tito's so many years ago. I will have to make do with this stuff until you can get Mom to send me the correct trunk. In the meantime, the Gungaris seem to be simply blown away by white satin, fox fur, and white ostrich plumes. When I pounced on Thomas and tried to give him holy hell, he rolled his eyes and said, "Oh, Mr. Jackie, you know how flighty I can be!" Just what arcane things did you do to our gardener? I can assure you that we will talk deeply on this matter when I return.

I was pretty sick the first few days here. I was nauseated and spent most of my time squatting behind a bush. And the bugs! Mosquitoes the size of woodpeckers! Spiders that can remove a finger with one bite. It was dreadful.

One of the Gungari women took me under her wing and taught me how to brew an all-purpose kind of tonic from roots, mushrooms, and berries. It tasted pretty good, too. After one dose of it, my stomach cleared right up. After I rubbed it all over my body, the insects stayed yards away from me. If we could sell this potion back home in the States, we would be rich beyond our wildest hopes.

I did that show-stopping section from "Mame" ("If He Walked Into My life Today") for the tribe at the Sabbath meeting. They LOVE Broadway. They have built me a very nice tree house in the tip top of a mango tree and given me my very own pet leopard to keep the snakes out of my bed. I named her Neva Jean and she sleeps on the foot of my bed every night.

Snakes aren't the only thing I have to worry about getting into my bed. Just as I feared, Brother Jerimiah Flem does NOT have a pure heart. I think it was my "Mame" number that pushed him right over the edge. He follows me about like a hungry leech, his wet, squinty eyes constantly undressing me. I hang real close to Racquel, the chief's wife (who gave me the yummy recipe for the anti-bug, anti-diarrhea medication); keep Thomas close at hand with his rake handle/butcher knife spear; and, of course, stay near my leopard. But something must be done.

The only real dangers around here are Brother Flem, quicksand, and these huge red and blue piranha. Perhaps some combination of the last two could free me from the odious advances of the first.

You're probably wondering how I managed to get Thomas Blaylock to accompany me on my sortie into the rain forest. It was easy. I mentioned to Helen that some of the men in the village were furious at Thomas for appearing in their church with nothing but a few vines wrapped around his waist, and that there had been talk of paying Thomas a midnight visit. Perhaps manipulative, perhaps based on a slight warping of the truth, but, as you have always told me, "The ends justify the means as long as it is in the best interest of the victim."

Down from the Dog Star

The story was pure fabrication on my part. We never have and never will allow that sort of thing in Ludens Bend.

I must run. We're having a love feast of roast peccary and jungle yams. Sister Tara Wilcox painted a much harsher picture of life in the rain forest than was needed. There are a lot of yummy things to eat here. If one does not care for grubs and termites, one eats roast peccary, baked monkey, boiled jungle chicken, and fruits and veggies that we can't even get back home unless we drive to Atlanta!

Under separate cover I am sending you a packet of powdered herbs and berries. Why don't you make a nice cup of tea for Neva Jean out of this delightful herbal mixture. It tastes, they say, very pleasant and fruity. You don't need to mention where it came from, Junior, and for goodness sake, DON'T TASTE IT YOURSELF! Just tell her it's one of those international flavored coffees.

It will do her a lot of good.

Love from the treehouse,

Jackie

June 1

Sister Ling-Ling Tarwater
Missions Coordinator
Third Church of God Delivered
State Headquarters
2021 Montgomery Highway
Birmingham, Alabama.

Dear Sister Ling-Ling,

I surely miss the Ladies of the Church. How is Sister Vernette and Old Mrs. Grant? I know your dear friend Tara is just as sweet as always. Did that unfortunate incident at the state prison for women affect her at all?

Now Sister Ling Ling, I want you to know that you need feel no guilt. That accidental incarceration gave Sister Tara six months in which to spread the message of the true cross to inmates. SHANDILEAVA! Do forgive me. When the spirit falls, tongues will roll.

Life here in the Amazon is just ducky! I have a stunning treehouse, which deserves a small comment. When Thomas Blaylock and I arrived in the Amazon, and the helicopter pilot dropped us in the clearing where we were supposed to meet the Gungaris, our spirits were high.

The day was sunny and clear, the breeze blowing across our faces cool and refreshing. The spot on which we landed was well-cleared land, not a bug or reptile in sight. It resembled nothing so much as one of our bottom-land pastures at Quarter Pine.

Thomas Blaylock and I sat there happily (fool's paradise!) on our luggage, waiting for our guides to appear. The first small sign that trouble was brewing was a light nip given to me by a tiny, inconsequential insect.

To be so petite, this bug packed an incredible wallop. Within seconds, there was an egg-size welt forming where the creature had bitten me. Frantically looking for the bug spray I'd packed was when I discovered the trunks had been switched. Thomas Blaylock, naturally, was immune to insects and evil plants. I made him suffer in other ways. It's my job.

The Gungaris materialized around us like caramel fog, at their head, the redoubtable Jerimiah Flem, their spiritual leader. More about Jerry later.

As I said, in the clearing, life seemed vaguely normal. Then we set off into the jungle.

BUGS! Big bugs. Black bugs, red bugs, blue bugs. I hate bugs. Always have, always will. They were everywhere, every size, and every shape. They flew, walked, crawled, and their main desire in life seemed to be to reach me. And snakes . . . You know those old Tarzan movies on television on Sunday afternoons? Just like that. Mud and rain. Mud that sucked the boots right off my feet. I had not yet reached exalted status, so I was forced to slog along with the rest. But, just like Scarlett, I swore, that at some point in life, I'd never be muddy again!

My life in the jungle looked pretty bad to me at first, but then I met Racquel. Racquel is the wife of the Chief of all the Gungaris and a powerful medicine woman in her own right. She took one look at the ostrich feather-silver-spangled headdress from the second-act show stopper number (Angela Lansbury, herself, had given me this headdress) and fell in love. I made her a gift of this object and she became my jungle mentor.

Racquel organized the women into a massively efficient team, and within a day, I had my very own three-level, river-view, penthouse apartment, high in the top of the jungle. The Gungaris even gave me indoor plumbing, using clever water wheels and long, bamboo tubing. The natives make wonderful fabrics, and their mosquito netting made my petite Shangri La insect-proof and, as a side effect, very pretty. A sturdy elevator powered by two, sleek native teenagers completed my home.

Of course we spend most of our time in prayer and contemplation of the true way, but every now and then we break away for appropriate fun. Perhaps we do charades of old testament prophets, perhaps we have gospel sing-a-longs. I put together a very nice gospel quartet indeed. We have a coconut rhythm section and the portable keyboard you sent is just grand for gospel music. Of course my favorite is the impromptu shows I put on for the natives. They are so uplifting and bring the Gungaris even closer to civilization.

Brother Flem! What CAN I say?! He is truly the most holy and charismatic messenger of the word that I have ever had the privilege of serving. We could not do without him. I worry about his health. He drives himself so very hard, following me about the jungle to see to my safety. The good man cares nothing at all for HIS personal safety. He skitters about the jungle at breakneck speed, ministering to the Gungaris.

There is one particular place that concerns me: a rickety log that Brother Jerimiah uses to cross a nasty stretch of the stream that borders the mission. I have warned him how dangerous it looks. As soon as I finish this hasty note to you, I will take Thomas and we will do something to that bridge.

What with fever, wild leopards, and deadly serpents surrounding us at all times I often wonder how we survive.

The Gungaris have run low on footgear. Could you Church Ladies whip up a few pairs of flip-flops? The ones on which Sister Vernette stenciled Moses parting the Red Sea seem particularly attractive to the Indians. Also please send a few yards of gold lame; some size fourteen slingbacks, clear lucite, spike-heeled bedroom slippers, and a flask of olive oil. The first items you can get from Junior Wulmothe, and you have a ton of olive oil at the cafe.

I am developing a marvelous rapport with the Gungaris.

God forbid that it should ever happen, but if Brother Jerimiah ever decides to retire, OR IF YOU THINK HIS TALENTS CAN BEST BE USED ELSEWHERE, I would deem it the greatest honor to be considered for some small part in the Gungari Ministry. Not that I could ever match Brother Flem's light. Only Sweet Jesus Himself could do that.

By the way, I understand The Eternal Life Cafe and Souvenir Shop for Jesus has a lease renewal coming up. Mother mentioned it and asked me what she thought we should do. You know me! Business just passes right through my head! Why don't you write and tell me what you think should be done about the lease?

    I am Yours, Sister Ling-Ling,
    In the bosom of Sweet Jesus,

                Sincerely,
                Brother Jackie Luden

June 1

Penny Warshack
22 Castlerock
Scottsdale Arizona

Dearest Penny,

Below is the new address at which you may write me. You can also send letters to me at Quarter Pine and Mother will forward them here.

Jackie Luden,
Assistant to The Director
Gungari Indian Outreach in the Amazon
c/o: Third Church of God Delivered
2021 Montgomery Highway
Birmingham, Alabama

You might be wondering how I ended up a missionary in the Amazon. I have always been open to adventure, and anyway, things around Quarter Pine were getting a mite too hectic for me. Too much tension and dissension from friends, neighbors, and even the police.

Yes, the police! Can you believe the police would try and implicate me in the disappearance of Jimmy Pierson? No, I am not trying to avoid the police, but absence doesn't make the heart grow fonder, it makes everybody forget you.

It's not so bad here. In fact, this place is a paradise. The Gungaris treat me like royalty. I bonded quickly with the Chief's wife. Her name, oddly enough, is Racquel, and she is teaching me jungle lore. The food is wonderful, if one learns what to harvest, and the tree house the Gungaris built for me has a nice balcony overlooking the river by which we camp.

Down from the Dog Star

My only real problem is Brother Flem. He does not understand the word "no." The poor little man had a nasty accident a couple of days ago. A log bridge on which he toddles back and forth across the Blue Li Popo river snapped just as he reached the middle of said stream. We screamed in despair! We thought it was finished with Brother Flem. You see, this stream is infamous for the huge flesh-eating piranha fish that patrol its depths. We feared that we had lost our leader.

Imagine our happiness when Brother Jerimiah emerged from the stream. That little man is so rancid that even piranha won't touch him. At least he smells a whiff less horrid.

As one can see from my letterhead, I have been made his assistant. Dear Sister Ling Ling Tarwater granted me this singular honor. I do my best.

I have begun the process of starting a twelve-step meeting in the jungle based roughly on our program. We will use brightly colored snail shells for chips. I've taken the liberty of printing up an appropriate format and the readings. I will write World Service for a start-up kit. The only problem I'm having is finding something to which the Gungaris are addicted.

I've noticed that a lot of our program deals with getting rid of secrets, and processing resentments. It's not my secrets that keep me sick, it's the process of holding the secrets that keep me so unhealthy. It's not the resentments that keep me so angry, it's the process of maintaining those resentments that hurt me so much. Each time I give up a secret, each time I process a resentment, I become a little healthier.

Not that I have any secrets or resentments. When I have a resentment against somebody, I have a very special method of dealing with the situation. It is a solution that I developed myself and may not follow program guidelines, but it is very effective.

Junior Wulmothe has been invited to Hollywood to explain a new concept for a series to the people at Fox! He wrote me all about it and asked my opinion. I encouraged him to follow his dreams. "Go west, young man!" I told him. I don't know how real all this is. He may be locked up again back at Clarion.

But the idea is sound: a new comedy series called BESWITCHED. It is about a semi-sinister, semi-wacky witch who is deeply involved in S&M. The pilot show's title is BONDAGE & BEELZEBUB. This is a very perky witch, too. By day she works in a plant, assembling word processors. At night she roams the halls of congress dressed all in . . . But you get the picture.

I told him that no, I did not think that Neva Jean would be appropriate for the role. She certainly has all the characteristics for the part but those studio lights are hot and you do know that she dresses only in the purest petroleum products.

Cemetery Golf is taking off. I talk to Mother and Helen every night via my mini solar-powered satellite dish that Dr. Wulmothe invented. Mother and Helen jumped right in when I made my quick-hurried trip to the Amazon. They even came up with a marvelous decoration scheme for The Perpetual Chapel To View The Departed And Rent Golfing Equipment. They are using sort of a camping/fly fishing motif. They found a stash of canvas and bamboo out in the barn and of course, they believe in putting to use natural materials. Ecologically friendly! That's my motto! I hated to testify against Neva Jean at her ecology hearing, but honesty is my greatest virtue.

I was lying out in my hammock yesterday with a Tupperware bowl full of Fruit Loops. Groggy from the heat, it took me a few minutes to observe that a yellow jacket had landed in my cereal. I watched it nibble away at the tiny pastel circles and suddenly realized that it was making a CRUNCHING noise. It's minuscule mouth parts were capable of rasping away cereal! I thought about the miracle of nature. Even here in the Amazon, thousands of miles away from the States, there are insects who like the same food as we. I extrapolated further that if that little wasp could crunch cereal it could probably bite the holy piss out of me! I slowly and carefully replaced the cover on my bowl and popped it shut. Then I shook the bowl, for about five minutes, like a mariachi player on pure meth. After the buzzing inside the bowl stopped, I removed the lid. The insect was not in the least damaged. It was a bit dizzy and it was coated in bright green, yellow and red pastel powder, but it was alive and well.

After it cleared the confection from its wings, it flew away. I visualized it arriving at the nest covered in colored sugar. I imagined all the other wasps gathering around in wonder at the bounty the bug brought home. I wondered if it would be given special honors by the queen or be torn to shreds as a new and unusual snack food. I wondered if it would lead a flock of killer, demented wasps back to my bowl and possibly to me. They are carnivorous, you know. I once watched a yellow jacket neatly dissect one of its dead friends and take it, piece by piece back to its nest. I dumped the cereal in a nearby bush and quickly (but of course gracefully) retreated to my tree house.

There may be something odder than usual going on around here. I keep thinking I hear airplanes buzzing about at night. Racquel just murmurs something about "Federal Express" and changes the subject. Racquel is too valuable a friend to alienate so I don't push it.

I hope I haven't stumbled onto a coke farm. The Indians get a lot of natural pharmaceuticals from local flora but they use it only in ceremony and very rarely.

Someone in the program once just loved peyote. He got clean but still wanted his peyote, so he became an American Indian and started chewing on the cacti during meetings. I don't know what became of him.

You never mentioned anything about Nelson. Does being one-eyed indeed limit his stalking prowess? Did you sue the store? I am dealing with a stalker now. Brother Flem learned nothing from his experience in the river. Can he avoid the quicksand?

Hugs and Kisses,

Jackie

June 1

Doctor Jack Kevorkian
c/o Minnesota Medical Center
Portsmouth, Minnesota

Dear Dr. Kevorkian,

I saw you on television recently.

I am writing to ask you for some information about your lawyer with whom I saw you on your interview with Andy Rooney.

Is he married? Is he in a relationship? What's his name?

In the face, he resembled a rather handsome mule or perhaps horse. To your knowledge, can this be turned into a line of deductive reasoning?

I would like to meet with you when I return from the Amazon. I have some techniques that, although rather blunt, may help you in your work.

Enclosed is a packet of powdered herbs and berries. It makes a tea that they say tastes fruity and pleasant. Sort of like an international coffee. It should be invaluable in your work.

Sincerely,
Jackson K. Luden

c/o: Mrs. Minerva Luden
Quarter Pine Farm
Ludens Bend, Alabama

Down from the Dog Star

June 1

Attention: Department of Exotic Animals
The Ralston and Purina Company
Raleigh, South Carolina

Dear Sirs,

I am writing to inquire about the possibility of your designing a line of Leopard Chow.

You may already have such a product.

If not, I have some colorful suggestions for packaging, contents and name.

We have always used your puppy and dog chow. Our animals always thrived.

Except one. Perhaps I will visit you one day and we will discuss that a bit further.

Sincerely,

Jackson K. Luden

c/o: Mrs. Minerva Luden
Quarter Pine Farm
Ludens Bend, Alabama

June 1

Lynda Verlance
6462 Marlette Lane
Glendale Arizona

Hello Lynda,

It was so good to get your nice letter. Did you get my Amazon address from Penny or Becky? How ever, it's just so darn good to see your handwriting.

Sad news, but not too amazing, that you have been removed as treasurer from your home group. It may be just as well. Really big problems could arise from your revenge hotline. Your new idea for a modeling/escort service is interesting. If done tastefully it could be a real asset to the community.

Tell me about the somewhat impromptu trip you gifted upon Kevin. It is tempting to try to keep newcomers out of relationships, but sailing Kevin across the church parking lot and into that big cactus patch could have done him some serious damage.

Could you elaborate on the mechanism of the catapult? Where, exactly, did Penny get those big rubber bands? Was Pirelli written anywhere on them? Perhaps whatever markings they might have had had been sanded or scraped off. You can trust me with this info, darling. You know I never gossip. Or say anything tacky.

You asked about an average day for me in the jungle. There is no such thing as as average day here. Every day is startlingly different. It takes a great deal of preparation and work to live well in the Amazon.

We arise at sun-up and go to bed shortly before dark. This is really not so bad as we have fourteen to sixteen hours of sunlight a day. The

Down from the Dog Star

Gungaris are a very organized group of people. We all have jobs to do and we do them. They are not "noble savages" nor are they "child-like natives."

We are speaking of aboriginal people with an advanced culture with emphasis on art, sciences, and law. They have a written language and make exquisite paper and textiles from the inner barks of various trees. The colors that they produce for dying these papers and textiles are vivid and varied: pastels to primary reds, greens, and yellows.

For the most part, the Gungaris are tall, and slender. Their skin tones range anywhere from copper bronze to milk and honey. They have occasional lapses into cannibalism but they never eat members of their own tribe. The last few people they have eaten were white. They say we are not true humans and so it doesn't matter.

The work we do is at times hard. We are broken up into different guilds or crews and one usually stays in that guild from birth to death. There is no lateral movement in the society. There is very little upward mobility either. The emphasis here is surviving and doing it in comfort.

We have hunters who bring in meat. Peccary is my favorite of all, but I do enjoy a nice roast jungle chicken. We have people who gather vegetables and berries. These folk also gather fruits, nuts, and the greatest prize of all, honey.

Then there is a group of men and women who work to gather drugs for their religious ceremonies. One day, while they were processing a sticky orange sap till it became a dry orange powder, I asked Racquel what it was used for. She told me it was a mild euphoric. She called it a feel-good medicine. But Gungaris don't use it a lot. It causes breast development in men. I asked her why they were making so much of it. There were big bales of the stuff lying around the clearing. She just mumbled "Federal Express" and led me away to see a new baby that had been born the night before.

That night, as I was drifting off to sleep, pieces began to fit in new and funky ways. The powder was orange. So was my Whackazoid-D. The powder had antidepressant properties. So did my Whackazoid-D. The powder caused breast enlargement in men. So did....

But no, that's absurd. No connection possible. Federal Express?

It may seem out of character for me to suddenly be doing missions work, but mysterious ways are afoot. This is a near perfect life. I even have a pet that I'm learning to love—not as much as Honey, but strongly. She is a nice little leopard. I named her Neva Jean, but after a few days, realized she was too sweet and playful to have that name so I changed it to Bonnie. She sleeps in my tree house at night and is very useful in keeping out snakes and preachers. Sometime she sleeps on the foot of my bed curled up on my bathrobe, but her favorite place to be is up in the rafters over the head of my bed. She has a good view up there.

She has taken a quick and instinctive dislike of Brother Jerimiah. She nearly made a meal of him one night when he mistook my treehouse (which is forty feet above the ground) for his humble grass hut on the banks of the river. I would have let her, but Bonnie is far too lovable to swallow vermin.

Here's a program joke for you: I sponsor 375 men, but only one calls me. Familiar? So many men — SO many men — ask me to sponsor them and then *never* call. I hate it!

Write me, dearheart,

> Love Ya, See Ya, Bye!
> Jackie

Tony O'Brien
4610 19th Avenue, N.
Phoenix, Arizona

Dear Tony,

Is your business taking off? I met a woman before I left Phoenix who did a similar job. She also decorated the homes of people too rich and busy to take that level of interest in Christmas. She is an interior decorator (or Environmental Coordinator, as she named herself) so she has some connections to those Christmas jobs.

Junior Wulmothe had an idea like yours, but it involved some elements that were dangerous and others that could get one federal time.

It would be great if you were here. Events are occurring that don't make a lot of sense. Yesterday, it seemed as if Uncle Wooley was peeking at me from a clump of trees. I turned to get Racquel's attention, and when I looked again, he was gone. Racquel said I was getting too much sun (it was raining at the time) and almost forcibly led me back to my treehouse, dosed me with one of her elixirs, and put me to bed. The brew knocked me right out, putting me under for a couple of days and nights. It's hard to tell, as we don't use calendars or clocks, but my beard was a shade heavy for an overnight nap, and Bonnie, my leopard, was very agitated.

You once told me that I should be thankful for my "privileged upbringing." Let me respond to that.

The first thought that pops into my mind is, "Please don't tell me how I should feel."

Born and reared in a small southern town, I grew up in a time when everybody had to be as alike as peanuts. If one did not dress, move, speak, and, at least, appear to think like everybody else, life could be hell.

There was nobody on that big, lonely farm but two women — who spoiled me wonderfully — and a few farm hands, with whom I had no contact. When my father did emerge occasionally from his office, he had nothing to give me but money and shame.

My earlier memories involve having to run home through the woods from school, because if the other kids caught me, they would rock me home. Having never been taught how to throw anything heavier than a tantrum, retaliation, on my part, was not possible.

While most little boys were watching their dads fix lawn mowers, I was in the house watching Helen cook. While most boys were out playing catch with their dads, I was sitting on the floor at my mother's dressing table learning how she applied her makeup.

All the money and privilege of my family could do nothing to help me because, at the time, I did not know how to use those tools.

It's different now. A singular joy can be derived from driving a big black Seville past the trailers and shacks of the men who once tormented me. They now have slatternly wives and snot-nosed brats who can hardly read. I have Quarter Pine.

It was not all bad. There were a lot of good, peaceful times, alone on the creek banks, alone in the woods. The happiest time of my life was the summer Pauly and Jim came into my life.

They lived across the creek from us. They were dirt poor. For some reason they took me as a brother and protected me from bullies. One of them I worshipped, but he brought out feelings that mystified me totally. He had a need and a desire for sex that had not yet come to me. My refusals angered and alienated him. He grew up, married, became a raging alcoholic and was killed in a bloody, senseless car wreck.

But sometimes when things are very quiet and I am drowsy, I can see him walking up the creek path to the back door of Quarter Pine, coming to get me, coming to take me camping.

My feelings for other men have never been the same since he died. My first and last human love.

There was a a polo team we put together when I was a teenager. The boys in the town who had horses or ponies (there was even one mule) got together in a fairly flat pasture at the Piersons' old homeplace, using brooms and an old basketball for equipment. We didn't have any rules except you could swat people with said broom anywhere but on the head. And it was considered the worst form possible to abuse another's mount.

Those were happy times. Then some boy's father spoiled it all by moving the event to the country club, getting proper equipment and uniforms, and hiring some pansy of an Englishman to teach us the "proper way to play."

What started out as a game for children that was fast, fun, and often hilarious, turned into something deadly serious. There's nothing worse than a redneck with a few extra coins jingling in his pocket.

I turned nineteen, developed an interest in the stage, and moved to Atlanta.

Don't talk about privilege unless you know about the pain that can go along with it.

I adore the young people today. Their odd little haircuts, the way they pierce any part of their body that they can, and their total disregard for what they or anybody wears is delightful to me.

I hung out with a bunch of these kids in Phoenix and never felt such love. I believe they have some how perfected what our generation from the '60s attempted: love and acceptance.

I will close now. Brother Jerimiah's invited for a bite of lunch and I must prepare. Poor Brother Jerimiah has been looking pale lately. He developed a nasty cough from his dip in the river. We must nurse him to the health that he deserves.

> Love you, Fish Boy,
> Jackie

June 10

Junior Wulmothe
Wulmothe Manor
Trimble Hill Road
Ludens Bend, Alabama

Dear Junior,

It's too bad that you and Mother are having such controversies over Cemetery Golf. She did, however, supply the land and money to get the project off the ground.

According to Sister Vernette, the decor she chose for the Chapel To View The Departed/Golf Equipment Rental Room is done in the very best of taste. Tell LZ that he's slipped a cog if he thinks the bamboo and canvas used in its construction has anything at all to do with those Scouts of his. You might also mention that the latest rumor about those goats is that they also love wallpaper when they can get it. That should give him something to ponder for a while.

I felt extremely fortunate to have Sister Vernette assist Mother in decorating the Eternal Hole-in-One Snack Bar. But I do hope that they can upgrade that to a nice restaurant. There is something just a scosh un-kosher about a few of the items they've put on the menu. "Chicken in a Casket" is not only trite, but it is predictable and dated. "Fries to Die For" is somewhat better. The only item I can really relate to is "Cryogenically Frozen Yogurt."

I will give Neva Jean's suggestion about the old freezers from the Dairy Queen consideration. I see no problem with offering the departed perpetual enfreezement. I'm assuming that YOU came up with the

Down from the Dog Star

phrase "perpetual enfreezement." It has style, it has class, it simply screams, "Junior!"

My only problem with perpetual enfreezement might be the way our electricity acts during thunderstorms. We would definitely need back-up generators. I think Cleatus McCloud has an old arc welder down at the garage. Is that anything like a generator? Uncle Wooley could probably make a few modifications.

Junior, has Uncle Wooley been out of town lately? I thought I saw him here recently. Silly, I know.

We are fortunate to have Sister Vernette and the church ladies in our corner. I toyed with the idea of asking them if they'd like to move their cafe to the Cemetery Golf Course. The only requirement for membership is the desire to be buried on a golf course. And to have a five thousand dollar membership fee.

But that's very reasonable when you consider all you get for five thousand dollars: a family plot that can hold four (eight if they're stylishly thin), opening and closing of the grave, embalming is included, and to be laid to rest with the strains of music from the Fighting Canecutters High School marching band! What more could any reasonable human want?

Some pundits in the program said that I took some of that directly from the readings, the ones that we do when we open our NA meetings, but I told them that what it actually was, was tough cookies.

I'm having trouble finding a sponsor here in the jungle. I hated that my last sponsor fell apart like that. He actually told me, right before his big breakdown, that, after being around for awhile, the steps just didn't work like they did at first. He's the only person I've met, so far, who worked a fine program and got sicker!

Brother Jerimiah Flem recovered from his chest cold. Even after I had him to lunch and fixed him my special version of flavored coffee. Remember that special coffee?

Bonnie likes him less and less. I would hate for my kitty cat to scratch the poor man. Considering that she weighs three hundred pounds and has six-inch claws, it could get messy. Brother Flem is getting better with boundaries, however. Racquel hates him and it is not wise to tamper with the emotions of a Gungari medicine woman.

Speaking of medicine, Junior, the people here are producing huge amounts of a substance that seems very similar to my last anti-depressant. I must snag a sample and see if the effects are similar. Gotta run. Bonnie is restless and needs exercise. I'm going to explore today. I believe there's an airfield near here. If so, it could be useful.

Don't let go five minutes before the miracle happens! I heard Neva screaming that from the back of Sheriff Beebus's squad car one night. I didn't know she was in the program . . .

Keep me informed,

Jackie

June 12

Sister Vernette McCloud
General Delivery
Ludens Bend, Alabama

Dear Sister Vernette,

We're very grateful that you are putting so much time and effort into helping Mother with the Cemetery Golf snack bar. Yes, I agree that "The Final Hole in One" is a better name than "The Eternal Hole in One." We already have The Eternal Life Cafe and Souvenir Shop for Jesus. This could confuse people as to our autonomy, and it could lead to problems when we go world-wide and start franchising Cemetery Golf.

Which brings up the subject of management. You have managed the church cafe for seven years now, and it has grown and prospered.

What I need to manage my cafe (yes, it is a snack bar now, but I plan to upgrade) is someone with your culinary skill, with your flash for mushroom soup, someone with their fingers on the pulse of the county. When we go worldwide I'll need someone to oversee the franchise.

You may name your salary, as long as it's not higher than I'm willing to pay.

Please tell Junior that I'm not sure about Hell Dogs. Not very positive. Slab o' Ribs is too common. Perhaps Ribs on a Slab?

Rigorsmorgasbord is nice. It is a bit ethnic—we only have one family of Swedes in the county and they're too busy with the Brookhaven Cheese Works to play golf. At least they'd better be. Our friend LZ thinks "Rigorsmorgasbord" ghoulish, but his sense of humor has been quite dull lately. You know he hangs wallpaper (he calls himself a wall covering engineer) and some fool started a rumor about the goats needing wallpaper for roughage and that they were busy digging a tunnel to Mountain Brook, where he does most of his work.

I offered him a free membership to Cemetery Golf, but he wasn't interested.

So, yes, go ahead and have "Rigorsmorgasbord" painted on the front of the snack bar.

Pre-registration looks good. Three hundred county families have signed up. And most of these people, contrary to vicious speculation, do NOT work for us.

I would like for you to check into the flag situation on the greens. Flags keep falling over in the empty graves. I am sure some simple engineering can solve this problem. Talk to LZ, as he so modestly has given himself this moniker.

Must run. The Gungaris are giving me my Indian name today. Thomas Blaylock suggested "Princess Swamp Water." Thomas Blaylock has not been all that helpful here at our outreach. He loafs in the shade all day, drinking fruit juice and telling outrageous lies to the young Gungaris about his role as a social leader in Jefferson County. Thomas needs some spiritual guidance.

Remember how the Catholics use to slaughter people in the name of religion? I may bring that back.

Dear Brother Jerimiah Flem has escaped death twice now. We are all so happy. Do you know Brother Flem's blood type? Just in case?

Let me know about your feelings and thoughts on a career change. Do come aboard the Cemetery Golf love boat! We need you!

Love,

Brother Jackie

Down from the Dog Star

June 14

Dr. Jack Kavorkian
c/o Minnesota State Medical University,
Portsmouth, Minnesota

Dear Jack,

Got your long, chatty letter.

I must say, we do see eye to eye on many things.

It's really too bad about your lawyer, Jack, but I told you distinctly what that packet of herbs was for. He seemed like a really personable fellow on television. Ten seconds from the time he drank it? Sounds like a record to me.

Have you had luck finding another simpatico attorney?

There's plenty of room here in the Amazon if you need a place to cool down for a time. And you could be very useful in a situation I have here with a co-worker.

Write soon,
Jackie Luden

June 22

Becky Bright
610 Lamont Street
Phoenix, Arizona

Hello Becky,

I'm glad things are going so well with your new family. Yes, I think
you did the next right thing when you turned in Lynda to the secretary
of your group. It was for her own good and will advance her spiritual
growth.

I would try and let go of any resentments you might have about your
new car burning up. You have no proof that Lynda burned it, although
her purse and house keys were found at the arson scene. She is so absent
minded she probably just left them on the hood of your car after the
meeting. She may have been in the middle of a spiritual awakening;
perhaps her emotional roller coaster collided with her pink cloud.

Still, it is interesting that she has second degree burns on her hands
and wrists. But if she said she got it from a toaster explosion, I believe she
got it from a toaster explosion.

We're all atwitter here in the jungle. My greatest hero, Nova
Meniere, is visiting me all the way from Paris. You may have heard me
talk about her before. If not, she's the woman who pioneered the concept
of pantyhose. Yes, she did. I am a bit rushed, so I'll tell you more about
Nova next letter.

You asked how I got started on drugs. It's the usual story.

My first drug of choice was fantasy. As a child, I had no friends, so
I developed a rich and wonderful inner world, full of imaginary play-
mates. Even now, I fantasize, but only allow myself three or four minutes

before I fall asleep at night. The world can go by, if I live in fantasy.

My second drug of choice was books. I found that, lost in a book, I didn't feel the spitballs hitting the back of my head, or hear, quite so clearly, the taunts my male classmates threw at me.

The next progression is so usual it's almost corny. Alcohol, then pot, then pills, then heroin.

All my life I had trouble entering a room full of people. When walking down a sidewalk, if I saw someone coming towards me, I would usually cross the street so that they could not see me, so I would not have to look them in the eye.

Then, one day in San Francisco, (I was twenty-four at the time), I had a tooth pulled. The dentist had prescribed a very mild pain medication. Never having had pain pills before, the results amazed me. Walking down the wet gray sidewalk, under a dull, gelid sky, towards a job I hated, my spirits began to soar! Smiling at strangers, walking with my head high and shoulders back, I was anxious to get to work and do a good job. Here's what's funny: I took that pill bottle out of my pocket, looked at it and said, "I love you. I'll have you with me forever."

Who knew? Even if I knew the hell I would suffer for years and years, I don't think I would done anything differently. My dope kept me alive for decades. Then it began to kill me. Then you guys came along.

It's important to ask what is appropriate for this section of life, and then act on it.

It sounds as though you are learning so much about yourself. This sounds like a healthy relationship to me. But remember, love means never having to ask permission.

Hugs and Kisses,

Jackie

June 22

Junior Wulmothe
Wulmothe Manor
Trimble Hill Road,
Ludens Bend, Alabama

Dearest, dearest, most scrumptious Junior,

I have news.

I have news that will bake your meringue-like heart into the frothiest of pink peaks.

The thought that drives my fear is that you will react in hurt and misery, which will then lead to insane jealousy. But we have had our share of that sort of thing before, and our friendship has remained firm.

No, it has nothing to do with Thomas Blaylock. I will gladly give you that nelly bitch when I make my triumphant return to Quarter Pine. I surprised that young man while he was trying to squeeze his six foot, six inch frame into my favorite "Mame" costume. "I don't want her, you can have her, she's too much for me," as the song goes.

It has nothing to do with marriage, money or, men, although it does start with the letter "M."

Have you suffered enough? Very well. Here it is: Nova Meniere. Yes. Our oldest and most spectacular of friends. Nova Meniere. The name positively drips from the tongue like *demi glas*. Nova Meniere. Coming all the way from Paris to visit her exiled friend in the Amazon.

I received her note in a most mysterious way. I knew it was from Nova even before I opened the letter—that classic pale lavender stationery, the smudged, spidery calligraphy, the smell of Chanel #5.

The note did not come in the usual way, by air drop or satellite relay.

It arrived like this: I picked a nosegay of tropical blossoms to add that certain touch to a party I was throwing in Racquel's, the Chief's wife's, honor. Yes, you often say that I'm just a name dropping fool, and that I social climb like a rabid monkey, but I simply can't be responsible for the superstars who flock to my banner.

As I was saying before you interrupted, Racquel is pregnant, and I wanted to show the Gungari women how to give a baby shower. They had never heard of such a thing. I had already taught them about Jello, Mahjongg and their favorite, show tunes of the forty's. Yes, I do believe I earn the money the church pays me.

I arranged the flowers in a wonderful art deco vase the Chief had given me, and just had to stand back and admire.

You know, what's interesting is, everyday I see flowers and plants growing wild here that we pay big bucks for back home. Could we export pine trees and kudzu to the jungle, do you think?

I was admiring my creation, when I noticed one rather large and unusual bud that seemed to be moving from side to side on its stem, almost as though it were searching for something. I didn't recognize the species, and I felt a bit nervous. Who knew? Anything could have been in that bud. There could have been a viper hibernating in that flower. There could have been a swarm of killer bees. Anything.

But what happened was even more astounding. The bud popped open, the scent of Chanel drenched the air and Nova's note dropped into my hand. This, Junior, is the gospel truth. You know I never exaggerate. Accuracy is one of my greatest strengths.

So Nova Meniere is coming for a visit. She didn't say for how long or how she was arriving. We will know when we know.

Do you remember the year we spent with Nova in Paris? Back in the sixties, wasn't it? Of course I was but a tiny child then and my memory is vague on some points. You, however, with your elephant-like intellect, and the twenty-or-so years that you have on me, should remember it all.

I do, however, remember that Nova, in our minds, is the undisputed inventor of the concept of panty hose. I remember her laboring round the clock in her lab, in that tiny garret, trying to create some new, enlightened twist for the fashion world. Fashion was so jaded then. Something had to be done. I'm sure her unrelenting work all that year is what finally broke her health. Work - and all that absinthe.

So there we were, me in my crib, you lounging about in your big felt bathrobe (where DID you get a robe that size?) and dear Nova sweating and moaning and gnashing her teeth in the throes of fashion conscious birth. I remember we were eating pizza that night. Nova had some crotchless red lace panties in one hand (they were trimmed in marabou) and some old argyle socks in the other. She had been hitting the absinthe pretty hard all that week and I remember how she collapsed in a miserable pile of despair in the corner of the room. The next day, she came to and looked about her.

There they were! Nova had rolled and thrashed in opium dreams all the long night, and the socks, the panties and the cheese from the pizza had blended into that most divine of all garments, the first recorded pair of panty hose.

If events had unfolded differently, we would all three be wealthy and famous. I say this, my friend, because you and I contributed directly to the discovery. The argyle socks were mine, the marabou britches were yours and we had split the cost of the pizza three ways.

It was while we were traipsing down to the French patent office that Nova's health finally snapped. We carried her, kicking and screaming, into a Sisters of Mercy charity hospital, and explained to a large, hairy nun that we feared Nova had become suicidal. After seeing her safely tucked away in a latex-lined room, you and I, with only Nova's well being in mind, continued on our way to the patent office.

And then disaster struck. We were apprehended by the French immigration officers. They threw us onto a Greek freighter and waved good-bye. We were on that ghastly ship for ages!

Oh the abuse! Oh the degradation! They definitely had a name for it, and if they didn't, they pantomimed.

By the time we reached New York harbor, and those sailors managed to pry your fingers from the anchor chain, some little upstart had beat us to the patent office. She used nylon, no less.

Nova was years ahead of her time. Today one can find edible under wear in all the smart boutiques. No, not cheese flavored, but Nova was always a ground breaker.

I wonder what she wants. I wonder how she found me. I wonder what she plans to do to me?

That she was able to insert a letter into a flower bud from thousands of mile away speaks of eerie and massive power.

If I survive the meeting, I'll keep you informed.

Satellite reception is a bit sketchy today. Racquel blames it on sunspots. She says that when we have sunspot activity, I need to stay close to my tree house because, during these periods, the animals become unpredictable and treacherous. I asked her just when the various reptiles, man-eating fish, and carnivorous cats in the Amazon were supposed to be predictable and trustworthy. She didn't answer.

Junior, I swear she's starting to remind me of Natasha, Boris Badinov's side kick, from the old "Rocky and Bullwinkle Show." Sometimes I think she's up to something. She guides me away from areas that I'd like to explore and when I ask her certain questions, she loses all command of the English language. But she's very good to me. If it were not for Racquel, I wouldn't be living as well as I do.

I'm not one for revenge, but I know exactly what Scott Fitzgerald meant when he said, "Living well is the best revenge."

But now, Junior, I must speak to you in a stern tone of voice. I must speak to you as would a well-meaning father figure, and I must explain a very basic thing to you, for I fear the canoe of your life is heading towards the rapids.

Junior, I can not believe that for the third time, in less than a year, you have attempted to weigh your Miata on a road side truck scale. I believe you when you say you thought it was a toll booth, but listen carefully: THERE ARE NO TOLL BOOTHS IN JEFFERSON COUNTY, ALABAMA!!!

It is a dubious distinction, but you're fortunate the highway patrol men know you so well. I rather like your excuse. A toll booth would give us a bit of gloss, a touch of cosmopolitaneuity.

If memory serves, the first time you did this, you told the attendants that you thought the scale was the entrance to a rapid transit system. The second time, you told them that God had come to you in a vision and the ramp was actually an entrance into the promise land. At least, this time, you didn't back your car under the nose of a sixteen-wheeler.

Let's get real. (As real as we can be.)

You've been chasing truckers for years, and so far, to my knowledge, the only one you caught had green teeth, body odor, and what looked like scabies.

Give it up. Or get a job at a truck stop. If you like, I'll use my influence with the Church Ladies to have a diesel pump installed at the cafe and you can pump gas and cruise in safety.

Please stay off the freeways at midnight. I love you and worry about you. It's not a game without consequences.

Don't you remember what those two punks did to Lady Brenda? If you can't, or won't remember, I'll refresh your memory. They took her into the woods, tied her to a tree with barbed wire, soaked her with gasoline and, while she was very conscious, and very aware of what was going on, set her on fire. They burned her alive, Junior.

And how can you forget what happened to poor Miss Kimberly? She picked up a drunk Marine, and when he discovered Kimberly was a man, cut her up with a chain saw and strewed her body up and down I-20.

You're my best friend. I know you get lonely at Wulmothe Manor, but your behavior speaks more of illness than a desire for companionship.

Enough.

Let me comment on your plan to use sheep to keep the grass mowed at Cemetery Golf. No. I feel queasy, thinking of the possibilities. What if the sheep and the goats were to breed some dark night? Even worse, don't you remember the rumor about Beebus McCloud and barnyard animals? You must think of these things, Junior.

I understand that three hundred county families have signed up for Cemetery Golf. At five thousand dollars a pop, that comes to a nice bit of change. Who's smiling now? I really want to be there for the grand

Down from the Dog Star

opening, but there are matters that I must clear away, both here in the jungle, and at home.

Perhaps you can represent me.

You've told me nothing about the sinkhole behind your home. Did the police manage to explore it? If so, what did they find?

Write me, punkin.

I love you.
Jackie

June 28

Miss Penny Warshack
22 Castlerock
Phoenix, Arizona

Hello Penny,

So . . . Nelson has moved into your place with you? It should make his stalking so much easier. I can see him now, following you all about the condo, hiding behind the sofa, crouched behind the shower curtain.

Doesn't the guide dog hinder his stalking? I knew that he lost one eye in that green bean accident. You did not tell me he had only one eye to begin with. What with Beckie's boyfriend Fang, and your lover, Nelson, and Lynda's boyfriend Muley, one could almost build a complete human!

Tell me, Penny, just exactly why do they call him Muley? I understand that Lynda hired him to be an "Escort" for her new business, "Stranger Than The Night," and personally took him on a trial "Date." Six foot four, blonde and skinny. He sounds great. And from what Becky tells me, he's pretty normal, if one considers a confused bisexual who likes to ball Thanksgiving turkeys normal.

Enough of that. I want to tell you a surprising new development here in the Amazon.

Brother Jerry and I went fishing this morning. Brother Jerry has changed dramatically since I arrived. From being absolutely ga-ga over me, and chasing me about the jungle, he's lost at least fifty pounds. He's even started to maintain his personal cleanliness. He works out three days a week, has gotten rid of those awful khaki clothes, and wears tank tops and cut-off jeans. This man has turned into the ultimate fox. Hunkasaurus. Unfortunately, he's also beginning to develop self confidence and self esteem: two characteristics that I must stamp out if I want a decent

Down from the Dog Star

relationship with this man. The minute they think that you like them or that they're worth more than a pile of cat shit, they get arrogant and controlling. I must be the only gay man in the world who knows that he hates men.

This kind of stuff comes and goes. Only I am left. That's why I firmly believe that I am the center of my universe. That is why people seem so kleenxy to me.

I haven't had a chance to tell you about Nova Meniere, the unrecognized fashion maven of the universe, but I will fill you in. She's arriving soon.

As I said, Jer-Jer and I went fishing this morning. I used to hate fishing, but here, it is really necessary. I remember once, after a meeting, some big bruiser mentioned that he was a bass fisherman. I liked his looks and wanted to spend some time with him. I told him that I also was a bass fisherman and had won many tournaments. (I had seen a tournament once on "Fishing with Roland Martin") and he invited me to be his fishing partner at Smith Lake that coming Sunday. I eagerly agreed.

I had remembered some tackle of daddy's in the garage, but couldn't find it. What I found was a small, rusty tool box with some kite string in it and a bent hook. I did manage to find some fine bamboo, and stenciled it red and blue and painted dozens of tiny silver fish up and down its length.

When we met at dawn, he looked a bit regretful, but it was too late for him to do much about it. Bass fishermen have very tight boundaries, and never, never look at another fisherman's tackle or watch them when they pee over the edge of the boat. This guy was interesting in that he didn't even have to move from his seat to pee! Things were ok, until I caught a fish. The way fish look and feel give me the creeps. It makes my skin crawl to even think about touching one. Birds affect me the same way. I politely asked my fishing buddy if he would mind removing the fish from my hook. He did, but did it grudgingly. It was a sixty-two pound bass. A record, I understand. We won the tournament. The prize was a whole bunch of money and a baby blue, metal-flake bass boat. I still have the boat. Junior and I sometimes take it for a spin on the lake.

And so Jer-Jer and I were, as I said, fishing. We have a cute kayak made from canvas and bamboo, and the Gungaris have been teaching me to use a spear gun. I caught a really big fish. When we got it back to camp, none of the Gungaris could identify its species. We cleaned the fish and there, inside its stomach, was a menu from a restaurant I remembered in Paris, with the message: "Nova is on her way!" The fish's blood was pure Chanel #5.

How are your preparations for the World Convention? Are you considering my ideas for your costumes and music? Don't be concerned about anything anyone may ask you or mention to you about my hub caps or tires. You know I love you best of all. Even if you DID steal those tires and hubcaps, it just wouldn't matter. I was well insured, and if they were, perhaps, used to build that catapult, it was for the program. I am concerned that Becky has been using it to spread literature in downtown Phoenix. One might worry about littering and such.

No book yet. Much too busy.

Cemetery Golf is getting out of hand. Japanese and Arabian investors are clamoring for a piece of it. I am firm in my resolution to keep Cemetery Golf in the family and all-American. I've been trying to come up with some catchy names for the golf course and having little luck.

I sampled some of the strange orange powder the Gungaris are producing and, yes indeed, it has all the properties of Whackazoid-D. I can't take too much of it though. If I develop mammaries again, the Gungaris will know I took some, and they keep a pretty tight watch on it. Some really confusing things are going on around here. I hope Nova will be able to help me sort them out.

I feel just like Miss Davis in "Hush Hush Sweet Charlotte," waiting for her cousin Miriam to come and straighten everything out. But you know how that all turned out . . . I hope the chifonus Ms. Meniere knows how to practice forgiveness. She's been in the program for over thirty years.

Need to go. I'm having a fish-fry this afternoon.

Toodles

Jackie

Down from the Dog Star

June 28

Lawrence Reed
4835 17th street, South,
Birmingham, Alabama

LZ:

Mon cher! Tried to call you via satellite, but you are obviously, as always, in popular demand. How is Charlotte? Is she still busy gardening? None of my business, but when ARE you two going to get wise to the concept of chemical gardening? This is not pre-Columbian times, you know. Today, one can get potassium, nitrogen, and phosphorous out of sacks, instead of the wrong end of cows and horses.

Enclosed in this note, you will find a package of assorted plant and flower seeds that grow around our encampment. The four, large, nut-like seeds in the canvas pouch will produce an ornate vine. It has white flowers and a sticky, orange sap. The Gungaris find it to be medicinal. Be sure and plant them near a tree. They are fast growers and they get really big.

Have you any new hobbies? If you are heart-set on restoring old motor vehicles, why don't you collect old Buicks or Mercurys? They are very sturdy. Helen told me that you were considering a sailboat. It's none of my business. I have nothing to say about it. Mother mentioned that you had a few comments to make on the decor at the new Cemetery Golf range. I firmly deny any knowledge about that canvas. Mother probably got it at a yard sale and forgot about it. The poor dear is becoming so forgetful.

You know, I've been meaning to tell you for ages how much I enjoyed that twelve hours of sanding you treated me to. Someday, when we have time, I'll be sure and tell you all my true feelings on the subject.

I have made a fast new friend here in the jungle. Brother Jerry has made some changes for the better. He had two close brushes with death when we first arrived. It makes me feel a hint queasy when it occurs to me that I would never have found out the kind of man he really is, if he had not survived. LZ, I may have found something I've been hoping for for a long time. I'm trying not to get too excited. You know how much I loved Honey. I don't need to have my heart broken again.

Owned property, however, is owned property, and even if I don't want it, I don't think I'll let anybody else touch it. Thomas Blaylock keeps making sheepeyes at Jerry. A snake in my bosom! But, noblesse oblige.

What progress on your farm-treatment center? I was so pleased that the governor gave you a land grant and funding. I was blown away to hear your idea about the Twelve Steps for Growing Hay. Hiring Dr. Wulmothe as consulting physician is a coup. Fifty thousand acres of prime land, a contract with all the mounted police in the country, and clients coming directly from the prison system to produce the hay! AND *carte blanche* to use any techniques you think necessary to rehabilitate these men. Dr. Wulmothe is a genius with chemicals. He is the doctor who designed the chemical restraints to keep dear Sister Tara Wilcox from removing all her skin after that nasty brush with Poison Oak.

There are silly, nasty people who have said Dr. Wulmothe was involved in CIA mind control experiments. The only problem with that rumor is . . . Well who knows. All I know is, I trust him completely. And I miss him. Sometimes I think I can almost hear his voice. Oh how we used to love to eat at the Wulmothes!

It sounds as though you've finally found your niche in life. Not that I would care to go through your program. I don't need it.

As you probably have heard by now, my dear, dear special friend, the unrecognized queen of haute couture, is visiting me soon. I've been receiving clear messages from her in obscure fashion. Last night Racquel, Queen of Gungari-Land, had her first child. I had given her a sumptuous baby shower and a beaded diaper bag. The Gungaris insisted that I be present at the birth. At precisely three AM this morning Tula, Racquel's sister, came for me. She led me deep into the forest to a small, torch-lit clearing. Several women were gathered around Racquel: the head birthing woman, the head of the Animal People, and Tula, who does nothing but annoy Thomas Blaylock. She wants that man for a mate. Talk about wishful thinking!

Tula did, however, beat the birthing drum, I played my portable keyboard, and the birthing woman thumped Racquel briskly with a large stick. I think this last was a new technique the birthing woman improvised after she developed a severe resentment against Racquel.

For my birthing gift, I brought that charming red velvet cape with the blue velvet dice trim. Charlotte wanted that cape for her niece's debut into society, but unless some things are straightened out back home, I would never have been able to deliver it to her.

It was an easy birth, as such things go: a husky man-child named in my honor: Kavorkian, my adopted middle name.

The birthing women had me help deliver the child. I could not but notice that on the amniotic sack, in glowing smudged calligraphy, was the message: "Nova Meniere. Get ready! Arriving soon!" The amniotic fluid? Two liters of pure Chanel.

I found an airfield near our camp. It is very large. It could easily handle the Concorde, and is about a mile long. I found a few stubs of hand-rolled cigarillos sealed with pine resin.

Uncle Wooley is the only person I know who smokes them.

LZ, if you love me, please tell me something about the sinkhole at Wulmothe Manor. Despite some insignificant differences that we may have had, you know I love you best of all.

Don't worry about those goats or the wallpaper. I happen to know the kinds they like and the kinds they can't tolerate.

Excuse the blood on this note. I sustained a severe cut today while I was working in the yam field. A sharp stone or a sliver of wood gashed my palm badly while I was grubbing these big sweet potato-like tubers.

This is how we cook them. (Charlotte will be interested in this.)

Choose a nice big yam — five-pound yams are usually the best —

wash it and rub all the skin off with your rubbing stick. We use the jaw bone of a peccary. They have tiny, sharp teeth, and the jawbone is a very important tool for us. Pierce the yam all over with a sharp stick about the size of a pencil, and soak overnight in honey, natural chicle, cinnamon, and cloves. In the morning, wrap the yam in a non-poisonous leaf, encase the leaf, with the enclosed yam, in a shell of white clay. This is then buried under the cooking fire where it slowly and quietly bakes all day. By supper time they are tender and sweet. Heartbreakingly delicious.

That reminds me. I once told a dude in Canada that something I had seen was heartbreakingly beautiful. Rather a common phrase, I think. He looked at me and asked me how anything could be "heartbreakingly beautiful." He said the terms were contradictory. I wanted to tell him that if he had the sense of a goat and the sensitivity that God gave a fencepost he would understand. But he had been as kind to me as he knew how to be. We were just two very different humans. I have heard that he is now successful in his chosen field, has found the love of his life, and is generally joyful. I am glad for him, but to be honest with you, I was a smidgen disappointed in not snaring him myself. It would never have worked. He needs stability and I need chaos.

Did you hear about Mrs. Grant's narrow escape from the aliens? Her old, three-legged hound dog, Peanut, saved her. He also got a large mouthful of alien flesh, which I plan to display in a showcase at my Viewing Room for the Departed/Golf Equipment Rental Room. (Autographed golf balls, $25.00 each.)

I will tell you all about the aliens next note. Love you, miss you, goodnight,

Jackie

Down from the Dog Star

June 30

Becky Bright
610 Lamont Street,
Phoenix, Arizona

Dear Becky,

That sounded like an interesting meeting. Sometimes an angry meeting can be more productive than those nice, mellow, laid back ones. Still, so much anger over coffee that was a little too strong? I remember one meeting when I said that I had a sponsor from our fellowship, and my sponsor had a sponsor from our fellowship, and so forth and so on. Then Don, my sponsor, said words to the same effect, about continuity of message being so important. At that point Joel, the man to whom you are referring, stood up and began waving his hands in the air and bellowing that it was such elitist, cliquish, bullshit as this that drove people back out again. He was so offensive and spooky, that most of us got up and walked out into the parking lot. Indirectly, it would seem, we WERE driven out by my sharing. Have another cup of java, Joey!

Joel has about fifteen years. If I'm that miserable an asshole at fifteen years, I think I'd rather be back out there.

That's another thing. "She went back out!" or "He's back out there using!" or "I hit my knees!" Is such trite, dramatic language necessary?

How about "He relapsed." or, "I prayed."

I don't pray on my knees. It doesn't seem to me that my particular God wants me crawling around like a worm. That's how I've spent most of my life, in one way or another.

How are the triplets? I'm sorry you and Hematite are having such problems finding your separate duties and roles in the relationship. I would suggest to have no roles, and to share all duties.

Poor old Sister Amy Grant was nearly taken by the aliens last week.

It's true. The story came straight from Sister Vernette, via satellite. Except for the snakes, I have never known her to distort the truth.

This is what happened: Sister Amy had been to the big closing night of The Third Church of God Delivered Rattle Snake Round Up Revival. James Randal, one of Sister Amy's grandchildren, has landed a new job at the zoo and has been smuggling real rattlesnakes home for church services. Sister Amy had been severely bitten by a twelve-foot timber rattler.

She then had the clear choice of either rushing to the emergency room, thereby showing her lack of faith, or sitting quietly to await developments.

Nothing developed. She seemed fine.

They closed the service and everyone went home. But during the night, Sister Amy began to feel odd. Peanut, her three-legged hound dog, began to growl softly and to scratch at the door. Sister Amy thought it was just a cat or one of the grandkids come to check on her. But when she peeked out the door, nobody was there. She went to bed, her Bible in one hand, her twelve-gauge in the other, and waited for sleep.

A short time after retiring for the night, she suddenly felt very lightheaded, as though she could float. The next thing she knew she WAS floating towards her bedroom window, which had mysteriously opened. There were two small men, with large heads, big blue eyes, and overbites, standing on either side of the window! They were reaching for her with long, skinny fingers and about to push her out the window, when Peanut leaped from behind the door, slobbering and screaming death.

Let me tell you about Peanut and Sister Amy. Peanut is a big, beautiful, Brindle-hound. This breed of dog is rare, indeed. They are descended from Gaze-hounds, made famous in the days of King Arthur the Pendragon. Peanut weighs about seventy-five pounds and has the sweetest nature that a dog could have. The numerous grandchildren and great-grandchildren in the Grant family ride him, roll on him, the girls dress him up and the boys use him as the monster in their games. When he was a pup, someone shot him. He had to have most of his back left leg

Down from the Dog Star

removed. The men in the family wanted to put him to sleep, but Sister Amy would not hear of it. She nursed him in a basket beside her bed until he was strong and frisky. Peanut worships sister Amy the way Sister Amy worships God.

And so, when Peanut saw something trying to do something strange and dangerous-looking to his Mistress, he lost it.

He came scrabbling from behind the door like the original Hound of the Baskerville. Sister Amy said one of the Aliens pointed what looked like some sort of a ray gun at Peanut, but for once, the aliens were too slow. Peanut grabbed the weapon with his gaping, rabbit-gulping mouth, and swallowed it. Sister Amy said that she distinctly heard the other alien call the weapon loser a "schmuck" before he jumped out the window. Sister Amy thought the word schmuck must have been the Alien equivalent of "RUN!" and I won't disillusion her. Before the small saucer person could get away, Peanut latched onto one shiny, white thigh and tore out a hunk of flesh. Sister Amy then floated back to her bed and gently fell into a dreamless sleep.

Some questions remain. What will the effect be of a ray gun in Peanut's belly? What will happen to the alien meat? Sister Vernette wants it for the church, Sister Tara wants it for her lecture tour, Dr. Wulmothe wants it for experimental purposes, and I want it for an exhibit at Cemetery Golf. If the government hears about it we will all lose.

Except for Uncle Wooley. If he knows, I have a feeling that the government (some government) will soon know also. I observed, on the little satellite dish, which he claimed to have invented, a spot that had been sanded, as though to remove a logo. When I splashed a little of Nova's mystic Chanel #5 on the spot, the words, "Property of the CIA" appeared. I don't like the way the puzzle is starting to fit together.

Tula, Racquel's baby sister, has come for me. She says a boat with lavender sails was approaching! Could It be? Could Nova Meniere have arrived? Be still my heart! And God, let her be in a good mood.

Will write soon,

You ARE my little porcupine!

Jackie

June 30

Sheriff Beebus McCloud (HA!)
Town Hall
Ludens Bend, Alabama

Beebus,

Listen, you raunchy. white trash bastard, my family gave your mother the roof over her head and the very food in your ungrateful mouth when your failure of a drunk old man (I won't dignify him with the title of "father") ran away from Ludens Bend on your third birthday.

Do you, by any chance, remember the first pair of shoes you ever wore? Do you remember the Christmas presents under your tree? Do you remember who paid to bury your mother and who, before that, kept her in the most expensive nursing home in the county?

Well, asshole, it was Luden money that made your life, and I promise, it's Luden money that can take it right back.

Do I sound a smidgin perturbed? Guess why.

Shape up or get ready for a coming out party like the county has never seen.

Yours.
Guess who?

Down from the Dog Star

July 1

Junior Wulmothe
Wulmothe Manor
Trimble Hill Road
Ludens Bend, Alabama

Dear Junior,

Do you remember anything odd about Nova? I mean REALLY odd. Not just the way she looked. You once said she looked like an anorectic flamingo in a bad trench coat. I am still a member of the "can't be too rich or thin" school. Despite the unkind things most people said about Nova's appearance, I thought she was grand.

Even when she was on the very bottom, and eked out a living catching snails for the petit bistros on the streets of Paris, she always had time for me. When she was living in that horrid attic room, she made space for both you and me. When she finally made the big time, all I could do was cheer.

No, I never discovered how she made her money. It happened when you and I were cruising the Mediterranean on that Greek freighter. Do you remember the captain's monkey? Remember how the little fellow would tease me by biting me and then running up the radar antenna? Remember how delicious he was in that soup I made? Those sailors would eat anything.

Now, MY memories of our last day with Nova may be a shade different than your or her memories, and for both our goods, I think we should, rather than spread discord and confusion, tastefully coordinate the tale.

This is what happened: Nova awoke very groggy, with slurred speech and possibly, a very high fever. We (you and I) carried her in our own four hands to a hospital where the DOCTORS insisted that she stay. It was the DOCTORS who took the prototype panty hose into custody. You and I were captured by the authorities and the rest you should have no problem remembering correctly.

Do you Understand? I don't know what Nova has become, but I've had three spooky communiques from the woman, and I'm prepared for anything.

I thought she had arrived a couple a days ago, but it was a just a scare. Tula came to tell me that a boat was at the dock, a boat with Lavender sails and a creamy white hull. It sounded as though it could have been Nova, but to me it just didn't seem dramatic enough an entrance.

It was the Japanese. They are frantic for a piece of Cemetery Golf. They want to invest so badly they risked the piranha, the quicksand, the cannibals, all the things that keep sane men away. They offered me millions for a tiny percentage. Thank God I took out a patent on the concept.

I said "No!" to the Japanese and they seemed really miffed. They made no threats, but with my superb ability to read body language (an ability no doubt acquired from years of cruising crotches in the closing circle at meetings) I knew what they were up to. I sent them on their way and even gave them a royal Gungari escort party, with a map to get them back to the coast.

My Gungari friends returned, two days later, with a lot of unusual cameras, and bellies that were sticking far further out than usual. They were hungry again, a few hours later.

Junior, keep alert. With Neva Jean, the CIA, the Japanese, the police, the goats, an unbalanced LZ, Sister Tara Wilcox — and now according to Sister Amy, the aliens — all milling about, and God only knows in what relationships, we must be cautious.

Speaking of the aliens, is it true that Peanut belched at Sheriff Beebus and removed the sheriff's right ear and both eyebrows? I'd give anything to have Peanut here, with me. I would strongly advise you to make fast friends with this glorious dog. He could be very helpful to you some day.

Down from the Dog Star

Junior, with all the confusion going on here, I'm tempted just to come home. I could bring Jerry, Bonnie, and a few of my Gungari friends might be lured to come along for the ride.

And now Nova. You and I both know how unpredictable she can be.

By the way, I got a really tacky note from Neva Jean. She said to make sure that you were buried face up at Cemetery Golf or we'd lose a lot of golf balls forever. The same might be said of her, only that we must make sure that she's buried on her stomach.

Enough cattiness. At times it seems life will go on forever. Sometimes it doesn't seem important to stop and smile at someone I know, because they are familiar, and therefore, they are devalued in my mind.

But Junior, one story ends and another story begins. It has always been so and will always be so. I would like each new story to be a little brighter, a little kinder.

Can't wait for you to meet Bonnie,

KISS KISS,

Jackie

July 14

Mr. Don Johnstone
1717 Horsecollar Lane,
Phoenix, Arizona

Hi, Don,

I may be seeing you soon. I hope so. I do so need to get home and take up the reins of my golf course. It is in good hands, but any enterprise profits from the owner's presence.

Also, I want to get up to Kentucky to see my buddy Stephanie. Bill, her husband, was in a terrible accident involving his Harley and a 240-volt extension cord attached to the Harley's seat by their youngest child, Logan.

Then again Blaire, their oldest child, a ravishing teeny-bopper, may have it in for me. One dark night, when she was a bit younger, I dressed up like a dancing bear, and surprised her in the back yard. The costume consisted of a large bear mask made from a grocery sack (Steffie said it looked more like a werewolf), Steffie's purple fur coat, and Bill's big, black leather gloves, which I wore on my feet.

We had expected Blaire to giggle, but she nearly died of fright. So I need to watch my back around the child.

Steffie and I plan to drive over to the college to see Professor Carlilse, the world's leading expert on pawpaws. Great Grandfather Luden once developed a cure for the blind staggers using the pulp of the pawpaw fruit. After taking it, his son, Laramie — who was a raging alcoholic — never drank alcohol again. He did, however, become so addicted to the pawpaw extract that he never managed to leave Quarter Pine, or for that matter, his bedroom again. Side effects, side effects . . .

Down from the Dog Star

After meeting with Dr. Carlilse, we will drive to the World Convention of NA. I will see a lot of friends. And of course the exquisite, though kleptomaniacal, Miss Penny will speak. Penny needs me. I am afraid, unless I am there, she will simply sink into the same old blah blah story that we always tell when we speak: "What it was like, how I got here, what it's like now." I have a special costume for her, and I believe, if we're lucky, my friend, Nova Meniere, will be there to help coordinate it all.

After World, I will ride with Penny back to Phoenix. Either in her truck or in an ambulance. Lynda tells me the catapult is becoming less accurate with age.

How's Lynda's escort service doing? I understand that Muley has really been attracting a lot of business. What did you mean by "Put it under your arm and giggle"?

My friend, Jerry, showed me an interesting trick involving ten silver dollars, and an unusual way to support them. You'll like Jerry. He's developing a nice sense of humor.

Racquel, the chief's wife, is talking about sunspots again. Every time she sees sunspots she doses me with some mixture of herbs that puts me under for hours. I'm gonna fool her this time. Knowing where she keeps the mixture, I'm pulling a switch. I want to see what happens when she has me doped.

And I think that that is what it amounts to, Don. Evidence is stacking up that says the Gungaris are acting in collusion with somebody to keep me in the dark. It involves the airfield, and, I believe, the Whackazoid-D. Last time she slipped me my "Sleepy Time Medicine," as she calls it, when I awoke, I noticed that the bales of orange powder, which the Gungaris had been warehousing, were gone. I drifted out to the airfield and observed a burned circle in its center, and a large pile of Uncle Wooley's cigarillos.

No sign yet of Nova. Our fingers are crossed.

I've been talking to Jerry about returning to Quarter Pine with me. I think we've done all that we can do for the Gungaris.

LZ wrote and told me that the Atlanta Fire Commando Rescue Team had explored the Wulmothe Manor sinkhole. Supposedly, there was nothing in it but a few animal droppings and lots of tiny hoof prints.

Neither Jimmy Pierson's body, nor any charred remains, were found. You realize, of course, that this means I can come home.

Until I get definite confirmation of this from Helen, Mother, and at least three Church Ladies, I am staying here. Not that LZ would play any little tricks on me. I trust him completely, but . . .

Racquel is down at the video shack picking up a movie. Her trashy, younger sister is with her, so this is a good time to exchange her knock-out drops for something drug free.

You know I miss you.

Jackie K

July 26

Sister Amy Grant
General Delivery,
Ludens Bend, Alabama

Dear Sister Amy,

I wanted to write and thank you for all the lovely things you sent.

As always, the flip-flops are not only welcome, but also needed badly. The Gungaris are making remarkable progress along the road to freedom. We can only thank Brother Jerimiah for his constant work. I am doing my best to help him in his ministry and I felt so honored to officially be made his assistant.

Is the church moving along? You know, I am sure, that we at Quarter Pine will always be there to support you in your projects.

I never gossip, or even listen when Satan tries to speak (just like two of the three monkeys!) but I would surely like to hear more about Sister Tara Wilcox and her brush with prison. I understand, that through some odd computer glitch, she was kept for six months at the Livingston Women's Correctional Facility, after taking the message of the Lord in to the inmates. Is it true that the guards found a file, a hand grenade, and forty feet of rope in her flannel-board supplies?

And is it also true that Sister Ling-Ling was the one who packed those supplies? Personally, I like the flannel board. It's very appropriate for the little children in church. It tells the story in ways the kids can understand and enjoy. If you want a dog to take its medicine, sometimes you have to put a dollop of peanut butter on it.

I'm not sure, however, how useful it is to women in solitary confinement.

I understand that Sister Tara made the best of her prison experience. She uses it for a whole new lecture series. Sister Vernette told me that Sister Tara got a big appliance box from the dumpster, cut slits in it, to look like a jail cell, and combines her prison experience with the story of "Daniel in the Lions' Den."

I support her completely, but it might be confusing, to the children, to see her cross-dressing in a costume, mixing ancient biblical garb (a big felt bathrobe), a crew cut, tattoos, and an orange prison jump suit.

It was a touch of brilliance on your part, however, to tie a mop head around Peanut's neck and have him play the part of the lion. How long did it take Peanut to learn to walk after he lost his leg?

You know, Sister Amy, I don't open up to very many people. If you don't already know me, it's not likely that you're going to. But you know me.

It was your house to which I always ran when things got too horrible for me to stand. It was your lap I cried into, when the kids had thrown just one too many rocks at me. When they screamed sissy, or queer, till I thought I would die, it was your house in which I hid. So you know me.

I put the picture you sent me, of you and Peanut, in a gold locket. I wear it around my neck and always will. Thank you.

Enough emotion. I want to hear the real story behind "The Great Cavity Miracle." (No, not Neva Jean's cavity. Nothing will fill that.) I want to hear about Sister Macey and her teeth.

This is what I know so far: Sister Macey had awful, black cavities across the front of her mouth. I never understood why she didn't get them fixed. Since we got that jackass of a president out of Washington, got our man in and passed socialized medical and dental care, she could have had them fixed for free. Maybe she's afraid of doctors.

The way I hear it, she stood up during "Praise-the-Lord-and-Shame the-Devil" time at church, and claimed that the Lord had filled her cavities with Jewels!

Now this brings up an interesting thought. We aren't allowed to wear jewelry, and we constantly testify about how we don't want or need wealth or gold and silver. Then how come we have songs singing about mansions over the hilltop, and streets paved with gold, and wearing crowns in heaven? If jewelry is such a no-no, how come it was just fine and dandy for Sister Macey to look as though she'd had breakfast, lunch AND dinner at Tiffany's?

I understand that Reverend Cooper called her up to the podium and had her speak a few minutes on healing and salvation. Her teeth sparkled and glittered like a Miss Alabama tiara. The audience was in the palm of her hand and she was about to be made a Saint of God, when the sound system began to act peculiar. There was a blinding flash of light! I heard that Sister Macey was blasted to the floor and was out cold for at least an hour.

It appears that Sister Macey had stuffed her cavities with bits of scrunched up, colored tin foil. While crying, slobbering, and in general, putting on the kind of show dearly loved in the Third Church of God Delivered, she shorted out the microphone with these copious bodily secretions.

She made an incredible comeback. She said the Lord had changed the jewels to tinfoil to punish her for the sin of pride. Since she probably knows more dirt on the other church ladies than anybody else in Ludens Bend, they bought the story.

But you know, Sister Amy, and I believe this with all my heart, unless we relax our policies a touch, our church doors will eventually close forever. I can see the rationale for some of them, but not to be allowed to wear jewelry and makeup? This will chase our young people right out the door. We must keep up with the world or we will vanish.

I'm sorry Peanut has been ill, but throwing up is not such a big deal to a dog. A long time ago, before dogs came into man's houses, a mother dog would catch something, eat a lot of it, take it home, and regurgitate part of it for her pups. Dogs did not have hands in which to carry food to their babies, so they developed this technique. Their digestive system is very different from ours.

Enclosed is packet of leaves. The Gungaris use a tea made from this to tonic their dogs when the dogs look ill. Steep one leaf in a bowl of warm water and give it to him each morning.

Yes, the Gungaris have dogs. They are treated like family members. They have their own dishes, their own beds, and are honored above all other animals.

My leopard, Bonnie, loves dogs. She likes to lie on the ground, in the evening, when we sit around the community fire to sing story songs, and let the pups roll about on her. She teases them with her tail. She'll tap a puppy on the head with her tail, and then jerk it away, so that the dog doesn't see what tickled it. I think Bonnie would like some babies of her own, but she might be a little young, yet. I will close now. I need to find a nice ripe coconut. Here is the recipe for a good sun screen: take one cup of clarified peccary fat, one half cup of reduced coconut milk (boil the milk until about the consistency of cream cheese), mix together and chill. This screen keeps me from burning, but lets me turn a lovely shade of gold.

Yes, I am still a little vain. But I really like me. I have dropped all that weight, my muscles are rock hard, and I manage to maintain my blonde hair with a very effective bleach the Gungaris make from plants. (Now that's our little secret. I would only trust you with the fact that I am not a totally, natural beauty!)

It's hard to believe that Brunetta is out of high school and about to enter nursing school. Mother's promise will certainly hold good. That girl maintained an A average all through junior and senior high school, and we, at Quarter Pine, will make sure she has any moneys that she needs to get her degree.

Love,

Jackie

Down from the Dog Star

August 4

Junior Wulmothe
Wulmothe Manor
Trimble Hill Road
Ludens Bend, Alabama

Junior,

I'll be brief. Things are moving quickly.

Last night, I exchanged Racquel's knock-out drops for some mango nectar. In the past, whenever she mentioned sunspots, I ended up sleeping for days. I am just now tuning in to how crafty she can be.

This is what happened: Racquel brought what she thought was her sleeping potion, and I drank it. Feigning sleep, I waited for the camp to empty.

I tracked the Gungaris to the airstrip, waiting for a plane, or perhaps a super-copter, to appear. What actually came, was a saucer. That's right, an extraterrestrial craft. It was big, Junior. It was easily the size of two football fields. It was white, saucer shaped, and perfectly featureless.

It hovered a few feet above the ground, and a small ramp descended from its belly. The Gungaris carried bale after bale of jungle pharmaceuticals into the ship, and unloaded box after mysterious box.

And then Uncle Wooley and Nova Meniere strutted down the ramp! That's right! Nova Meniere is somehow involved in this jungle drug scam.

I sneaked back to camp, put myself to bed, and pretended to sleep. Actually, as soon as my head hit the pillow, I passed out from sheer exhaustion. Today seems normal. I will explore a bit more tonight.

Pray for me, Junior,

Jackie

PART THREE

QUARTER PINE

TWIN BED

When you said
That the floor was too hard
For my soft bones,
Come up here
To my twin bed,
I wondered what message you were sending.
When I awoke in the night
My arm around your waist
I jumped in fear,
Wondering what message you were receiving.
My friend,
I was dreaming of amber,
A string of yellow amber beads
As soft and buttery
As the flesh above your heart.
The next morning you smiled and said,
"I knew your intentions,
And it gave you comfort....
Someday you may know me."

August 6

Stephanie Cost
The Willows Treatment Center
Sprongville, Kentucky

Hello Steff,

How's treatment? Co-dependency treatment is very popular, but you're the least co-dependent person I've ever met. Just the opposite.

Excellent documentation for this might be the time you left Bill in jail for six days, because paying his bail would have kept you from tanning and getting manicures for a month.

Another memorable occasion was when your mom was stuck in Lexington, in a blizzard without a coat, and going to get her would have caused you to miss the Movie of the Week on television.

It's OK. If you need a little rest, label it anything you please.

I guess you've already seen the headlines and, of course, my interview with Barbara Walters.

Did you ever dream such things would happen to me when you met me, five years ago, at that convention? No, I never expected to go quite this far, but we've often heard people say that if they had made a list of what they wanted from recovery, and compared it to what they got, they would have short changed themselves.

The media doesn't have the full story on what happened with the aliens. The one most responsible for our finally contacting them is Peanut, Sister Amy Grant's hound.

Let me explain. As you know from my last letter, I had tracked the Gungaris to the landing field, and discovered the ship.

Yes!

The aliens have been trading with the Gungaris for years, taking bales of strange, orange powder, which, at the same time, Dr. Wulmothe was testing for its anti-depressant properties. Dr. Wooley got it from Jerry, via Sister Vernette.

That night, I made another exploratory journey, but this time I ran straight into the arms of six little men, with large heads, big, blue eyes, and overbites.

They floated me back to their ship and strapped me to a cold, hard table. I knew for certain that I was about to be used to create an alien-human baby.

While removing my clothing, they discovered the locket containing the picture of Peanut and Sister Amy.

Now, Steffie, I know I have often scoffed at newcomer men who come in covered in gold chains and rings in the shape of hood ornaments. From time to time, I have commented on the women who come into the rooms of NA with their vaginas pinned to their shoulders like brightly colored corsages, but, for once, wearing a trifle too much jewelry was useful.

The sleek creatures popped open the locket and out leaped the picture of Peanut, the Alien Snapper.

Peanut has a powerful reputation among the aliens. I was released, and given an honored position in the ship.

The aliens have become very useful to me at Cemetery Golf. They're about the only thing that can keep the Japanese away.

Slow drowsy day. I need a nap.

The ever watchful,

Jackie

Down from the Dog Star

August 8

Noland "Junior" Wulmothe
Building C, Room #238
Clarion Sanitarium
Tuscaloosa, Alabama

Dearest Junior,

Sorry you're back at Clarion. Along with this letter, I'm sending you a big box of goodies. You'll find, inside, a butterscotch, pineapple upside down cake. I made it myself. Don't lose my Tupperware! It's hard to get this particular cake carrier. Helen sent the ham. She baked it in that honey/clove sauce you like so much. Your Aunt Minnie (Mom, to me, although at present we aren't speaking, thus, "Your Aunt Minnie") sends the fuzzy slippers.

It's just awful without you, Junior. I miss you.

If you are attempting to hide from Nova, I can honestly assure you that there is no need for such action.

In the first place, Nova has forgiven you for your unsuccessful attempt to have her locked away by the Parisian Sisters of Mercy. If it wasn't for that, she would never have met the true love of her life.

"Who might that be?" you ask.

"Doctor Wulliam Wulmothe." I answer. Yes, Junior. Uncle Wooley has been carrying on a passionate secret affair, all these years, with Nova Meniere. It seems that he was doing a psych rotation at the Sisters of Mercy, in Paris, when you attempted to put Nova away and steal her pantyhose concept.

You may think that you remember that I had some part in that affair, but you must be realistic. I was hardly old enough to even walk then, much less carry a grown (though stylishly thin) woman down six flights of stairs, across five city blocks, and into a hospital.

No, Junior, I fear that Neva Jean may be right about your failing mentation. I had nothing to do with it. Nothing at all.

So, Nova is ensconced at Wulmothe Manor with Uncle Wooley. The Gungaris are busy working at Cemetery Golf. The aliens (they prefer to be called "The Friends") are fitting nicely into county life. Since they resemble the product of generations of inbreeding, and as they have a superb grasp of the unknown tongue, they are right at home here.

It's too bad that you weren't here for the grand opening of Cemetery Golf. There was some controversy at first about who would do what, but the event was so large, everybody got to participate.

Mother, Helen, Uncle Wooley, the Church Ladies, Jerry Flem, Racquel, the Chief, three aliens, and, of course, I sat in the review stand.

Beebus escorted the lovely Nova and the glamorous Neva out onto the first tee, and there Neva Jean broke a bottle of Yoo-Hoo over the nose of the first golf cart to leave the club house. I must say Junior, that although severely impaired, you do have brilliant ideas. Designing golf carts to look like tiny black hearses! What can we say! And your new idea of Ice Cream with Hearsey Sauce is right over the top.

Nova threw out the first golf ball of the season. Mother and Helen have been working for months stenciling (with sister Vernette's help) tiny skulls on the golf balls they keep finding. The first five hundred are signed, and will be sold, at hefty prices, as collectors' items.

I had feared conflict between Nova and Neva Jean. Was there room, in Ludens Bend, for two such Divas? I am amazed at how well the two complement each other. According to Nova, Neva Jean is a fashion "DO," not a fashion "DON'T." Nova is in Hog Heaven. Neva Jean has turned her on to Wal-Mart. I fear that we shall all have to reevaluate our closets.

Speaking of closets, thank God for them! Some people owe a debt to society to stay in! I could give you a list, but I'll just talk about Thomas Blaylock and his red dog.

No, I won't talk about his little red dog. Suffice it to say, that while

Down from the Dog Star

in the Amazon, Thomas acquired a darling Chow/Retriever mix. Tula, his great love, gave it to him as a wedding gift. This wedding came about rather quickly, on the mother ship, actually. It seems that when Thomas found out we were returning to Alabama, he got real straight, real fast. Tula had been pursuing him hot and heavy. So . . . A marriage of convenience? Who knows the truth. All I know is that I get awfully tired of having everybody under the sun come to me asking if he's straight or gay. I don't have an answer. He looks happy. Tula looks happy, and most importantly, their little red dog looks happy.

Cemetery Golf is getting too large for me to handle. I'm grateful the Friends are pitching in to help. I'd much rather sell them shares rather than some foreign country. The aliens are planning to take Cemetery Golf galaxy wide. As soon as the news media picked up the story about me and the Friends, they also picked up on Cemetery Golf.

Golf courses all over the planet are closing for lack of business. Humans on this planet see a better way. If they want to survive, they must convert and, of course, we hold the patent. If it were not for the Friends supercomputer and communications technology, I wouldn't be able to move so quickly.

You might be wondering what the Friends have been up to all these years. I can explain some of that.

There are many groups of aliens. They are related, but by no means do they all have the same agendas.

The more sinister of these people are, indeed, doing research to develop human/alien hybrid babies. It is rumored that LZ is one of these experiments gone bad.

A lot of aliens are just tourists taking in local color.

Our batch of Friends are traders. They've been coming to Earth for many years, dealing with the Gungari. The orange powder that Uncle Wooley was testing as a medication, the Friends use as a spice.

If you remember your history, you may recall that hundreds of years ago, explorers sailed all over the planet looking for pepper. Same with the Friends. They get tremendously high prices for the spices they take from Earth.

And what do they give the Gungari in Exchange?

Celestial Flip-Flops, of course.

Aunt Bessie is giving her first party in over fifteen years. We're all so excited. Oh, how we used to love to eat at the Wulmothes!

By the by, guess who's back. Your special friend Ronnie! He dumped that cheap floozy somewhere near Macon, Georgia (that's HIS story), and returned to the bosom of The Tender Tendrils.

It's entirely up to you, Junior. He says he's waiting for you to come home, but if you ask me, there's plenty of room left in the sinkhole.

We'll all be down to see you Sunday. No, don't worry about Nova. You know she loves you best of all. And she never gossips. Or says anything tacky.

I love you and miss you, buddy,

Jackie

August 18

Penny Warshack
22 Castlerock,
Scottsdale, Arizona

Dearest Penny,

I spoke to my surgeon in Phoenix, yesterday, about Nelson's eye (eyes?) and the good doctor thinks he can help your friend.

As you know, when I first came to Phoenix, I was practically blind. Do you remember those glasses I use to wear? Even my contacts were about three inches thick. Dr. Perk said, that as long as Nelson has a shred of eyeball left, his new laser-vacuum technique should be able to restore Nelson's sight.

Were you being facetious when you said that his guide dog ran away because it thought Nelson was stalking it? Perhaps Nelson could get a spot of counseling.

You were asking about Cemetery Golf. It's gone world-, and now, galaxy-wide. Yes, the Friends have taken it to several civilized planets in other solar systems, and it's thriving.

Cemetery Golf is allowing me to fulfill my greatest dream. I will elucidate. The Friends tell us that those Egyptian temples were actually animal shelters for dogs and cats that had no homes. That led me to fantasize a bit about our homeless animals here, in this part of the universe. This is how 1-800-DOG-STAR was born.

We're socking most of the U.S. monetary returns from Cemetery Golf into a charitable trust designed to drive a giant animal shelter.

We'll buy five hundred acres of land, build shelters, hire vets, and what I call "play therapists," for the pooches and kitties, and open our help line. If anybody in the state has a puppy or kitten, or any kind of animal they no longer want, all they'll have to do is call 1-800- DOG-STAR, and we'll go get it.

I believe we'll have trouble keeping animals. Everybody will want a Dog Town pet!

If Nelson's guide dog shows up, I'll let you know.

Here's some exciting news: Aunt Bessie Wulmothe is giving a party! The first party at Wulmothe Manor since her goats vanished, fifteen long years ago.

I believe part of the reason she's coming back into society is that the peccaries have given her spirits a big boost.

Racquel and her husband, The Chief, brought a pack of peccaries back to Ludens Bend from the Amazon. They breed like wildfire and so practically everybody in the county has one or two. Aunt Bessie fell deeply in love with them. She now has around thirty of the creatures. The grounds of Wulmothe, which had finally begun to prosper after the goats' disappearance, are once again ravaged. But Junior doesn't mind the peccaries, or perhaps he simply doesn't want to make any more animal enemies.

If you've never seen peccaries, I'll describe them for you.

Peccaries are about the size of a Cocker Spaniel. They rather resemble a pecan in color and shape, thus, their name. Their fur is a rich brown, with red, cream and black stripes running down their backs. They have tiny hooves, long floppy ears, and the females have pouches, in which they carry their young, or anything else that may interest them. In the jungle, we ate them, used them for watch-pets, and sometimes trained them to do tricks. They're darling! I expect them to become as popular as pizza! They certainly revived Aunt Bessie Wulmothe.

Wulmothe Manor is the jewel in the crown, so to speak, of Ludens Bend, of Jefferson County, perhaps the entire South. Until the goats vanished and Aunt Bessie got testy, tour buses from all over the nation would come to see the estate.

The house was built in the seventeen hundreds by crafty, Norwegian immigrants, imported by Aunt Bessie's Greatgrandfather, the original

Wulliam Wulmothe. This is how LZ's ancestors came to this country.

The house took nearly fifty years to complete. The raw materials came, for the most part, from the state of Alabama.

Wulmothe Manor is built of nearly indestructible granite, taken from the great quarries on the northern slopes of Sand Mountain, Alabama. LZ's staunch forefathers ripped the stone from the Earth, floated it down the Warrior River on rafts made of pig bladders, and then carried it, by ox sled, through the virgin forests of Jefferson County, to its present site.

From the foot of the massive mountain range which divides Alabama into equal thirds, beams of oak were harvested. (This took place before the glacier of '47 wiped out the timber business in northern Alabama.)

The glass factories of Huntsville produced the stained glass for its windows and the prisms for its chandeliers. The house is a monstrous, square, gray pile of stone. Its corridors, basements and sub-basements go on for what seems like miles.

Thomas Blaylock once delivered some eggs to Aunt Bessie and was lost for three weeks in the house.

Many of the rooms are closed. Most of the windows are shuttered. Junior and I have often talked of bringing the old house back to life, but Junior has told me stories of how, in the past, the place had a habit of sucking the joy out of anybody who cared too much about it. Desire is Pain . . .

Enclosed is a snap shot of the Gungaris, Bonnie, some Aliens and myself, at a convention. Fun in the Sun will never be the same.

I must run, precious. Between the golf course and Dog Town, my days are pretty hectic.

BUT! BUT!! BUT!!! Here's a bit of trash that I can't leave for later. I was browsing through Nova Meniere's jewelry box yesterday, (no, I was not snooping. I was merely looking for the perfect ornament to set off Nova's classic profile for the new Dog Town brochure. Nova has agreed to be the spokesperson for the agency), when I came upon an old locket. The initials on the locket are N.J.W. Inside, was a picture of two little girls. Twin girls. And a lock of strange, pale brown fur, very similar to the Afghan fur given to me by Helen.

Neva Jean Wulmothe.

Nova Jean Wulmothe?

Could Nova Meniere actually be the lost twin of Wulmothe Manor? If so, will she and Uncle Wooley be persecuted and ostracized for their incestuous love affair?

Only time will tell. Time, and the DNA test I'm secretly having run on some hair samples I lifted from those two.

It may come in handy.

Love you, punkalicious!
Jackie.

Down from the Dog Star

August 22

Becky Bright
610 Lamont Lane
Phoenix, Arizona

Dear Becky,

It is evening, here at Quarter Pine. Cool and damp. We had a really bad drought, and some of our people lost a lot of their crops. As soon as the fields of produce were safely dead, it began to rain. It rained for two weeks, and anything that wasn't nailed down washed away. The Friends tell us that the planet is in deep trouble, that global warming isn't something a hundred years away, that it's here now.

People seem to have the attitude that, since we've made contact, and since the Friends are not hostile, our many problems can be solved with the flip of an alien switch.

Not so. The Friends say they can do very little to help. This is one problem that they've seen time and time again. Only by drastic changes in all our lifestyles can anything be accomplished.

My good friend Eric, the captain of the saucer that brought us all home, tells me that it may be too late.

"Captain" and "he" are not accurate words for what Eric is. There are no actual leaders, and gender lines are very complicated. These people communicate through body language and thought. They act as one, and they're not willing to give us any juicy tricks of technology to save our collective asses. The best way to describe the group that I've met is to call them observer-traders.

They want spice. The main thing they have to offer, in trade, is philosophy.

You see, their technology has nothing in common with ours. They're more spirit than matter.

Electricity? Atomics? Iron? Oh, no . . . . Their ships are powered by forces that have nothing to do with our dimension. They're vastly old, Becky. They've seen it all. They say our candles are flickering. We may have a few millennia left. And it's not a definite thing.

Politely, I tell Eric to get screwed (in a kind and loving way.) I believe it's totally our choice. Something negative about our Eric.

Other groups of Friends have been transplanting earth people to other places for generations. That's nice.

Eric is a good companion. He's helped me to get a better insight into my feelings about Honey's death. He even offered to clone her from a clump of her fur that I kept. But he advised against it. I have learned to pay attention to his suggestions.

Bonnie is doing well. She fits in nicely here on the farm. I was concerned that neighbors would be afraid of her, but we have so many other freaky things going on that, I guess, they're just too busy to notice one little leopard. Of course, the most fascinating event on the calendar is the open-house Aunt Bessie Wulmothe is preparing. Mysterious trucks from Atlanta, bales and bundles from UPS, a new staff hired from the people around Ludens Bend . . . just getting the place open and fresh again will be a project in itself.

Sister Vernette has been hired as housekeeper for the Manor. She told me, in confidence, that it's difficult to keep workers. New things disappear, old things reappear.

The stone goats, rampant, flanking the bronze entrance doors, seem to be looking in one direction one day and in another the next.

And people get lost. People get lost simply going from one room to another. Time doesn't always work quite right there. One can enter Wulmothe at nine AM and leave there at seven AM of the same day.

And people forget. People forget things that they need to remember, and they remember things that they have spent years trying to forget. They remember things that their parents and their grandparents forgot.

I've been to Wulmothe Manor countless times. Junior and Neva

Down from the Dog Star

Jean and I spent our childhoods playing hide and seek in that dusty, old house, and sometimes, odd, inconsequential things would happen, but nothing like this.

Aunt Bessie just grins and says that the house is grumpy, that it's waking from a nap and that it would like to remain asleep.

Eric went with me once to take some roses to Aunt Bessie from Mother, and he said he definitely would not go back.

But Aunt Bessie said the house will calm down in time for her party. Junior and I have been spending hours in the library with Nova, designing the invitations.

I must run. LZ is picking me up for a meeting. I feel zingy and really need one.

I wish you were here. It's peaceful tonight. Mother and Helen are sitting on the back porch having their altar. Every night they read a chapter from the Bible that belonged to Grandmother Luden. They discuss it, sing a hymn and say a prayer.

No snakes, though. No snakes.

See you in the fall,

Jackson

September 2

Stephanie Cost
6465 Tiverton Court
Louisville Kentucky

Hey Steffie!

Your python returned. How nice! I was never really comfortable with reptiles until you desensitized me.

Sister Vernette always kept her snakes to herself. She would take them to services in a wicker laundry hamper, get them out, and do her thing up on stage, carefully keeping the other members of the church at a safe distance. She always said that this was strictly for spiritual reasons. Now we know that she just didn't want anybody to get too close a look at her pets.

Remember your first snake? It was a red corn snake. It escaped from its cage and we thought the cats had gotten it. Do you remember the white mouse that you had planned to feed it? With no corn snake, the mouse became one of the kids' pets.

About two months after the snake vanished, you found it while you were cleaning Blaire's room. It had been living quietly all around the house and had about tripled in size. What did that snake eat for those two months? You're a pretty good housekeeper, and I've never seen bugs or anything like that in your house. It's a mystery.

How's Bill? I called the other night to see how you all were. The news said a tornado had destroyed a lot of Louisville and I was scared it had gotten you guys. There were pictures, on the news, of block after block of houses that had been swooped away.

Bill sounded a bit amused at my concern. He said that the tornado

154   *Down from the Dog Star*

had not come anywhere near your neighborhood. What a relief!

So the marriage is still working? You needed somebody and so did the kids. And Bill needed you and the kids. You know, I never told you this, because my pride and stubborn nature would not let me speak the truth, but I was pretty jealous of Bill. I didn't think you would have room in your heart for me, after you married. I guess I was wrong.

Aunt Bessandra Wulmothe is preparing a party. She hasn't entertained for fifteen years. She closed most of the house down and was rarely seen in Ludens Bend. When Junior got rid of her goats, I think it took a lot of her joy of life away.

Now, she has peccaries. We brought a few back from the Amazon and they've been breeding like crazy. Aunt Bessie has a flock of thirty. They're a lot more civilized than goats. They can be kept as pets, they can be housebroken, and Aunt Bessie had Cleatus McCloud build a swinging pet entrance into her kitchen door. The peccaries scoot in and out of the house at will, just like puppies. One of the best thing about peccaries is that they hate snakes and are good at keeping them away.

We never had a problem with poisonous reptiles until the Driving Club was built across the road from Quarter Pine.

A construction company bought the range of hills that used to overlook our farm, blasted the top off the mountains and extracted all the coal from the ground. They then used the money that they made from the coal to build their golf course.

They didn't know, or didn't care, that they were destroying an ancient Cherokee Indian burial ground.

Quarter Pine is built on what was once their camp grounds. When we used to plow, we would usually find arrow heads and spear points. We never felt badly about living on an old Indian home place. My people have always respected and cared for this land. We never over-planted and we rotated our crops.

Blowing up the graves of the Indians is an entirely different matter. When the Driving Club opened, unpleasant things began to happen. Certain snakes, such as Rattlers and Copper Heads, like to live in the hills, where it is sunny and dry. Other snakes, mainly Water Moccasins and Blue Snakes, prefer to live along creek bottoms. With their mountains blasted away, the hill-loving snakes had nowhere to live. They migrated down to the river lands.

Quarter Pine and Wulmothe Manor are neighbors. Our western pastures snuggle right up against Wulmothe's eastern pasture land. Our combined northern borders are defined by a stream named Canecutter Creek. Our land lies between the driving Club and this river land, right in the path the snakes had to take to find new housing.

For the last few years, our land has been a snake freeway. I'm grateful to say that nobody, and none of our livestock, has been bitten, but we still feel a touch nervous with all these homeless critters creeping about. This is why we love the peccaries. They use their sharp hoofs and leathery snouts to kill stray serpents.

The man who owned the construction company that desecrated the burial grounds is, so far, the only snake-fatality.

It was at the opening of the Driving Club. He knocked a ball into the rough, and while he was scrabbling around searching for it was bitten by an eight-foot Water Moccasin.

The Water Moccasin is the most deadly snake in Alabama. It is never seen far away from water, and so it was thought odd that this snake was on a hill top on a hot summer day.

But the Driving Club prospered. I would never have thought that a golf course could survive out here in the country. The "good old boys," as we call us, took right to it. In the evenings, Mother and I used to see them, when we sat out on the front veranda. We could see their golf carts rolling up and down the hills on the horizon, like tiny, cartoon-figure ants. We would hear them hoot and holler and give Rebel yells. Beer is as important to these boys as are their golf clubs. The drunker they got, the louder they got, and of course, the more inaccurate they became.

This thrilled Mother and Helen. On a good day when the fellows were really loaded, Mom and Helen could gather phenomenal numbers of golf balls from the sides of the road below the course.

Since Cemetery Golf has become so popular, the Driving Club has lost most of its clientele.

Steffie, its owners have approached us requesting a franchise of Cemetery Golf. Mother, Jerry, Helen and I have talked it over, and we don't think that we're going to sell them one. We don't want to be part of something that further dishonors a burial ground. On the other hand, the Driving Club employed a great many men and women from Ludens Bend.

It's time for our evening walk. Mother, Jerry, Helen, and I go for a long stroll every evening after it cools down. Sometimes we go early in the morning.

Jerry is the first friend I've ever had that Mom approves of. He's living here at Quarter Pine with us. Steff, I may have fallen into the first decent relationship of my life. I really love my friend. He's a decent man. He never tries to control what I do. He's not a jealous person, and he has a life of his own. I guess I'll just have to wait and see.

Speaking of murder, guess who returned to the living. Little Jimmy Pierson is back. He was not killed when he had his unfortunate slip into the sinkhole. He slithered down into the mines and has been lost, underground, all this time. How fitting. He was in pretty bad shape when he emerged, and his hair will never grow back. He says that he lived with the goats and that they took good care of him. He ate what the goats ate, fungus and moss, and occasionally the goats would bring him vegetables that they stole from people's gardens. He says that he can't remember how he got into the mines.

Strictly out of Christian duty, I paid him a visit while he was recovering in the hospital. He reacted strangely, yelling and running around his room, as if in fear. Can't figure it out.

I'm glad he survived, Steffie. He poisoned Honey, but I believe murder would have weighed heavy on my conscience. Eventually.

Yes, I'm laughing with God before he laughs at me.

Now why on Earth would I say that? My HP is pretty neat. My fear is talking. I don't want more surgery, don't want more stainless steel rods and joints in my body. You know, I wanted to be cremated, and had a great NA funeral planned. My friends would do the readings, my sponsor would shout, "He worked the steps," and my ashes would be spread on the parking lot at Denny's.

But Junior told me that Cleatus McCloud would probably use all my steel joints and rods to replace somebody's universal joint.

Jerry is calling. It's time for our walk. Such a gentle, sweet period of time in our lives. Please, may it last.

I love you, sweetie,

Jackie

September 10

Miss Penny Warshack
22 Castlerock
Scottsdale, Arizona

Hi Penny,

The town is agog at the prospect of Wulmothe Manor opening its doors for the first time in fifteen years.

Helen and Mother pitched in by sending Aunt Bessie some of their favorite furniture polish. It's an old, old recipe, very fragrant, and even if it does give a mellow, deep sheen to wood, it's the devil to apply.

Here's how it's made. Save four dozen lemon peels and dry in a warm, shady place. The sun must not touch these peelings. Store them in a cedar box for at least six months. Prepare one pound of bees' wax. Cook gently in a copper pot until the honey and insect larvae have floated to the top. Skim carefully until the wax is clear. Grind the lemon peels in a mortar to the consistency of talcum powder. Slowly mix a half-pint of pure linseed oil with powdered lemon peels. Pass the bees wax through a sieve until it has the shape of angel hair pasta. Knead wax, linseed oil/ lemon peel mixture, and a few drops of clove/geranium oil on a cold marble slab for at least one hour until the mixture is the color and consistency of soft taffy. Divide the polish into twelve equal parts, form into cylinders, and allow to cure in a cool dark place for a couple of months before using.

What's the latest with Nelson? Did Dr. Perk's vacuum/laser procedure help him? You know, Penny, it's none of my business, but with his record, do you think it wise to improve his vision? I mean, really, if his guide dog actually ran away, he can't be all that healthy a human.

You once told me that we tend to attract people as healthy or as unhealthy as we are, so you didn't want to be in a relationship because you didn't want to be with somebody that sick. I love you, Penny.

My disease tells me that if somebody likes me, they can't really be worth much, or they are worth far too much to talk to me. When does it stop chattering? It gets tiresome.

I was talking to Junior the other day, and he said the biggest problem about the party was the guest list. Almost everybody in Ludens Bend is related in some way, and everybody wants to go.

I suggested a formal, sit-down dinner for thirty or so of the elite (me definitely being the elitist), and an open house, dance/buffet afterward.

Junior said there would still be feelings hurt. It may turn out to be, simply, a ball, so that all feel equal.

Of course, that won't fool anybody. Only people in the deepest denial, or in the rosiest blush of idiocy believe in equality. Some are definitely more equal than others.

Sister Amy Grant is among this category. Ever since her brush with the Aliens, she's been sitting in the catbird seat, indeed. The aliens hired her, at an exorbitant salary, to be a facilitator at their communications seminars.

It turns out that the unknown tongue is actually a lost language similar to Greek, and Sister Grant has the knack of teaching it.

What's interesting is the discovery that if those blue-light-special announcements at K-Mart are recorded, and played backwards, they're perfect Rosetta stones for interpretation. Sister Grant discovered this when she was shopping for a wedding present for one of her granddaughters.

Ever since Peanut bit the alien and saved Sister Amy, he rarely leaves her side. He goes to church with her and sits outside the church window, guarding her from possible harm. He followed her to Wal-Mart one morning. That was a seven-mile trip and, as you know, Peanut only has three legs. He managed to get through the doors of the store and track Sister Amy to the fabric department.

The manager, a fine man who attends church with Sister Amy, tried to expel Peanut from the sacred halls. Sister Amy told him, flatly, that after Peanut tracked her seven miles on three legs, she wasn't about to let him be thrown into the streets. She further threatened to boycott the store if the manager didn't retract his threat at once.

Sister Grant is the matriarch of a widespread, extended family. The manager knew that, if she said the word, Wal-Mart as he knew it would cease to exist. He compromised by allowing Peanut to stay, if he would ride peacefully about the store in the shopping cart.

Peanut LOVED it. It was Nirvana to him. It seemed to be what he had always been searching for. He cruised at eye level with all the fascinating merchandise. Occasionally, he would stick his long, pretty snout into displays of corncurls, or into the cheap, polyester lingerie sets that cause Sister Amy to set her jaw and mutter about immorality and her sixteen-year-old nephew, James Randal, to blush with pagan dreams worthy of de Sade.

When Sister Amy was ready to go home, Peanut refused to jump down from the shopping cart. He cowered in the bottom of the shiny, chrome vehicle, and made pathetic, yammering sounds.

So Sister Amy bought the cart. James Randal loaded it, with Peanut happily ensconced, into the back of his Silverado and took it home.

When Sister Amy got home, she discovered that Peanut had shop-lifted a shiny, lurex bow-tie: peacock blue with strands of silver worked throughout the fabric. She attached it to his collar and it has added a certain continental air to his demeanor.

Peanut sleeps in the shopping cart and, daily, Sister Grant or one of the grand kids can be seen taking him out for an airing.

I must run. I promised Junior that I would help him coordinate an outfit for the gala evening at the Manor.

Penny, you know that I never say cruel things about friends, but Junior is now tipping the scales at three hundred pounds. I can't think of anything to do except maybe get him upholstered.

Helen said that might be too tempting to the goats.

Jerry grinned, and said I was just jealous because Junior was getting so much attention.

Mother suggested that we make him hoop skirts out of some canvas and bamboo that we had left over from decorating the Cemetery Golf Viewing/Equipment Room.

Perhaps I am jealous. Junior and I have the most complex relationship that any two humans could have. And yet, after all the times we have attempted to sabotage, embarrass, or thwart one another, we remain close.

Write and tell me how World went. I just wasn't able to make it. Lynda sent me pictures of you in the costume I sent and, I must say, you looked smashing.

Much Love,

Jackie

Down from the Dog Star

September 10

Dr. Richard Carlilse
University of Southern Kentucky
Department of Horticulture
Old Minway Road
Level, Kentucky

Dear Dr. Carlilse,

We so enjoyed your visit to Ludens Bend. I want to apologize for your nasty run-in with Miss Wulmothe. I also want to deeply apologize for the strip/cavity search Sheriff McCloud inflicted on you at the airport. I had nothing to do with it. But, I must say, I felt hurt and shocked that you would try and smuggle our special strain of pawpaws out of Ludens Bend and back to Kentucky.

Did Neva Jean insert those seeds for you? What a novel way to transport agricultural supplies! Helen said that if you showed your face around here again, she would make sure you carried a bale of hay home the same way.

This may interest you: Junior Wulmothe has developed a new product based on pawpaw extract, coconut milk, and Peccary fat. He calls it "bi-racial sunblock." I believe there's a market. It also makes a tasty party dip.

I'm sorry we won't be seeing you again, but perhaps you should let things cool down around here for a time.

Good luck,

Jackie

September 15

Tony O'Brian
4610 19th Avenue North
Phoenix, Arizona

Hello Tony,

Not such a chipper letter. Some kids, playing down in the bottom-
land, found what was left of Beebus McCloud. He'd been cored like an
apple. The Canecutters aren't animals to be trifled with. Beebus knew
that. Anybody who grew up near the swamp knows not to hunt
Canecutters.

I know you folks out West have never had to deal with a Canecutter.
Even here, in the South, they're rare. A Canecutter can best be compared,
in shape, with a rabbit, but a rabbit weighing over a hundred pounds.
They feed on the vast groves of cane that grow in our bottom lands.
Canecutters have a temperament that has nothing to do with rabbits.
They have the heart and fighting spirit of a lion, stringy muscles, amber-
red eyes, the claws of a cat, and razor-like teeth. These spooky animals are
at home on land and in water. If they were aggressive, we'd be in trouble.
Luckily for us, they just want to be left alone.

But they're tasty and that fool was trying to show off for Neva Jean.
He promised Aunt Bessie a brace of Canecutters for her big party.

I was sitting there with Junior, looking at some old photographs of
Uncle Wooley and Aunt Bessie. The pictures were posed on one of those
big paper moons that they used to use as props at carnivals. Junior and I
were blown away by how truly lovely Aunt Bessie had been. Uncle
Wooley had a mustache and was carrying a big stuffed animal that he
may have won.

Junior and I were involved, true, but we know better than to ever be at ease when Neva Jean is around.

And so there sat Beebus, rattling his spear and shaking his game bag for Neva's (and my) benefit. Aunt Bessie was making sounds of protest that didn't fool anybody. Aunt Bessie is a dear, but nobody has served Canecutter since Greatgrandfather Luden accidentally caught one in a bear trap. The Canecutter destroyed the trap, chewed it right in half, and tracked Gramp Lude back to the farm house.

His alcoholic son, Laramie, happened to be sober (an extremely rare occurrence, according to Mother) and luckily, was on the way out the door with a shotgun. It was quail season and Laramie was going hunting. The Canecutter came creeping around the corner of the house, snuffling the ground in pursuit of my grandpa, and Laramie happened to spot it before it spotted him. It was sheer luck that he was able to kill it before it slaughtered him and the rest of the family. And then, of course, there were weeks of ceremony and sacrifice to appease the Canecutter's relatives.

Although Aunt Bessie knew that she would be sending Beebus to a just about certain death, she did so want her party to be nice.

Neva Jean was sitting on a rose-tinted, tufted, silk ottoman at Sheriff Beebus's feet. She was attempting to portray the Southern Belle that she had been about twenty years ago. Neva was pumping his ego the way a coal-town whore moves her hips on Friday pay-night. She told him how brave and strong he must be, and covertly promised him the rewards of Eden for just one, itsy-bitsy Canecutter.

Junior knows me pretty well. He knew that although Beebus had forced me to the Amazon over Jimmy Pierson's supposed death, and, worse than that, had betrayed my tender feelings by skipping between mine and Neva's beds like the goat that he was, I wouldn't sit still for sending Beebus off into the swamp to please two vain, silly women.

I started to rise from my seat at the card table on which Junior had spread the old photos, and a very odd thing happened. Junior, under the cover of the table, put his hand on my knee, leaned forward with his mouth slightly open and looked quietly into my eyes.

He said nothing. I said nothing. And yet, years of shared pain and bitterness passed between us.

Junior closed his mouth, removed his hand from my knee, and pointed out a picture of Uncle Wooley and some obscure relatives at what appeared to be a Sunday picnic, complete with striped jackets and smart straw hats.

I felt wrapped in sheets of cotton candy. I couldn't have spoken if I had wanted to. The moment was gone and Beebus was good as dead.

The afternoon passed, warm and drowsy, sweet and slow, a bit decayed at the edges, until supper, when Beebus decided to go.

Neva walked him to the door, and Junior and I could see their reflections in the pierpont mirrors that line the entry hall.

She kissed him goodnight. It was a very chaste, almost sisterly kiss, that left Beebus looking puzzled and somehow cheated. She shut the door behind him. I shivered, and felt the hairs on my arms rise when I heard the long, drawn-out rasp of the big, iron bolt being thrust into its socket.

She knew that Junior and I had been watching this last performance, this uncharacteristically gentle peck on the cheek with which she had parted. She paused in the doorway of the dining room, smiled brilliantly at the three of us and said, "I do so hate to kiss the dead."

So Beebus McCloud is no more. He took his old thirty-ought-six deer rifle down to our swamp, a Canecutter jumped him, tore out his guts, and burrowed straight to his still-beating heart before he even had a chance to slam a round into the chamber.

Junior and I have been wrangling, wondering what his last word was. Whose face flashed across the blackening brainpan of his mind before the Canecutters' flat, chisel-like teeth crushed the blood from his heart?

Junior says it was probably Neva Jean's name. Yes, I bet he died cursing her.

But I like to think it was my face he saw outlined against that perfect blue September sky. I hope that he saw the Luden jaw painted in bold, fearless strokes, the Luden eyes, cobalt against blue, the lips . . . the lips. I can't imagine a better sight to take into death. Can you?

Down from the Dog Star

I have to run, buddy. Helen and Mother want me to drive them over to Atlanta today for new funeral dresses.

You haven't written in a while. I hope you're ok. My invitation still stands, you know. Say the word and we'll kill the fatted calf for you. Or something.

Love,

Jackie

September 20

Miss Penny Warshack
22 Castlerock
Scottsdale, Arizona

Hello, Penny,

A cool, dry morning. A perfect day for harvesting the various mints and herbs that go into the making of our Christmas Tea. I write it with capital letters because it is such an important part of the Christmas Season here in Ludens Bend.

We've always drunk the Christmas Tea. Each family has a slightly different recipe and each family is sure their version is the best, but the three central ingredients are always the same and always mixed in the proportion of thirds.

September seems a lot closer to December now-a-days. I can remember, when we were small, how Neva, Junior and I would start, right about now, hinting for our presents and how we would lie, outrageously, to each other about the things we had been promised.

One thing for sure, no matter what, or how much, I got for Christmas, it was never enough. Never enough lights on the tree or holly on the rafters. Never enough eggs at Easter or candy on Halloween. There was never enough love or laughter.

About five years ago, I started this journey towards enoughness. Last night I was driving home from what we call an "eatin' meetin'." This is simply a pot luck dinner my home group throws once a month. There was an empty casserole dish on the seat beside me. It suddenly occurred to me that I was going home and the evening had been enough. This wouldn't sound very profound or amazing to a non-addict, but you know what I mean, don't you? Sometimes, when trying to talk to people who aren't in recovery (and it can be recovery from anything), it feels like we're talking two different languages.

There seems to be basically three topics of conversation in the world. Conversations about stuff, like cars and clothes and houses, conversations about people and what they're up to, or conversations about my feelings, my thoughts, and the way they mesh with the world and those around me.

At one time in my life, dope was my only interest: where I got it, how good or bad it was, how it made me feel and how to get more. I shudder at the memory. Who was that man? Not me, surely.

Anyway, the Christmas Tea:

one cup white cedar leaves (leaves only)

one cup pine tops

one cup catnip

one tablespoon valerian

one cup lemon balm

one tablespoon Mexican damiana

one tablespoon saw palmetto berries

Pour one gallon boiling water over herbs, steep for twenty minutes. Sweeten with honey. Serve hot at night before bed with slices of lemon and orange studded with cloves.

Don't plan to leave the house after you drink it and be sure your object of desire is near!

Write me,

love,

Jackie

September 22

Stephanie Cost
6455 Tiverton Court
Louisville, Kentucky

Hello Steffie,

I'm grinding my teeth. We went to Sheriff Beebus's funeral this morning, and it was hideous.

Despite my success with Cemetery Golf, I don't like funerals and rarely go to them. Neither does Mom. Helen thrives on them. She goes to the funerals of people to whom she has never even spoken. To me, this is a mystery. It's almost impossible to get a straight answer from Helen on some matters. She and Racquel have hit it off like bandits. They putter around Quarter Pine, often not talking, just observing and existing. Every now and then, when something amuses them, they'll glance at one another and murmur, "Federal Express" under their breaths and break into peals of laughter. They especially like to do this when I'm present. Oh well . . .

To me, funerals are ugly, even at Cemetery Golf, but funerals are especially trying when it rains. We've had a long stretch of crisp, cloudless days this September, and of course, the day we buried Beebus, the skies opened. This was not a genteel sprinkle, which could, after all, have added an Amadeus-like patina to the day, but a raw, raunchy thunder storm that turned Beebus's grave into a dismal, soupy lake.

Mother and Helen spent the morning on the phone deciding how to accessorize their smart new dresses bought especially for Beebus's bon voyage event. Jerry and I simply stuffed ourselves into hot, itchy wool straitjackets. We both despise dressing in suits and ties.

Down from the Dog Star

Helen came over about ten, and we loaded ourselves into Mother's Town Car, and headed down the drive. Mother and Helen were in the back, looking decorously solemn, Jerry was driving (my driving scares the hell out of Mother), and Helen's little dog, Killer, was snoozing on seat between the two women.

We pulled out of the front gates and Mother's car died. It wouldn't make a squeak. Mother and Helen trudged back up the drive. Jerry and I pushed the big, battleship of an automobile across the road and parked it crookedly, but fairly out of traffic's way, on the verge.

As I said, it was raining buckets, so by the time we were gathered in the house, we were soaked. Everyone changed clothes, Helen borrowing a frock from Mother, and we looked about for transportation. Helen will not ride in my Seville because my dad died in it. The coroner called it an unfortunate carbon monoxide accident. I've driven it since the day we buried him and, so far, I'm breathing fine.

Mother called the Wulmothes and, luckily, they had not yet left the Manor. Thirty minutes or so later, we heard Uncle Wooley's '26 Packard chugging up the drive. We four prized ourselves into the car and wedged ourselves among the various Wulmothes. There was no room for Killer.

So far, though the day had been ugly, it was bearable. But when I got in Uncle Wooley's car, the first thing I saw was Neva Jean's hat! You will not believe this, but after Neva practically single-handedly murdered Beebus, she had the gall to wear a VEIL! Yes, I know it sounds incredible, but she did. It was a black pancake of velvet with a tiny wisp of gauze just grazing her eyebrows.

Junior's mouth was down around his ankles with disapproval. We certainly have told no one about her part in Beebus's hunting trip. Not that too many people would give a rat's ass. Beebus had his fingers in too many pies.

The problem is, Beebus, although seemingly illiterate, kept a journal. Junior and I, under cover of dark, rummaged through his house in search of it. Although we found some pretty esoteric things in Beebus's surprisingly fussy, frame bungalow, we found no diary. If that thing ever turns up, this town may go up in flames.

We got to the graveyard without too much bickering, and sloshed through the downpour to the graveside. Uncle Wooley had been asked to speak the final words before Beebus was drop-kicked into eternity.

While Uncle Wooley orated, Neva Jean moaned and whimpered, attempting to rest her head on Junior's corpulent shoulder. Junior kept edging away from Neva until he was about twenty feet from the grave. Nobody even noticed.

This big, root-a-toot ugly, gas-powered pump had been set up to suck the water out of the hole in which Beebus was destined to rest, and it made so much noise that we weren't able to hear a word of Uncle Wooley's tribute to Beebus. This was a blessing, because there was absolutely nothing both kind and true that could have been said about the sheriff.

The funeral party straggled back to Quarter Pine to partake of the funeral feast. Jerry and I had decorated the dining room with pine and cedar and black silk ribbons. The table was near collapse with food from the community. I particularly liked the center piece: Junior had created a masterpiece, a lime Jello mold filled with fruit cocktail. I can't imagine where he got a mold of a Canecutter, but, one must admit, it was appropriate.

A new man in Ludens Bend, one who had only lived here for about twenty years, was babbling about getting a bunch of men together and "cleaning out those Canecutters."

He fails to understand that we have lived peacefully with those animals ever since Ludens Bend was settled. We don't bother them and they don't bother us.

After the funeral, I took the small Ford tractor down to the edge of the swamp to see what I could see. Beebus's hat and a few scraps of his shirt were lying in a trampled patch of rain-soaked, blood-tinged grass. (The hat will make an excellent surprise Christmas present for Neva.)

I sat quietly by the last trace Beebus had left on the planet, and waited. Two auburn eyes stared intently at me from a patch of cane; then four, then eight. They were watching to see what I would do. One by one, they slipped away, satisfied as to my intentions. No, I'm not afraid

Down from the Dog Star

of Canecutters. They know their friends and they know I'm a Luden.

Junior told the newcomer that, if he wanted to go hunting, go, but not to expect any support.

This man is a doctor, an optometrist-gynecologist. He has a clinic on the square called "Gynecology-Vision." The motto he chose is, "Gynecology-vision . . . We care, inside out." He does a thriving business. Neva Jean is his biggest customer. Now you know I don't gossip, but it's rumored that Neva Jean has the healthiest female parts in the county, no doubt from all the exercise they get, and that she only goes to Dr. Giddeon because of some special technique he developed for synchronized checking of eyes and vaginas.

I, of course, have never been. Junior and I have talked about getting into costume, just to check the place out, but have never had time to do it.

It's been a stressful day. I wish I were sitting with you in the green room watching the kids destroy video games and the snakes gobbling rats. I'd like to sit out on the patio with you and see Bill and Tony and Brian dissect their Harleys and lubricate the air, and each other, with those huge clouds of testosterone and thirty-weight motor oil, of which they are such masters. Perhaps in a month or so . . .

Right now, we have to repair the ravages the funeral party left at Quarter Pine. No one touched Junior's Canecutter Jello mold. I don't know what the heck to do with thirty pounds of fruit and gelatin. Helen told me to throw it down the sinkhole, but Mother warned of retribution from the goats.

Much Love

Jackie

Jackson K. Luden
Quarter Pine Farm
Ludens Bend, Alabama

September 22

Marty Stouffer
c/o PBS Channel 10
Birmingham, Al.

Dear Mr. Stouffer:

We, here in Ludens Bend, have had a town meeting and decided to boycott your show. We are tired of seeing such smut and violence on television and decided to make some changes on a grassroots level, beginning with you.

In the first place, every time your show comes on, those poor animals are either eaten by something or soundly fucked by what is supposed to be an animal of the same species. We believe that you have one universal, hungry, horny animal that you simply dress up to play different parts. This is not acceptable.

We also think that you must either drug or tie the eaten animals with twine so that they can be caught. I know that if I were a hippity-hoppity bunny, or a sleek antelope, I could get the heck out of the way of a fox or a cougar.

Mr. Stouffer. Now here this: NO MORE CHEAP ANIMAL SEX! NO MORE ANIMALS AS FASTFOOD!

You have a grave responsibility to the youth of this country. There are consequences for pornography and cruelty to animals.

Here is a list of guidelines that we have developed for your show. Please follow them.

GUIDELINES

1. If an animal must appear, whose genitals stand the slightest chance

Down from the Dog Star

of popping out at us, the viewers, put either slacks or a tasteful skirt on these creatures. Nothing split up the hip, and for God's sake, no culottes.

2. If you absolutely MUST show an animal eating something, you may show it eating grass or perhaps nuts and berries. No carnivores. If one of these meat-eaters slips into your program, you may feed it a Big Mac or perhaps a sausage. Just make sure we can see that it's commercial beef. (No, you can't put a weeny on a string and drag it about the forest trolling for predators, and you'd better not be throwing baloney, like a Frisbee, into the maws of wolves.)

3. About those mountain goats . . . I know about goats, Marty. You paint a very innocent picture of a very sinister animal. Show those goats as they really are.

Marty, we've had it. We simply won't take such tasteless viewing any longer. Shape up or ship out!

On the other hand, we have some interesting animals here, in Ludens Bend, that may interest you. They're called Canecutters, and are the ultimate cuddle-bunny. If you'd like to film these beauties, arrangements could be made.

Give us some feed-back.

Sincerely,
Jackson K. Luden

J.L.:jw

Jackson K. Luden
Quarter Pine Farm
Ludens Bend, Alabama

September 25

Dr. Jack Kavorkian
Portsmouth Medical Center
Portsmouth, Minnesota

Hello Jack,

Junior and I were chatting about you just this morning. Imagine my surprise when I got your telegram! We're so excited about your coming to visit.

We're busy preparing a guest room and organizing a party in your honor.

I need to comment on some things going on around Ludens Bend that may interest you. You have some competition. Dr. Gideon, the man who pioneered the concept of the Gynecology-Vision Center here in our town, has added a new area to his clinic. He calls it "The Hammer of Death: Alternative Death Styles."

He tried to get us to let him install a branch at Cemetery Golf, but we, of course, are faithful to you.

I must say, however, that he does offer some fascinating and chic methods for "dispatchal," as he calls it. I particularly like the deluxe package that involves a night on the town, a date with the super-model of ones' choice, and a surprise ending. The neat thing about this combo is, one doesn't know exactly when, where or how ones' "dispatchal" will take place.

It could be from poison in the consommé or a quick hit-and-run outside the restaurant. It could involve Cleatus McCloud and a high-powered deer rifle. If one likes adventure, this is the way to go.

Down from the Dog Star

He sent one of his circulars to Aunt Bessie Wulmothe, which was a serious mistake. Aunt Bessie had Junior drive her over to the clinic and she cleaned Dr. Gideon's clock.

She said that she was very healthy, thank you, and that if she did ever decide to end her life, she had a nice .38 caliber pistol in her bedside table that would do nicely, thank you, and if she did ever come to this decision, she planned on taking a lot of "friends" with her and that Dr. Gideon would be the first to accompany her. Thank you.

Mother said that "The Hammer of Death Clinic" was too commercial to be in the best of taste.

Helen said that that fat honkey better keep the —— out of her face or she'd send Killer right up his anus and out the top of his head.

Jerry just chuckled. He's still not plugged into the lifestyle of Ludens Bend. I seem to be protecting Jerry from the truth of this place as my mother protected my father.

Junior wants a job at the clinic. I told him that he could use Uncle Wooley's Packard for the hit-and-runs, and I had some international coffee left over from the Amazon.

So, when you arrive, you'll have a lot to keep you busy.

I can't imagine what it will be like to have two such superstars of "dispatchal" in the same town.

Call and let us know the particulars of your journey.

Deepest respects,
Jackson K. Luden

Jackson K. Luden
Quarter Pine Farm
Ludens Bend, Alabama

October 2

Doctor Featherengill Gideon
Gynecology-Vision
The Square
Ludens Bend, Alabama

Doctor Gideon,

I could have called or dropped by, or gotten this information to you in a dozen different ways. This news is of such import, I knew that you would want documentation for your memoirs and, most certainly, that you would want a letter in order that you might have it matted and framed.

Having neither a vagina nor poor vision, I haven't had the need to visit your establishment, but I've seen your charming sign on the village square, and my dear cousin, Neva Jean, speaks of you often and with deep appreciation.

There will be a reception at Wulmothe Manor to celebrate, among many other things, the arrrival of one of your colleagues to Ludens Bend, and you are invited. I'll save his name for last. First, I feel the need to talk with you on a very personal level. You have no mentor here in Ludens Bend, and so, you may be having a difficult time feeling at home.

As you're sure to know, Ludens Bend was founded by my greatgrandfather, Jackson Luden, about two hundred years ago. As the only scion of the original family, I have a duty to help newcomers metastasize throughout our community.

To be blunt, Dr. Gideon, although your Gynecology-Vision Center, and now, perhaps, The Hammer of Death Dispatchal Center, are greatly successful, I understand that you haven't been reaping the benefits of an active social life.

Junior Wulmothe, another member of a founding family (although nowhere near as illustrious or ancient as the Luden clan), and I, have taken the time and trouble to analyze your somewhat scabby social life and formulate a plan to help you achieve the rewards of assimilation into Ludens Bend.

First, stop taking that "taster-cat" everywhere you go. In the days of the Borgia it was necessary to have one's food tasted, but in this era, and in this place, it can be construed as rather insulting to take a "taster cat" to the Eternal Life Cafe and Souvenir Shop for Jesus. (Now selling diesel.)

A cat, in a small wire cage which you stuff with food and then wait twenty minutes to see said cat's reaction, could, possibly, allow people to think you a bit paranoid. Besides that, some poisons, some mushrooms, for instance can take up to three days to kill. Leave the cat at home.

Second, disparaging comments about Doctor Wulliam Wulmothe will not be tolerated. It came to our attention that you said Dr. Wulmothe was an insult to the medical profession and that if he had a diploma, he either stole it or bought it on the black market.

We don't have a black market here in Ludens Bend. We are totally integrated, due, in part to Helen Luden, my mother's companion of seventy years. Helen, by the way, is anxious to meet you. She has a dog that she thinks could benefit you greatly. Stop badmouthing Dr. Wulmothe.

Third, about your clothes. A white vinyl lab coat and those matching hip-boots may be appropriate for some areas of your medical practice, but not for the streets of Ludens Bend. And get a haircut.

Fourth, STOP galloping up to people, like the Rickety-Racehorse at the Doomsday Carnival, with those fliers. A physician may not advertise and still be thought of as a professional. His name may appear on a small, tastefully engraved plaque by his office door, and in the white pages of the phone book. Word of mouth is the only acceptable means of advertisement. Anything else pushes one right over the edge into the land of the used car salesman, or even worse, one of those rebuilt, mattress/furniture warehouse stores. Lose the fliers. There are countless other tips that we could offer, but for right now, these will suffice. Take them.

Now for the news.

That Grand Old Man of Euthanasia, that Kaiser of Kill, the future talk-show host of heaven — that's right, Dr. Jack Kavorkian — is coming to visit us in Ludens Bend. He will be staying at Quarter Pine, and we will offer a reception and buffet with receiving line.

Here is the protocol that Junior and I have designed for this night. When you see the Doctor, stand very still, bow slightly from the waste and wait (with a polite, interested look on your face) for him to speak first. Do NOT offer your hand. Do NOT attempt to hand him a flyer. Do NOT make that repulsive choking sound that you make.

What IS that sound? Some say it is a laugh, some call it a shriek of fear. Whatever, don't do it. IF the Doctor speaks to you, you may reply only in a definite answer to his question. If he asks a question. He probably won't. No off-the-wall comments about weather and no attempt at shop talk will be allowed. You are dealing with American royalty here. After all, the man HAS been on "Sixty Minutes."

Aunt Bessie Wulmothe has graciously agreed to be your observer for the evening. She'll monitor you at all times as sort of an impropriety detectorate. (The word "detectorate" was invented by Junior Wulmothe. Credit where credit is due and all that.)

Aunt Bessie will communicate any displeasure in your deportment and discourse directly to you. We've left the method entirely in her hands, but she has spoken of a friend that she keeps always near. Very cryptic, no?

Please take this letter in the spirit in which it was written, a spirit of concern and desire for your advancement in our community.

By the way, exactly where did you go to medical school? The university mentioned on the diploma in your office has no record of your attendance.

Sincerely,
Jackson Kavorkian Luden

October 4

Becky Bright
610 Lamont Lane
Phoenix, Arizona

Hello, Becky

The ball at Wulmothe Manor was, to say the least, a masterpiece. I had a small part in the planning and execution.

We had a very exciting receiving line. Aunt Bessie, Uncle Wooley, Junior, and Neva Jean stood in the entrance hall and made gracious comments to all those who entered.

Aunt Bessie wore a dramatic black gown, circa 1910, and a tiara. This piece of jewelry deserves a bit of explanation. Like many of our Southern Belles, Neva Jean had pretensions of becoming Miss Alabama. Indeed, this was what she had been groomed for since birth. Even at her christening, there had been touches of pageantry. It will always be a mystery how Aunt Bessandra managed to get Uncle Wooley to sing "There She Is, Miss America" as Neva was carried down the aisle to the Baptistery Font. Her entire childhood was colored by dance and music lessons. Every Sunday of her young life was spent at deportment class. She was a beauty pageant machine, and only sabotage of the worst kind kept her from walking away with the title of Miss Alabama. No, she didn't win. But as the young lady who had won was making her peregrination down the runway, Neva Jean snatched the crown from the reigning queen's head, and fled from the building into Beebus McCloud's squad car. I think those two had it planned all along.

Aunt Bessie saw it and wanted it. She doesn't usually make demands, so when she asked Neva Jean for the rhinestone chapeau, and commented that Neva Jean should be grateful for all the years of food, shelter, and protection afforded her by Aunt Bessie, Neva gracefully gave it to her. It's also out of character for Neva Jean to ever give up anything, so we don't know what other machinations Aunt Bessie brought into play.

At the reception, Neva was wearing her charming sky-blue ensemble, with matching blue mesh mitts, her fake-fur stole and a silver lurex snood. Junior and Uncle Wooley had to be content with plain, black and white. Tuxedos and all that. How Boring! Junior rebelled a bit and complemented his ensemble with a plaid cummerbund and bow tie.

The entire community was invited and they came. You wouldn't believe the diverse finery scratched from trunks and the backs of closets.

Even Peanut came. He was wearing his blue lurex bow tie and Sister Amy had sewn him a darling pair of silver satin Bermuda shorts. People get a bit nervous around him since he removed the ear and eyebrows of a local man. The ray gun is firmly lodged in Peanut's digestive track. It seems to be doing no harm to Peanut, but every time he burps, coughs, or barks, chunks of Ludens Bend disappear. The Friends won't go near Peanut. Nobody's been killed, so I think Peanut has some idea of his powers.

I wore my white satin evening jacket, blood red slacks and a charming pair of burnt orange and blue platform shoes. (Waste not, etc.) When I shook hands with Junior in the receiving line, he grinned like a maniac and bowed from the waist. I made a very genteel curtsy and everybody in the receiving line followed suit. Junior told me later that he thought that it added a rather royal air to the proceedings, that certain clat de elan for which the party screamed.

The food was exquisite. The centerpiece, once again, was a lime Jello mold of a Canecutter. There were unusual trays of veggies, carved into the shapes of ducks, peacocks, and geese, and a three hundred pound ice carving of the letter "W," surrounded by silver, crystal-lined bowls of black and red caviar. Most of the guests ignored the caviar, and if I know Junior, that's exactly what he had in mind when he ordered it. We both became violently ill from scarfing the salty, pearl-like globes by the tablespoon-full. What a wonderful way to get sick! I contributed my

Down from the Dog Star

butterscotch pineapple upside down cake that I had formed into the shape of the state of Alabama.

The house behaved itself. Everyone went out that had come in.

There was one nasty moment between Doctor Kavorkian and Doctor Gideon. I had written some guidelines for Doctor Gideon to follow but, of course, he ignored them. He tried to hand a flier for The Hammer of Death Dispatchal Center to Jack. Jack glimpsed the gist of the flier, smiled, and offered Doctor Gideon a cocktail. Aunt Bessie gave her usual predacious grin. I knew something bad was going down. It wasn't my party, so there wasn't a lot that I could do.

Dr. Gideon had that damned cat under his lab coat, so he was saved a painful demise. He will, however, have to get a new cat. He also had to be rushed to the hospital for stitches and a transfusion. The cat died in horrendous convulsions and Doctor Gideon was carrying the creature down the front of his pants in his jockey shorts.

Neva Jean will have to find a new Gynecologist-Optometrist.

We danced the night away. The Fighting Canecutter Marching Band entertained. They played chamber music. Nothing like Mozart played by a marching band.

After the party, Jerry had a glazed look in his eyes. I hate for him to be exposed to the true side of Ludens Bend, but he lives here and it will be safer for him.

I must close, love. Big day today. We're planning our Dooms Day Carnival, and I want first dibs on Sarah as the Rickety Racehorse.

Much love,

Jackie

Jackson K. Luden
Quarter Pine Farm
Ludens Bend, Alabama

October 4

Colon Pile
The Pentagon
Washington, DC

Dear Mr. Pile,

Here's a tip. I was considering voting for you, but I began to wonder what kind of sadistic parents would name their child after the last five or six feet of the alimentary canal, and how stable a child, with this burden of a name, would be.

Not that I would actually vote for anybody (true aristocrats NEVER vote) but a few minutes of fantasy every now and then is so restful to the overworked mind.

Junior Wulmothe, however, admires you, name and all. Of course, he's been extremely anal-retentive ever since toilet training, so it's understandable that he might be strongly attracted to names suggestive of the digestive tract.

I'm more than miffed at Junior. He's stolen my house guest, Dr. Jack, and I'm in a tizzy! I don't know what Junior did or promised to Dr. Jack to lure him away from the safety of my home, but I awoke this morning and found my friend absconded from the premises. The gracious guest room, which we had prepared for him, was empty. I don't mean just his clothing and personal effects were gone, I mean everything was missing—the four-poster bed, the knotty pine dresser and chest, the bedside tables, the carpet, the deer head collection that I had hung over his bed, Helen's collection of cuckoo clocks that all actually cuckooed, though not always precisely at the same time, and worst of all, the big papier-maché chandelier in the shape of the heads of the last five presidents. I was particularly proud of Jack Kennedy's. He visited here, before he was president. Junior said it wasn't actually him—what would a presidential hopeful be doing hitchhiking up Highway 78 in tight Levis, a black t-shirt with a pack of Camels in the sleeve, and a tattoo saying "BORN TO RAISE HELL" on his bicep? I told Junior that he was just a jealous bitch and reminded him of a certain depraved trucker he had lured to Wulmothe Manor when Aunt Bessie was in the hospital with gall bladder surgery, and he told me that was totally irrelevant, and that trucker was actually royalty in disguise. I naturally mentioned to Ronnie, Junior's "special friend," about Junior's dangerous liaison with the trucker, and this is when Ronnie ran off with Sue-Lyn, the manicurist at The Tender Tendrils.

And so, Junior has not been totally in my corner, so to speak, for a while now, and I think this is why he stole my house guest.

Of course, Dr. Jack might have been offended by Dr. Gideon at the reception at Wulmothe Manor, but I believe he is a bigger man than that. At any rate, Neva Jean, Nova and I are having a spot of lunch and a shopping spree at the Galleria this afternoon, so I will certainly get to the bottom of things.

I seem to have gotten a bit off-track here. What I had planned to do was give you some feedback on your name and make a few suggestions on how to fix it.

Now you could put a "Y" on the end of your first name and become Colony Pile. You could put a cedilla over the "E" in Pile and attain a nice Jamaican slant. Better still, you could do some major surgery on that dreadful name and become Collie Pup! You would get a lot more votes. Not mine, of course. As I said (I always like to teach), true aristocrats don't vote. A law unto ourselves.

By the way, exactly who are you and for what office are you running? Nobody here seems to know. I put in a call to my friend LZ, to find out, (LZ knows everything), but he hasn't returned my call. Charlotte got really tired of his pomposity and left him. She is now residing with her mother in Albertville, and I imagine he misses his captive audience.

Literally, captive. They had some controversy over a workshop Charlotte wanted to take in Canada. It was a feminist workshop kind of thing, put on by a group of militant Canadian Lesbians, and was scheduled to last six months, during which time the women were sworn to have no contact with men. I seem to be getting an overflow of anger from the tautly stretched LZ, which is OK. He's been a bit testy ever since his Scouts were vandalized.

You know, I just realized that those people actually have a dog named Scout. I had not picked up on that till just this minute.

I'll close now, Mr. Pile. I hope my suggestions are valuable to you. If you can get your name under control in time, I might be able to get you a speaker's engagement at our Dooms Day Carnival.

Cordially,
Jackson K. Luden

October 6

Mr. Donald Johnstone
1717 Horsecollar Lane
Phoenix, Arizona 70762

Dear Don,

Things are moving as smoothly as they ever do down here in the land of cotton. Actually, we no longer grow that much cotton in Alabama. Soybeans and pine trees are our major crops now. Here at Quarter Pine, there was nothing but fields of sweet potatoes, peanuts, and corn, for miles around. That was way back when. Mom can just barely remember when the farm was really a farm. Now we raise CDs and rents. Sorry to disillusion you.

Speaking of being disillusioned, Junior's finally pushed the envelope a few inches too far. He has what he claims to be a "foreign exchange student" living with him at the Manor. HA!!! First of all, Junior had no student to exchange. Second, this pseudo-exchange student doesn't go to school, although school is definitely in session. Third, who ever heard of a Yankee exchange student. You'd think with all those "dems" and "dos" coming from this child's mouth, that you were watching a really bad version of "The Champ" with Mickey Rooney.

This young man does look foreign. He has curly black hair, big brown eyes and is the color of a sweet potato. But I think Junior finally struck Inca gold on the I-20 highway. Not that I'm jealous. I'm not the least bit concerned that Jerry might be interested in this extremely young, extremely pretty man. I'll just wait things out. You know me, patience is my greatest spiritual strength. Besides, I am totally confident in my friend's faithfulness.

Plans for the Dooms Day Carnival go forward. I had considered Sarah for the part of the Rickety Racehorse, but that part is usually played by a nervous, thin horse with a reputation for biting (the fiercer, the better). The Rickety Racehorse is always dosed with a special potion made of loco weed and brugmanzia sap to give it an edge. Well, Sarah is about as fierce and dangerous as a big, over-stuffed barca lounger, and her teeth are worn down to nubs, so I decided against Sarah for the honor, and lobbied for Lobo-the-Teeth, a young, rangy quarter horse that has badly injured its last three trainers.

We always put the Rickety Racehorse out to pasture after the Carnival, into a pleasant, hopefully long, retirement.

I've decided that Paulo, Junior's house guest, might be appropriate for the one who will be stalking the Rickety Racehorse. As always, we will keep the name of the Rickety Racehorse a surprise. Junior thinks it's going to be Sarah. What a surprise!

My choice of Paulo for the Carnival is not, as some might think, based on jealousy. The simple truth is, Paulo has been verbally, and possibly physically, abusing Junior. I won't have that. I love Junior, as much as I'm capable of loving any human.

I need to get cracking on my costume. I thought I'd do sort of a cross between Rhett Butler and Tina Turner this year.

Much Love

Jackie

October 6

Stephanie Cost
6455 Tiverton Court
Louisville Kentucky

Hi Steffie,

A slow, pleasant day. I wrote a nice letter to Child Protective Services about Junior's exchange student. They sent a social worker out to check on the situation. It could have gotten nasty (!!!), but Junior's amorata had a driver's license which proved him to be twenty-six years old. Junior was saved, but Nova told me he had a dreadful shock this morning. He awoke in a bed full of blood. Nova said he was caterwauling like a man who just discovered he has cancer, running naked through the house (My God, what a hideous sight that must have been!), in search of a mirror large enough to get a full view of his body.

At this point, in Nova's narrative, Neva Jean broke in and said that only the Hubble Telescope had a mirror that might — just might — be large enough. Junior was eavesdropping in the next room and stormed in, ready to throttle us all. He got sidetracked by some left over butterscotch pineapple upside cake and just sat there, glowering and stuffing his face. At any rate, he had been standing naked in the entry hall, twisting and writhing about trying to find the site of leakage. His lily white body didn't seem to have any holes in it, so Neva Jean said that he had finally gotten his period, and she would set up an appointment with Dr. Gideon just as soon as he got out of intensive care.

It turned out that Junior had fallen asleep with a red magic marker in his bed, and had wallowed about on it during the night.

Neva and I came up with a really funny trick. As you know, the

Olympics are coming next summer. Neva used her computer to print up some official looking Olympic stationary. We typed a nice letter to Junior on this paper, telling him that he had been chosen to host the Bulgarian hockey team. We let Nova and Aunt Bessie in our little prank. Junior is busy painting five multicolored circles on everything he owns. He used an entirely different pallette of colors than the authentic Olympics logo, and I think it makes quite a statement.

Junior even went to a sporting goods store to find all about the correct way to launder soccer uniforms and jocks. That idiot even bought a jock and is so proud of it. He drops his pants and shows it off to anybody foolish enough to talk to him. Really! We won't tell him the truth till he's calmed down a bit.

Write me, sweety. Jerry and I are driving into town to look for a book that he needs for his English class. He teaches at the junior college and seems to love it. You know, at first I had planned on doing my usual number and sabotaging his self-esteem and self-worth, but he proved too centered. So far, I've had no problems with him, but I'm watching.

Love you,
Jackie

October 12

Charlotte Heywoode
112 Coffeeden
Albertville, Alabama

Dearest Charlotte,

A girl's gotta do what a girl's gotta do. That's true. And I support you completely in your decision to take a sabbatical to Albertville. How's your lovely mother? Thank her for me, for those cuttings.

Don't worry about LZ and friends. Those fellows will be fine. The house is a disaster, with all those savage men dwelling there, but you know how men love to roll about in their own squalor. At least they can cook, so if they don't die from some rare tropical mold or fungus, they will survive. I don't go there anymore. We had a tiff, he apologized, but he apologized for entirely the wrong thing. It's hopeless.

My biggest regret is that you missed out on the Dooms Day Carnival. I videotaped the highlights for you . . .

At six AM, on the day of the carnival, the Rickety Racehorse was given his loco weed/brugmanzia cocktail, and left alone to come to a boil. At twelve noon our new sheriff, Little Willie, hung by his heels from the rafters of the barn and opened its stall door. Willie is making a good sheriff. He's not as interesting as Sheriff Beebus, but he's honest and kind. Let's see how long he keeps those characteristics in Ludens Bend.

At this point, no one but me knew who the Rickety Racehorse's Stalker would be. Imagine Junior's surprise when I announced Paulo's name over the Big Red Bullhorn. Junior, Nova, Neva Jean, Jerry, Eric, Peanut, and moi were on the roof of the cafe, to get a good view (and to keep out of the way of Mr. Horse), when Paulo was led from the cafe in the traditional Stalker's costume: a black, silk skeleton suit, a skull mask, hobbles and bells. It has always seemed odd to me that this person is called a Stalker. I know, basically, how the ceremony evolved, and it's all pretty logical, as far as things here go, but still . . . . Traditionally, we used rope to hobble the Stalker's feet, but now we use a pair of handcuffs. Ten years ago the Stalker chewed through his ropes, and if the Rickety Racehorse hadn't been really a splendid animal that year, his victim might have gotten out of the valley.

Junior just about threw himself off the top of the cafe to save his true love, but Nova and Neva grabbed him by the arms and held him back. His histrionics were just for show. Junior loves the finale of the Dooms Day Carnival as much as any of us. After the festivities this year he would get to moon around wearing black and looking tragic (he always does, anyway), and have people make a big fuss over him. He's really quite strong, so those two skinny women couldn't have held him back if he hadn't wanted them to.

Jerry, at this point, hadn't a clue as to what was about to happen. It terrified me to think what his reaction would be. I'm pleased to report that he's still here.

The girls were dressed beautifully in matching ensembles, sort of a mother-daughter look, though we never got deeply into the subject of who was the mother and who was the daughter.

I had on my favorite dress-up clothes: that white satin dinner jacket and my red golfing pants. I also had Helen's camcorder, and a fine picnic lunch.

Everybody in Ludens Bend was either hiding behind locked doors, or safely on rooftops to observe the feast. It was quick, this year. The Rickety Racehorse found Paulo within five minutes, stamped him into the ground and proceeded to gobble the boy down al fresco. Paulo spotted El Lobo the Teeth just as the horse came thundering around the corner of the cafe. I couldn't resist getting Paulo's attention. I had to see the look in his eyes as R. R. took the first bite from that sleazy tramp's throat.

I lifted the Big Red Bullhorn to my lips, smiled at Junior, and yelled

192

Down from the Dog Star

"QUACKKKKK" directly into the horrified eyes of le slut just as he spotted his doom on four hooves.

Cleatus then shot a strong tranquilizer dart into Lobo's flank, and led him off to retirement.

Here's a copy of the video I took of the day's festivities. I wouldn't advise showing it to your mom. It was unusually bloody this year, probably because I added a handful of black beauties, from our pharmacy, to the usual tonic that we give the Rickety Racehorse.

People think this is an ancient ceremony, but it's not. Jackson Luden, my greatgrandfather, made the whole darned thing up to get rid of a farmer in the next valley so he could add a few more acres to Quarter Pine. He told everybody that it was a Celtic method of insuring fertility in the women and in the crops. People will believe almost anything if it offers a break from ennui.

Good Lord, Precious! The sun is coming up outside. Let me get a nap. I'm exhausted.

Is it as cool in Albertville as it is here?

Love you, dear heart,
Jackie K.

October 28

Miss Laura Martin
457 Gay Street
Auburn, Alabama

Dear Laura,

I'm too scattered to know the exact date, (which, to say the least, is pretty darned arbitrary), and besides that, after chasing this dog around all day, I'm exhausted, and perturbed.

What I wanted was a cute ball of fur to cuddle on my pillow every night, (as I did Honey), and I hoped for a female dog. Mother thinks male dogs are SO vulgar, with those floppy male parts bouncing and jouncing all over the place.

When we got to the breeders, what they had left were two male dogs, and these dogs were three months old, and nearly as big as Scout, LZ's hound. The one we chose has feet bigger than mine. I can deal with this. I told mother that once a dog was "fixed" as we so genteely call it, their penises shrink down to practically nothing and they will NOT give themselves cheap fellatio right when the bridge club is breaking for lunch. Not that we have a bridge club, but I'm sure you get the picture. And not that I would dare say "penis" in front of mother. She abhors the word and prefers euphemisms I don't fear the word at all. PENIS PENIS PENIS!!! See? I am fearless. Mother wouldn't say "penis" if she grew one.

I certainly don't go around flashing mine the way Junior does. This behavior of his started when he got the idea that he was to host the Bulgarian soccer team for the Summer Olympics. This erroneous bit of information may have come to him via a phony letter someone whipped up on their computer. I really don't care to comment on this.

Junior immediately went out and bought a jock (!) and flashes it to anybody dumb enough to give him the chance.

When he showed it to me, I acted very blasé and told him I had one just like it, but had had to get a much larger size. I don't really own one. Those things have always intimidated me.

Where were we? Oh yes. The dog. We brought the dog home and he immediately ran under the porch and WOULD NOT COME OUT! I put his food under there and he gobbled it down. He comes out when I go inside the house and runs back under when I come outside. He dug a hole under the porch, and all I can see of him are his gigantic, bat-like ears sticking up. He looks at me with terror in his eyes. I'm really disgusted and disappointed. My anger is, as usual, based on fear, unforgiveness, and not getting my own way.

Gay Street? Is that some sort of joke? I bet you actually sought out an address on Gay Street to persecute me, sitting out here in the country. I'm not offended. At least it's not Queer Court or, God forbid, Faggot Freeway. That's probably next.

The Summer Solstice ceremony was lovely. I would loved to have a s'more, but I have to watch my weight. I don't know how I missed out on the recipe for s'mores. The combination of chocolate, toasted marsh-mallows, and Graham crackers looked divine.

When are you coming back out? Perhaps you could come to the farm and meet the dog. We haven't named it. I don't particularly like the Goddamned mutt. There. I said it. I don't like the dog. He's nothing like Honey, and will never be anything like Honey. I may take him back to the kennel. Probably not. I am really confused about my feelings, but I know that I need to take this as a separate event. As I have often said, "I can't make the same magic twice, exactly the same way . . . only different magic."

> Love you,
> Jackie

Jackson K. Luden
Quarter Pine Farm
Ludens Bend, Alabama

October 29

Marty Stouffer,
c/o PBS Channel 10
Birmingham, Alabama

So, Mr. Stouffer, you have ignored our suggestions. These simple guidelines could have brought you into the realm of realism, and would have placed you within the protection of the moral majority.

The Committee To Regenerate Wild America (or CRAW, as we call it) voted to wait for four weeks after we sent you our letter of protest, because we thought you would need time to gear up for the new format.

And here, four weeks later, you're still showing those nymphomaniacal, slavering, wild-eyed, starving coyotes gobbling French Poodles.

This letter may seem a touch terse, a smidgen short. I am under pressure.

Yesterday, Mom and I went puppy shopping. We picked a male, three-month-old German Shepherd. When we got him home, he ran under the back porch, dug a hole, and crouched in it for several hours. At two PM, he crept up onto the porch, and hid behind the wrought iron queen's chair. No amount of coaxing or wheedling could get him to emerge and be petted. He spent a restless night out there. I know this for a fact, because every time I checked him during the night, he was wide awake and chewing on his chew-toy.

He eats like a pig and, for some obscure reason, puts his huge feet in his water dish, and splashes the water out onto the floor. Then he barks angrily until I fill his dish again.

I left the kitchen door open for a second, to take my Night-blooming Cerus cactus outside for some sun, and before I knew it, Hiser —

Down from the Dog Star

pronounced "Highsir" — jumped into the kitchen and began to explore the house. He would run like hell if I went anywhere near him. I sneaked up on him in the main hallway, and grabbed him, in order to pet him. He screamed bloody murder, but finally submitted to an ear scratching. Hiser then meandered into Mom's bedroom and hid behind her bed. First, however, he had to fight his way past a floor length mirror, where he saw his reflection. He growled and the fur on his back stood on end. That's where he is now, in seclusion in my mother's bedroom. He won't come out.

Do you think I should take him back to the kennel and swap him for another pup? Should I slip a Valium into his food? My so-called friend, Junior Wulmothe, says if he were a dog, he wouldn't come near me either. Of course Hiser looks at Junior with a look of deep trust and affection in his eyes, almost a promise of licks to come. Hiser IS a male dog and Junior IS a real bitch. Nevertheless . . .

So here's my deal, Marty. If you come to Ludens Bend and tame this animal for me, I will hold the Committee in check until you can get your shit together. You might want to bring an anesthetic dart or, perhaps, a net in which to capture Hiser.

I'll also point you in the direction of some Canecutters. You'll have to take your dart gun, because they're very helpless and timid.

You may call me at Quarter Pine. You missed our Dooms Day Carnival, but there's always next year. If we interact the way I think we will, I could probably get you a really important role for next year's event.

I'm awaiting your reply with bated breath.

Sincerely,
Jackie Luden

October 30

Miss Penny Warshack
22 Castlerock
Scottsdale, Arizona

My Dear Penny,

I haven't heard from you in a good while. Are you still there? I wanted to make World Convention very badly, but so much has been happening.

My life is perfect: I have everything that I need. I also have everything that I want. I have fallen into that place of balance where my needs and wants have merged. Or perhaps I just, finally, got over wanting everything that I see.

We are finally slowing down. The Doomsday Carnival is over, the Wulmothe party is behind us, Cemetery Golf is being managed by an excellent team of Gungaris and Friends, the Church is prospering, and the goats are calm. Somebody finally got the idea to throw car upholstery down the sinkhole, so that the goats wouldn't emerge as often. They still come out.

We're cranking it down for a long, peaceful winter. Christmas is the next thing to handle. I would LOVE to manipulate Junior into playing the Christmas Fool, but he knows too much about the hot molasses and the Big Brass Funnel. Oh well. Perhaps Marty Stouffer . . .

Here's something new to think about: I was sitting around the dining room table the night of Summer Solstice with "the kids" (it's funny how anybody under thirty has become "kids") after supper, and Shea, L.Z.'s son, began talking about a spiritual awakening he had in a Mexican restaurant the day before. Listening to the waiters talking, he came to believe that if he could just get past the idea that he did not understand Spanish, not only would he be able to understand it, but he would also be able to speak it.

We carried the progression forward into playing musical instruments, and even flying without a plane or hang-glider. LZ called it something like the power of positive thinking.

Well, Eric the alien and I were buzzing around the farm on the smaller, red Ford tractor the next day, and I mentioned this theory to him. He gave the equivalent of an alien laugh and told me that that was exactly how they powered their ships! WHOA!

More good news: I have a puppy. At first he was scared of me and ran whenever I tried to pet him. He's still shy, but this morning he licked me on the nose. Helen was watching from the kitchen window. She came storming out and told me that was how people caught "Zoo Nose." I didn't figure out, until an hour later, that she was trying to say "Zoonosis." Zoonosis is a term meaning the acquisition, by man, of an animal disease.

I'm still anxious for you to come out and visit. Why don't you, Becky, Lynda, and Don jump in a car and come on down? We'll treat y'all fine! And there are no festivals to distract us from a nice time together.

I'm gonna go see where Hiser Van Luden (the pup) is. He got the telephone book and tore it to shreds last night.

Much Love,
Jackson

October 30

Doctor Jack "Snuggles" Kavorkian
c/o Minnesota Medical Center
Portsmouth, Minnesota

Dearest Jack,

No, you mustn't worry about our relationship becoming public. I can see how it might hurt your credibility. It was just a Summer Love, a last fling on your part. I plan to have a lot more flings before I get in the Big-Black-Boat. I feel hurt that you would be ashamed of our "Great Passion," as you put it in your brief note.

I don't care how good a doctor you are, you can never prove that I drugged you and "had my way" with you. Really Jack, you need to be less dramatic when you write letters. And a bit more tactful.

Let's say, for instance, that a certain piece of video tape existed that documented the true story of your "rape" (!!!) as you called it. Not that it does, but if it did, Sixty Minutes would eat you alive.

I have nothing but affection for you. But if I don't get a letter of apology really fast, you (and viewing America) might get a major surprise. After all, as you may know, I have total control of the programming on "America Wild."

Yes, I know most people think of it as a show about animals, but I think it could use some human interest, too.

Mother is getting paranoid. She walks around the house at night closing drapes and locking windows. I ask her why, and she tells me that "they" might be watching us. Of course Helen had to pop off and tell us that if "they" saw Mr. Jackie naked "they'd" be blinded instantly, and not by his beauty.

I humor Mother, and help her close the house up tight at night. No matter how odd her requests, she's my mother, she's getting along in years, and I won't have her with me forever. And who knows, maybe there are some "theys" out there, panting and manipulating their appendages in the dark, as I slide my perfect body into my pink, silk pajamas.

Sorry, Jack. It's unfair for me to remind you of the "splendor in the grass" that we shared. At least I think you said grass. You'd better have said grass.

Dr. Gideon is recovering from his taster cat's clawing. Mother said that now, at least, a gynecologist would know how those "simple, painless" pelvic exams really feel. Dr. Gideon was talking about opening a new clinic called "Veterinary Carwash." I think it was the morphine talking. I told him that if he even looked like he was going to start such a sacrilege in Ludens Bend, the incident with his "Taster Cat" would seem like paradise when I got through with him. I don't give a bloody damn what people do to each other, but that bastard will NOT touch a dog and live. Really.

We do so want you to return to Quarter Pine soon. We are also curious about what happened to your bedroom furniture. Did it, perhaps, get eaten by the goats? Let us know.

Perhaps you could make it here for Christmas. We have a wondrous celebration with clowns and chariots and everything! There's a place for you, Jack! Do you like molasses?

Write me. Write me within ten minutes of getting this letter. I do so miss you.

Affectionately,
Jackie

Jackson K. Luden
Quarter Pine Farm
Ludens Bend, Alabama

October 30

The Coca-Cola Company
Atlanta, Georgia

Dear Sirs,

I have always drunk, and enjoyed, Coca-Cola. I love its sparkly taste!
However, there is always room for a new product.

I wanted to write and share with you this potential blockbuster, but
first, a little background.

My cousin, Junior Wulmothe, and I, recently made a trip to the zoo.
It was there that he saw his first mongoose.

I'm not saying that Junior is a copy cat, or a jealous kind of person,
but he was feeling left out that week. After the tragic loss of his friend
Paulo, and that incident with Dr. Jack (pure rejection!), Junior needed
some attention.

There was a tribe of Girl Scouts, and a few tourists from Alpha
Centauri, hanging around in front of the mongoose cage and the crowd
was going "OOH" and "AHH."

I don't know what possessed Junior, but he called James Randal
Grant over, (the zoo keeper), and demanded to be let into the cage with
the mongooses. He had in mind to do sort of a trained mongoose act. I
believe he either had a stroke, or was on powerful drugs.

He was wearing that ridiculous, claw hammer frock-coat, and a tall,
black, silk hat, his usual costume for progressions through the public
domain, and I must admit there was something Kafkaesque about the
scene. Tragic. Oak trees in Autumn.

Down from the Dog Star

Junior approached the group of animals. They stared up at him with their liquid, brown eyes. As one, the entire flock covered Junior and began to puncture his hide.

Junior ran from the cage, or tried to, but James Randal had locked the cage door and vanished.

We finally got him out. The only permanent damage, to Junior, was the loss of a couple of fingers. I'm sure Junior will pass it off as a war wound or, perhaps, a pirate attack.

But it set me to thinking. Mongoose Cola. So appropriate for the virile, macho nineties!

I'm busy working on a design for the label. Mongoose Cola. Just trips from the tongue, doesn't it?

You come up with the actual cola, and I'll supply the can. This is just an idea I've been kicking around.

By the way, yes, I am that Jackie Luden who pioneered Cemetery Golf.

Sincerely,
Jackson K Luden,

Jackson K. Luden
Quarter Pine Farm
Ludens Bend, Alabama

October 30

Mr. Walter Disney
c/o The Walt Disney Studios,
Hollywood, California

Dear Mr. Disney,

I realize that you are, at present, frozen like some divine Eskimo Pie, awaiting the cure for whatever ailed you, but I wanted you to have this letter when you are thawed.

I actually have experience with cryogenics. We offer Perpetual Enfreezement at all our Cemetery Golf courses. It was bumpy at first, but once we got the generators in place, we had no more problems with accidental thawation due to electrical cessation.

I thought about writing the executives at your studio, but they are so very temporary and you are so forever.

Here's what's going on: your people made an animated version of "The Hunchback of Notre Dame." They made the hunchback (I believe they call him "Juan," in the movie) into a rather attractive young man, with really nice clothes, excellent personal hygiene, and bright white teeth. He also sings like a mockingbird. Everybody is always hugging and kissing this creature. He has some friendly, animated gargoyles to party with, on top of the cathedral.

Now, first of all, nobody lives in the bell tower of a Catholic Church. Those people are so cheap they even charge the pigeons rent, and as QuasiMoto had no visible means of support, I don't think those priests would have let him live there. The same goes for his designer clothes and shockingly brilliant teeth. The real hunchback wore filthy rags, had black snags for teeth, and didn't use toilet paper, much less deodorant. Trust me when I say that nobody would have hugged him.

As for the gargoyles, I have experience with gargoyles. Junior Wulmothe has them on his roof at Wulmothe Manor. They are mean and nasty. They don't sing and dance. They just wait until dark and then, they get you.

Where'd he get that voice? I don't believe it's really him. I think some singer dubbed it.

I hate to see the Disney Studios create such drek. When you are popped into that big, Donald Duck Microwave at Epcot, and brought back to life, I hope you clean house.

Looking forward to meeting you,
Jackie K Luden

P.S. Did you ever have trouble getting Pluto to let you pet him? I'm sure Goofy beat the crap out of him regularly. I have a theory about Goofy's real character.

JKL

November 2

Tony O'Brian
19th Avenue North
Phoenix Arizona

Hello Tony!

A lot of good news. Enclosed, you'll find a drawing of our new
puppy, Hiser Van Luden. Mother named him after my good friend,
Mike. Jerry is terribly happy with the pup, Mother loves Hiser, and I am
making progress. At first, he wouldn't let me come near him. Now, he'll
walk up and lick my hand. He licked me on the nose a couple of times
yesterday, and today he actually accepted a piece of roast beef.

I was getting angry at Hiser, because he showed me no affection and
I didn't understand him. Eric asked me if this reminded me of anything.
I said "No," although it did. He came right out with it, and said that it
reminded him of my father and me. I told him that he hadn't been there
so how could he know. He said that he had always been there and
probably always would be.

He's right. My dad was distant and cold. I didn't get what I wanted
in a father and, God knows, he was shocked and disappointed in what he
got for a son. I think the real trouble began when, at the age of fourteen,
I wore a full face of makeup (with false eyelashes) to a deer hunt. Cosmo
was wrong. No matter how carefully you apply makeup, somebody is
gonna notice. I see my part in it and I am determined to do work on this.
He's dead. I can't hate him forever, because it hurts me, not him. He died
in my Seville from carbon monoxide poisoning. His car had three flat
tires; Mother and Helen were in town shopping for fabric, so I offered
him my car.

Down from the Dog Star

I know what you're thinking, but you're wrong. I was completely cleared at the inquest . . . and Sheriff Beebus was not involved in the proceedings in any way.

Here's another tidbit. Marty came to Quarter Pine to hunt for Canecutters. In real life, Marty is sweet as sugar. I couldn't do it. I told him the Canecutters had migrated.

However, he got so excited about Dog Town, that he's coming aboard. He'll be doing publicity on PBS. It may have helped, a bit, when I showed him the Hot Molasses and the Big Brass Funnel.

How's Kitty-Kitty? Are you coming to see me soon? I promise no one will hurt you, and Bonnie, my leopard, loves kittens and pups.

Love you, Fish Boy,
Jackie

November 6

Miss Penny Warshack
22 Castlerock
Scottsdale, Arizona

Dearest Penny,

Still no word, and I miss you.

I just wanted to send you a copy of a letter I received from Laura Martin, a new friend that I met over at LZ's and Charlotte's. This is a brilliant young woman, but more than that, she seems to have popped up right when I needed her.

My heart has been breaking because our new puppy has wanted nothing to do with me. Lo and behold, today he walked over to the big iron Queen's chair on the back porch, where I was sitting, and plopped down under my feet, rolled over on his back and waggled his feet at me, demanding a belly rub! I've been so jealous of Mother. He actually sleeps by her bed at night. Honey always slept by my bed or in the hall outside my door.

What I've come to realize is, Hiser is not Honey. I have to take this dog for who he is.

Anyway, here's the letter Laura sent me. I can't begin to tell you the healing I got from this poetry.

The funny thing is, LZ, my sponsor, the kennel master that sold us the dog, and the vet all told me the same thing, but in words I couldn't hear. I need to watch Laura very closely. She could change me for the better if I'm not careful.

down from the dog star
       down
              down
              no time to say "dear jackie"
              down from the dog star reeling and screaming
              adolescent towards
              uncertainty and my spirit sinks down
              down from the dog star
              hurling into furry thick flesh
              so heavy
              unwelcome weight of young scrotum
              so ugly and obvious
              and Sirius flings me down into clumsy young paws
              and unfamiliar ears and what choice have i,
              but to be reborn, and terrified by this new life
              this new body so unutterably male
              i hit the ground running loping really
              a break-neck, awkward lope
              toward the porch a darkness, one last retreat
              back to the void and hey it's cool under here
              and so comforting a distant reminder of my
              recent past life hidden, moist comfort of girlhood
              and here
              underneath this porch, I catch my breath
              and rest and wait for you to realize me
              to re-realize here in my new body
              but, while I'm resting,
              my memory begins to fade and slowly
              i'm becoming an entirely new dog
              i am entirely new and nameless
              god, birth is so scary name me call me
              i'm coming i'm here down from the dog star
Sincerely
The Innocent Shepherd Underneath Your House

   Exquisite, no?

How can I be so dense, sometimes? How come certain words go straight to my heart and others fly away. Some glad morning . . .

I went to my bone doctor today. He tells me the sickness, which kept me in bed for a whole Winter and Spring, appears to be returning. Hiser came along just in time. Penny, I don't want all that surgery again. I stayed clean through five major operations the last time, and I only had six months clean. I don't know if I can do it again.

It's about ten at night. Hiser is curled up in Mother's bed. He crawled up on her bed tonight and was asleep, with his head on her pillow, when I checked on her at nine. Mother woke and the first thing she saw was a HUGE, black, wet nose, and these giant, bat-like ears, about four inches from her face. She didn't like such an awakening, I tell you! She said, "Jackson Luden, get this beast off my bed!" I told her that Hiser was finally starting to love me and I wasn't about to alienate him. She swatted him on his butt with one of her silk roll pillows and he did his cringing puppy act. I guess he's still snuggled up to her.

Write me soon, love

Jackie

November 8

Charlotte Heywoode
Peti Pomfrietz Lodge
Brampton, Ontario Mv4 - 6015

Hi Charlotte,

Are you planning to come back home? The boys miss you, but more importantly, I miss you!

It may seem early, but believe me, when Winter comes, you'll be able to use the enclosed goodies. Aunt Bessie knitted this sweater, and the socks are pure cashmere. It will be colder than you can imagine. The electric blanket will probably disturb you (I'm sure it violates some unwritten rule of ecology or spirituality) but when it gets so cold that your urine freezes the second it leaves your body, I believe that you will appreciate it. I still have problems visualizing you, and a dozen Canadian Lesbians, huddled in the wilderness, raising your collective conscious-ness — it reminds me way to much of something out of a Lisa Althir novel — but you must follow your heart.

Saturday afternoon, over the phone, Laura Martin reported a dream to me that I wanted to tell you about. Earlier, I'd been busy rearranging my address book. Thomas Blaylock was trying to clean the gutters. Terrified of heights, he had clung to the ladder like some dark, exotic marsupial. It was pitiful! Thomas was whimpering about how dangerous the job was, and how he didn't want to break his poor head, especially after he had "saved Mr. Jackie's life in the Amazon." Mother and Helen were standing at the bottom of the ladder, ridiculing him. Helen even went so far as to bat him occasionally with her broom as Mother cheered her on. Junior was rummaging through my closet looking for a scarf that

I had told him a dozen times was not there, and Hiser was holed-up, under my bed, chewing my favorite belt into shreds. In general, there was too much confusion around the house for me to do any constructive work. I was pleased when Laura called to chat.

Laura told me she dreamed that she and her friend Shea were driving around in the country when they came to this church. Somehow, the ocean had found its way into the center of Alabama, (although Laura said it was a sea), and the congregation was standing on the shore, speaking in tongues, and fishing.

Laura said that she was standing, facing the sea, with her back to the church, watching the people fish. The church people were an older crowd, very rural, and very serious. The men were wearing what Laura called "old men's pants." I asked her if she meant those khaki pants with waistbands up under the breast and she said, "Yes, exactly." The women had high-stacked gray hair, and were wearing muted, simple dresses. She said what she noticed most about the women was the look of pure, frantic joy beaming from their eyes. The people would pray, they would shout in tongues, and the catfish would jump up out of the water and leap into wire baskets the people held. One of the women, wearing a pair of light blue, polyester pants and a short-sleeved, white shirt, with a pattern of tiny blue flowers that matched the pants exactly, handed Laura a basket. She began to fish. The catfish were so anxious to jump into the basket that they bit her thumbs with a not painful but unfamiliar, tingling sensation.

Laura told me that she awoke with the phrase "Pentecostal Catfishing" on her lips. She woke with a feeling of boundless joy. Her spirit felt so light that she knew it had been traveling, and was sure that somewhere, in some distant place, she had stood on the shore of the Alabama Sea, sharing sacred fish with the people of that land.

The poke salad berries are getting ready to pick and preserve. Junior gave me a lot of plain white muslin that I want to sew up into drapes for the den, and I plan to dye the fabric with poke berry juice. Alum makes the perfect fixative for this dye.

Try not to freeze. I remember what those Canadian Winters are like,

Down from the Dog Star

especially out in the wild. Of course, you are with friends, and I was trapped in a canvas tent with a mad-man. If he hadn't been so cheap, I might have stuck it out a little longer. Now that I think about it, he really wasn't cheap, he was just poor. It's hard for me to understand not being able to buy food and clothing.

EEK!!! Am I trying to talk myself into looking this dude up again? I am truly the definition of a revisionist!

Let me know if I can send you anything to make your life a little more comfortable.

Love

Jackie

(no date)

Miss Penny Warshack
22 Castlerock
Scottsdale, Arizona

Dear Penny,

Hello buddy. We just got off the phone, and talked for at least an hour, but I didn't say what was deeply in my mind, which is: "Thanks for being there for me."

We talked a lot about recovery. I am in a hard period of recovery now, having feelings of being neither fish nor fowl. I speak one language, but am living in a country where a different tongue is spoken.

Survival on this continent is hard. I need to be back there, with all of you. I feel like the last unicorn, looking for her people.

My mindset, at present, tells me meetings here suck. This self-talk is my disease trying to cut me out of the herd so it can eat me. Meetings are pretty much the same wherever I go. If I throw myself into life, into the program, into the fellowship, I can be pretty happy. If not, not.

For many years I pumped garbage out to the universe. The universe finally got tired, and started pumping garbage back to me. I eventually learned that if I pumped roses out, the universe would start pumping roses back.

Today, I prefer to leave the scent of roses behind me, when I leave a room — not garbage.

The last meeting I went to was a tag meeting. I hate those meetings, and flash back to that strange boy on the playground waiting to be chosen, hoping to be chosen, and never being chosen. The other piece of that is that I never wanted to play the games that I was hoping to be chosen for (I hated football and dodge ball), but I just wanted to be chosen.

So what's it all about? I believe "it" is all about my relationship with God. Or your relationship with God or their relationship with God. It's about a lot of things . . . It's about forgiving the perpetrators but not letting them off. It's about not becoming perpetrators ourselves. It's about understanding those flashbacks. When I'm tempted to play stupid, or act pretty, or kiss ass to appease the perpetrators, I must stop, find my courage, find my relationship with God, and say: "No! You can't ever hurt me again. I'm not afraid of you."

The perpetrators. The ones who twisted our hearts, and hurt our bodies, and fed us fear and despair with our morning cereal; the ones who taught us that it's an unsafe world and that there will never be enough food, enough sex, enough money, and never, never any love. Not just not enough love. No love at all.

It's about finding the truth, which is: it's a beautiful, joyous life, where we bathe daily in light and love.

Remember what I told you once about the filter? I will tell you again. At the top of my head there is a filter and before any information from the universe can get down into me, it has to go through this filter. My filter is tied deeply to the disease of addiction. It is tinted by a negative outlook on life. So, part of this work that I must do is what I call "filter clarification."

I will not see the world through dirt-tinted glasses. I will do this work, will find and communicate with the big me, the authentic me, and at the same time I will not be ashamed of the small me, the self-willing me because it is part of me. I will simply find that small me and say, "I know you are afraid. But I will not act out on your fear. I will take care of you. Nobody will ever hurt you again."

It's late. It's around three in the morning. Cool and drizzly outside, this is the kind of weather I like best. There's a really funky movie coming on at four AM, "The Stepford Wives." I would like to stay up and watch, but I also want to go to church tomorrow morning.

I felt so joyful for you when you told me about the relationship you have formed with your friend — and envious too. Enjoy the moment. There is a happy balance somewhere out there. May we find it now.

I so hope to be out there with you, some day, but I feel a chill.

Write me, love.
Jackie

Down from the Dog Star

November 12

Tony O'Brian
1416, 19th Avenue North
Phoenix, Arizona

Dear Tony,

Old friend, I got your note this morning. It cheered me immensely. How badly I miss you and that land of Unicorns, which is the fellowship in Phoenix. Perhaps Jerry and I will drive out and see you soon. I hope so.

Fairly early in the day before it got too warm, Mother, Helen, Jerry, and I went walking. Helen had her little dog, Killer on a leash. Bonnie crept quietly along the roadside, just out of sight in the kudzu. Mother had her trusty hockey stick, and Hiser trotted proudly along at her side. Not that there are any golf balls. Until the Driving Club can convert to Cemetery Golf, there will be no players to whack their golf balls off the greens and down into the ditches, to tantalize Mom and Helen.

What a strange convoy we must have seemed: an elderly woman, the enigma that is Helen, her fluffy little dog, a leopard, a young German Shepherd, a short, muscular man, and me.

And just who am I? Mother told me that I was developing a wattle, which is, as you know, jowls. I thought she said a waddle. That is something that a duck does. Neither of these prospects alarm me, very much.

If I have jowls, they are my jowls and probably the best looking jowls on the planet. And I love them.

If I waddle, it's my waddle, and would probably win the waddling Olympics, if there is such a thing.

It's not the money, not the lover, not the land. It's finally finding some God-shaped Stuff to put in my God-shaped hole, it's finding that circle of safety in which to stand.

And so, we seven caravan along an otherwise empty road. The sweet, grape-jelly smell of kudzu blossoms and the creek-bottom smell of water-willow curve directly into our hearts, stitching us together into the ultimate, Southern quilt.

Mother tells me that when she and Helen were girls, they walked on this road together, daydreaming about the future, and making patterns in the soft clay dust that perked up between their toes with every step.

It's hard for me to imagine all these roads as once having been unpaved.

Have you ever wondered about roads? Have you ever been curious about from where they came?

The animals. Every major road, every great highway, began as a deer trail. Very soon now, according to Eric, the busy roads of our planet will return to deer trails. But Eric's concept of time is not the same as ours. Vast and wheeling. Turning and gone.

It's about time for bed. Mother has already gone up for the night. Jerry is out on the back porch talking to Racquel and Junior, his deep, rich voice counterpointed by Racquel's musical ululations, and Junior's occasional, cello-like pronouncements. Oh, how I have learned to love these people.

Soon, Helen will move quietly around this warm, dim house, drawing drapes, lighting the fairy lamps, seeing that the animals have water, and that mother has her bell close at hand.

It's about time to go out onto the porch, say goodnight to our friends and draw my buddy into the only place where time stands still for me.

Thank God for these gifts. I did nothing to deserve this life. People might say that I was born on third base.

I may have hit my very first home run.

I love you, Honey,

Good Bye,
Jackie

BOOK TWO

A Few Other Opinions:

Who knows the truth? Who, knowing the truth, is willing to tell it? Perhaps the truth — of this story — is strictly a matter of opinion. Except for Honey. She knew everything, and, being a dog, was not afraid to tell it. So here are a few snips of the truth as seen through the eyes of those from the Bend.

You decide.

The beauty of our living tree,
Grafted by necessity
May bloom again in other lands
When I lie prone beneath your hands.

Excerpts from the

Journal of Beebus McCloud

MAY 1ST

Hell, most people look at me and all they see is a big old redneck sheriff with a beer belly. But I've got a journal. Not just any old country boy has a journal. Right?

Jackie sits up on that hill at Quarter Pine like the Queen Cat of the County and God knows anybody that crosses those people usually ends up missing or worse. It's been that way for as long as I can remember and my memory is long. They act like they run the whole show. Maybe they do, but Beebus knows where the bodies are buried.

Neva Jean came creeping by the house last night, not five minutes after Jackie left. Whew! All I need is to get those two under the same roof for a couple of minutes. Sometimes I feel like one of those jugglers you see on Circus of the Stars. Jackie on one hand, Neva Jean on the other, all the bullshit I have to deal with in this loony bin of a town, and now Mrs. Luden herself is breathing down my neck. She hasn't come right out with what she wants, but then again, she never does. Sent Helen by the office with a pie . . . Helen's a good woman.

She keeps a close mouth and you know she's Luden-faithful, but she's a good woman. That time Junior went crazy in the streets, and was running around screaming the goats were about to get him, and then locked himself in the Baptist Church bell tower with a rifle, it was Helen who talked him down before he hurt anybody. When I went to Quarter Pine to get Junior's "best friend" Jackie, Jackie just about busted a gut laughing and told me to ignore Junior, when he got hungry — and that shouldn't be too far off a time — he'd come down.

Jackie bills himself as Junior's closest friend, but as far as I can tell, Junior's just a joke to Jackie. Everything's a joke to Jackie. I try, but I can't get a handle on that boy. I don't understand him. Maybe it's better if I don't—get too close to a snake and . . . .

It was Helen who took off her apron, clapped her hat on her head, and crawled into the front seat of the squad car with me (old Mrs. Luden would have settled herself in the back of the car), and held her peace till we reached the church. Junior hadn't fired any shots, but the town knew he was up there and the streets were clear.

It looked funny to see the streets empty in broad daylight. On the other hand, it wasn't for that reason, but it was so hot and dusty that it made sense.

This was before Junior started eating everything in sight. He was a good-looking boy then, and I must admit I had given him a thought or two, but at the time I was completely wrapped up in Neva Jean. Lord, that girl was pretty back then and sweet as sugar. Of course the Wulmothes would as soon have died as see me publicly courting Neva. Neva didn't care. She would have run off with me any time I asked. I think she loved me. I think the stuff that went down between me and Jackie and Neva was what changed her, was what put a hard, sharp edge to her. I should have grabbed her when I had the chance and got her out of this town, but Mrs. Luden was always dangling the carrot out in front of my nose, always promising this and that, and always delivering. Back then, to a boy with a drunk for a dad, who had run off before I could even talk proper, and a mother who spent most of her days in the hospital, the prospect of someday being town sheriff looked pretty good.

Mrs. Luden sent me to school, clothed me, fed me, stood right behind me. Why shouldn't I look the other way, every now and then?

But that damn dog had to die. Jackie's crazy with grief. I told him that it was just a dog and I'd get him another one. That was a mistake. I've been afraid before—any man who says he hasn't been is a liar or a fool—but when that boy stuck his face up in mine and whispered what he was gonna do to whoever killed his pup, I had a hard time holding my water.

Now the truth is, I don't think anybody poisoned his dog. German Shepherds are high strung and fine tuned. Honey was a sweet dog and anybody who visited Quarter Pine was in great danger, not from being bitten, but from being licked to death.

According to Helen, the day before the dog took sick, Jackie had been unloading groceries and Honey had got her jaws wrapped around a four-quart carton of Frantically Fudgey Chocolate ice cream, and run under the house with it. Nobody even knew it was missing till Junior came up that evening to sit on the porch and gossip and munch with Jackie and Mrs. Luden. Jackie had gone to a lot of trouble to get that ice cream, it being both his and Junior's favorite flavor, and they wouldn't have known the dog had even gotten her paws on it if she hadn't picked that moment to throw up about a gallon of chocolate-y sludge all over the kitchen floor that Helen had just waxed.

Chocolate contains a chemical called theobromine. This is the chemical that the brain produces when people are in love. (Would a redneck sheriff know that?) This chemical, in large quantities, is deadly to dogs. Add that to the fact that milk gives dogs terrible stomach upsets and the truth of it is, Jackie was probably the one who killed his pup. This might be the thing that's pushing him over the edge. I don't know. I just plan to lie low and hope for the best.

I was talking about Junior in the bell tower. Like I said, this was around the time he started putting on weight and being so crazy about the goats. My motto is, leave the goats alone, and they'll leave me alone.

Helen spent a good hour talking to Junior. She never even acted like it was odd that Junior was up there in the bell tower with a rifle, him on one side of the dusty door, her on the other. She talked about ordinary, everyday things, sort of like they were sitting in the kitchen having cookies and milk. She mentioned that she had a red velvet cake in the oven and if they didn't get back to the house before long, Mr. Jackie would sure as heck have that cake gobbled down. Junior came out, handed me his .22 and we all headed for home, where Helen did, indeed, have a red velvet cake cooling on the window sill.

She wrapped a slab of it in waxed paper, put it in a sack and handed it to Junior right before the men from the Clarion insane asylum came sashaying in to take Junior away.

That's when Junior started eating.

MAY 2ND

Quiet as a tomb,
Doomed from the womb.

MAY 3RD

New tires for squad car. Broke up a fight at the Fuzzy Mule. James Randal Grant drunker than a lord. Took him to the office, sobered him up and took him home. Good kid. Hate to see him go the way of the rest of them.

MAY 4TH

A long time ago they had what they called the language of the flowers. A rose meant one thing, a carnation meant something else. A lily

Down from the Dog Star

meant this and a pansy meant that. I don't know the language of the flowers but I sure as hell know the language of the pies. After the many years of receiving pies from the hill and then putting each particular type of pie together with whatever happened to be going down around me, I came to some conclusions. If it was a peach cobbler, then Mrs. Luden was just feeling good and saying howdy. A sour apple pie meant I wasn't dancing quite as fast as she'd like to see me dance. A blackberry fried pie meant batten down the hatches, hell was nigh. But there's this one hellacious pie she bakes, sort of a pecan pie, sort of a fruit pie, sort of maple-y and very, very sweet, that I've only gotten twice before.

The first time was right after my mama died. I was young, only about twelve. Mrs. Luden sent her husband down to get me at the town hall, where Sheriff Grant was holding on to me till the county people could get there to take me to the boys' town. Mrs. Luden wasn't having none of it. She sent the message to Sheriff Grant that I was Luden Bend born, I would be Ludens Bend raised and I would be Ludens Bend buried.

Two out of three ain't bad.

They took me in up there. And the first thing I remember about that big, dark, lemony smelling house was the taste of her pecan-maple-fruit pie.

Not that I was raised at Quarter Pine. I am a McCloud. They are Ludens, and no one ever loses sight of these facts. I'm not bitter. I'm more than thankful for Mrs. Luden. God knows what would have become of me without her. But a dog is a dog, a cat is a cat.

I was farmed out to the preacher of the First Baptist Church of Ludens Bend, Alabama. What I got in that house was a lot of love, a lot of discipline, and a whole lot of good food. A boy could have done worse.

When I was old enough, Mrs. Luden packed me off to the police academy in Birmingham, where I learned the finer points of law enforcement. She was always cultivating. Cultivating the land, planting seeds in the minds and hearts of men for later harvest.

So that was my first brush with that strange, sweet pie. The second time I tasted it was when her husband, Black John, died.

You should have seen Jackie at the funeral. The perfect son, looking after his poor, weak, old mother, and treating her like spun glass. I was the only one there who knew he was so full of hydrocodone cough syrup that he gurgled when he walked. I know, because I'm the one that got it for him. Jackie was a lot easier to handle when he lived on diet pills and cough syrup. I'm really of two minds about this recovery stuff he's gotten into. He may live longer, but with a clear head, that boy's hell on wheels.

Anyway, the death of Black John Luden. His name wasn't Luden. It was O'Brian. But Mrs. Luden was the last child of the Luden family and part of the deal to get hitched to Mrs. Luden was to take the Luden name. Story goes he was handsome, she was lonely. The family needed children. It must have seemed like a fine deal to Black John, him a stranger to the Bend, and having no idea about what really went on here. I sincerely believe he lived in innocence of the valley till the day Jackie offered him the use of his car, he tooled off down the drive of Quarter Pine, and five miles down the way pulled over, lay his head on the leather-padded steering wheel and sank peacefully into that red-skinned sleep that tells the tale of carbon monoxide poisoning.

The first thing I saw when I pulled up behind the big, black, slant-back of a car — its engine rumbling and chuckling under a blindingly shiny hood — was Jackie's sky blue riding boots, poked out from under the rear of the Caddy. He slid out from under the car, grinned at me through my windshield and vanished into the woods by the side of the road. He was carrying a greasy sack with some sort of pipe or tubing dangling from its half-opened mouth, trailing in the breeze.

Say anything? You must be crazy. Black John was never one of us. His only purpose was to give us Jackie.

That evening Jackie knocked on the door of the house Mrs. Luden had given me as a graduation present from the academy. I knew what he had in his hand: one of those pies. The second pecan, mapley sweet fruit pie I had ever tasted.

He left right before dawn, right before I had to get up and file my report of what I thought had happened.

And now, today, I receive the third of those nameless, wonderful pies. Either something has gone down, something is going down, or something will be going down that will require me to either be somewhere else or see things a certain way.

What the hell.... a man can only sell his soul once. Right?

MAY 5TH

Nothing much.

MAY 6TH

Deader than hell.

MAY 7TH

Stayed off work today to plant my garden. Half dozen Better Boy tomatoes, half dozen Big Tom bell pepper plants, a bunch of green onions, some squash, pole beans and a couple of egg plants. It's late, but now I'll have food till frost.

MAY 8TH

Louise Pierson came by the office. Said her son hadn't come home last night. Jimmy is a big old boy, but he's not quite right. Not retarded or anything, just slow. I wouldn't worry about him, except he never does anything like this. The only problem I have with the boy is the way he hunts on private property. I've warned him half a dozen times and it just goes right through his head. They caught him up at Quarter Pine once and Jackie like unto scared him to death. I saw him pedaling hell-for-leather towards his house that day. He was crying so hard he couldn't hardly see the road. Said Jackie had got him down on the ground, held a knife in his crotch and told him if he ever caught him on his land again, he'd nut him like a pig.

There's not much to hunt around here, a few squirrels and quite a few rabbits, but the deer were hunted out years ago. Of course there's the Canecutters, but I can't think of a surer way for a man to commit suicide than to go after one of those. Old Sheriff Grant, the man who held this job before me, told me a way to safely hunt them, but it would take some real persuasion to send me into those swamps.

I got a bad feeling about Jimmy.

MAY 9TH

Came in from work today and found a real surprise. Neva and Junior had planted my window boxes full of red petunias and big, white geraniums. Just when I think I don't have a friend in the world, they go and do something like that.

Down from the Dog Star

MAY 10TH

No word on Jimmy Pierson. Searched around town and asked if anybody had seen him. His bike was found in the sinkhole. This looks rough.

MAY 11TH

My deputy just isn't working out. He's a real go-getter and doesn't seem to know how to ignore the things I tell him to ignore. Now I got this fellow at the request of Doc Wulmothe. The Doc usually has a good take on things but this time I think he made a mistake. I'll give him a few days, maybe a week and if he doesn't learn to listen, I'll have to replace him.

MAY 12TH

Went fishing. Didn't catch much but I was sitting out there in the boat and suddenly remembered Jackie's big bass tournament. Jackie hates fishing and hunting. He has a tender heart when it comes to animals, but he had his eye on Farley Westport, a fine fisherman and a pretty nice guy. Jackie wanted to spend time with Farley and filled him up with one of the biggest whoppers I ever heard come out of his mouth. Jackie told Farley he was a champion bass fisherman and Farley invited him to be his partner in the big tournament they have once a year at the lake. Jackie had something like a rusty safety pin and some kite string and I'll be damned if he didn't catch the champion fish that day! You should see him and Junior cruising the lake in the boat he won. When those two go riding around in that boat, they act like they're on an expedition to Mars. I watched Jackie packing his supplies for an overnight camping trip once, and he actually packed six strings of Christmas lights and a portable generator to run the lights, his microwave, and an electric blanket. Junior is always happy as a pig in shit when he's hanging out with Jackie. And food! Those two cook incredible meals when they go camping. I saw them baking a turkey once. Even had silver candlesticks and one of Mrs. Luden's good linen table cloths out there in the woods. Being in camp with those two is better than being in a Holiday Inn. Jackie loves his comfort.

MAY 15TH

Had to get rid of my deputy. Doc Wulmothe raised hell till I mentioned the problems the boy was causing me. Doc's got a few bones buried, too, you know.

Willie Gates is the perfect man for the job. He's right out of high school, clean living and empty-headed. Most importantly, his family's been in the Bend forever. We were talking on the square the other day about what he wanted to do with his life.

I didn't offer him the job, just planted the idea. When he comes around asking for work, old Sheriff Beebus will act undecided, let him stew a day or two, and then let him have it. He's a cute little rascal, kind of chubby but he smiles nice and seems easy going. The most important qualification for the job besides being Bend-born is to be teachable.

Louise Pierson's raising hell about her boy. Said she was going to the state police if he didn't show up pronto. I can handle the state boys but there's talk of a team coming over from Atlanta to explore the sinkhole.

Down from the Dog Star

MAY 21ST

Peaceful days. Took Willie fishing for an overnight. Definitely what I want for a deputy. Smart but obedient. Jackie called, acting real nasty, asked if I'd fried any fish for Willie. Gave me holy hell but agreed Willie was the man for the job. I managed to get a good jab at Jackie. I could hear him turning white over the phone when I mentioned the exploration team from Atlanta. I wonder what else he's thrown down that pit?

JUNE 2ND

Been concentrating on training Willie. Good fellow, picks it up fast. Jackie's been way too nice lately. He's up to something.

Got in touch with the lead fellow on the team that's coming to explore the sinkhole. According to my buddies in Hotlanta, he's covered to the ears in gambling debts. The boys are about to close in on him. We got it knocked!

SEPTEMBER 10TH

I've had it. I've took as much as a man can take, done everything they ever wanted me to do, crawled on my belly and took it up the ass my whole life. I won't do it no more. I asked Mrs. Luden just how long a man was supposed to be grateful, and she said, "Forever."

This new thing she wants me to do, for me, is undoable. She shouldn't have backed me into a corner this way. Tomorrow I'll go up there and put my foot down once and for all. There's enough evidence in my files on that crowd to put the lot of them in prison. I can send that sissy to the chair. There's proof, records, and witnesses.

Yes, sir, tomorrow there's gonna be some changes in the Bend. Somebody else is gonna be playing the music, and some high and mighty folks are gonna be dancing a different jig!

Can't wait to see the look on that old hellcat's face. And her whelp, too.

[ED. NOTE: There must have been more, but that was the last page of Beebus's journal that has been discovered. His body was found on September 15.]

Junior

Everybody thinks I was locked up at Clarion, down in Tuscaloosa all those times, because I was terrified of the goats. The first time I went away it might have been so, partly. I guess the real reason I spend so much time locked away, is that I'm just bored to tears most of the time, and the rest of the time tormented to tears by Miss Jackie and Neva Jean.

Jackie had it all wrong when he talked about my throwing bales of hay down the sinkhole. I was NOT trying to get those poor goats to commit suicide. I never really minded the goats. Aunt Bessie loved them and they kept her mind and hands occupied. What really happened with the hay was it was moldy. We had a barn full of hay that had gotten wet and then molded. Molded hay can kill cattle quicker than one might think and at the time we had some prize livestock at the Manor.

I knew it had to be disposed of in a way that would keep the cows from making lunch from it, and a huge hole full of smoke and fire seemed the perfect answer. It wasn't a few bales, either. The way Jackie talks, I carried a half dozen bales of hay down to the sinkhole and tossed them in. It was more like three hundred bales, and I had a lot of help from the farm hands we use to keep. It wasn't my fault that those silly goats took it into their heads to follow the hay down into the mines.

Jackie says a few goats escaped the fire and made their way underground. This is mostly true, but the goats weren't happy about it, I can tell you that! They made terrible sad bleating noises, as though asking to be rescued. It looks like a goat could make it back up such a slight slope as the sides of the sinkhole. What happened was, the goats had slipped down through the bottom of the pit. They became confused in the smoke. Luckily for them, unluckily for me, they made it safely into a branch of the old mines that had either burned out, or had never been rich enough in coal to catch fire.

Perhaps I tend towards being a bit too anthropomorphic, but I'm sure the goats were smart enough to put me, the hay, and their being caught underground together into a plot supreme.

Anyway, Jackie is the true anthropomorph around here. He actually changed that big dog's bandannas and collars everyday, sometimes twice a day, because he said it depressed Honey to be seen in the same outfit too often.

She *was* uncanny. I know for a fact that she understood everything anybody said, and I've seen her do things that a dog simply shouldn't be able to do. Once there was an incident with the remote control of Jackie's television. Perhaps I shouldn't tell about that. They might take me back to Clarion.

Honey put up with a lot but she drew the line when Jackie decided to pierce her ears. Jackie thought some diamond studs were just what the dog needed to give her that "Clat de Elan" (and I have no idea at all what that bit of bastardization of the French language means, it's one of Jackie's sayings) and he never stopped to think that diamond studs would be completely lost in the fur of her huge fuzzy ears. He might have gotten away with it, but he made the mistake of letting her see the needles, alcohol, ice, and Irish potato with which he planned to perform the operation.

That was one smart dog. She scooted under the house and didn't come out for two days. So Jackie decided that I needed pierced ears. That's why I have three holes per lobe. But Jackie explained that it wasn't anything he hadn't done to himself, and he promised me wonderful things to hang in my ears if I allowed him to perform the surgery. I have the earrings he gave me in a box on my dresser. Six matched, quarter-carat diamonds. He really is the ultimate bitch, but a generous bitch.

I miss him. Oh, he's still around in body, but the last few years have changed him. I'd like to blame it on that midget he brought back from the Amazon (although short as Jackie is, Jerry must look pretty tall), and I'd like to say it was Honey dying like that, but the truth is, people just change.

A gay man needs another gay man to talk to. Jackie and I used to be

Down from the Dog Star

able to just look at each other, say one or two words, and laugh ourselves silly because we knew exactly what the other meant. Whole series of events could be summed up in three words. Camping and carrying on (pronounce that campen 'n' carryen on) is what we call it. It doesn't work with a straight man. There's always that low-grade puzzlement, that faint, ever so faint condescension behind their eyes.

Jackie says straight men are wonderful, very useful for carrying heavy objects, and for adding a bit of terror to one's life, but useless for campy conversation. Straight women can sometimes pull it off, but they usually have hidden agendas.

He did organize the best Dooms Day Carnival that we've seen in a long time. I was getting pretty sick of Paulo. I knew if Jackie thought I was really happy with that little hustler, eventually, he'd get rid of him for me. When he let Lobo The Teeth eat the kid for the finale, I subtly let Jackie know that he had pleased me by my dramatic attempt at throwing myself off the roof of the cafe, and allowing the girls to "save" me. I could tell by the perturbed look on his face that he understood perfectly.

See what I mean?

There are so many misconceptions about gay people and how we live. Some of us are easy to spot and some of us are very predictable in our behaviors. But most of us go quietly about our lives, walking through the world, thinking our own thoughts and building our own realities.

The misinformation that annoys me most of all, is the idea that we are all slavering and gnashing at our psychic bits, with lust and perverted dreams about every guy on the planet.

I've known some hideous-looking losers who worry about one of us approaching them. PLEASE! I'm queer, not blind.

And straight friends will inevitably try and fix two gay people up with each other. They seem to think that our only requirement for a relationship (or a decent fuck) is that we both like men. There are all kinds of gay men and the diversity of their natures is important to a successful interaction.

Some people foolishly think that Jackie and I had a thing for each other. We are sisters. Both of us like very masculine, somewhat goofy, stupid guys. Jackie's theme song is that old tune by Wendy O'Williams and the Plasmatics whose chorus goes, "I like 'em big and stupid!" Me too. I don't know why. I don't care why. And both of us like those delectable emotionally and physically unavailable men. Jackie says he wouldn't want the Hope Diamond if he could afford it.

I was told once that we thought this way because we have a fear of commitment, a fear of getting too close. There may be some truth in that, but I think we're just repeating the patterns of our childhood. We seek what is familiar. Black John never touched Jackie. The only time he smiled at my poor cousin was when Jackie goofed up some way. Jackie took exquisite pleasure in torturing his father with being homosexual. I admire Jackie's chutzpah. He went deer hunting with a bunch of macho, moronic men that had what they called a "deer club." He wore a full face of make up. Nobody said a word. If they had, Black John would have had to kick somebody's ass, and it would definitely not have been his son's, because Black John knew Aunt Minnie would have slaughtered him like a hog.

In my own case, I never knew a father. All I had for a masculine role model was Uncle Wooley. I could have learned how to manipulate God Herself from Doctor Wulliam Wulmothe, I could have learned how to take out an appendix, I could have learned how to smile like a tiger while I was cutting your throat. But that was not my nature. Neva and I had Uncle Wooley's number practically from birth. Neva once said to me, "I love Uncle Wooley. He's divine. He reminds me of one of those tiny dancers on the top of a music box."

"What?" I asked in non-comprehension.

Neva simpered and said, "Why, sugar, he's completely artificial and always looks like he's got a stick stuck up his ass."

Neva profited from Uncle Wooley's tutelage. She had to learn fast. What a childhood she must have had. Uncle Wooley on one side trying to indoctrinate her with his evil, and Aunt Bessie on the other trying to match her with Jackie.

The plan was for a child from the union of the Wulmothes and the Ludens. Yes, that would have been quite a match, if one ignored the age difference between Jackie and Neva Jean and the fact that they are first cousins. Luckily for them, Jackie developed a case of "the love that dares not speak its name" (although he spoke it loudly and longly every chance he got), and Neva fell in love with Beebus McCloud. Beebus broke her heart, ruined her.

Let's hear it for the Canecutter!

At least let's hear it for whatever gutted Beebus. The pool of blood in which Beebus was lying was too dark and viscous to be human blood. I'm the only one who seems to have noted that. It looked like hog blood to me.

The Blaylock family were slaughtering that week and some folks wondered why they were killing pigs before frost.

Prophecies. All prophecies.

One would think that only original, fresh lines would really twink my jaded sense of humor, but when Jackson lisped, "I thought it was a deer," I rolled across the gold-and-cream Aubusson in his living room and couldn't get to my hands and knees for a good five minutes.

That deer hunt. No, nobody commented on his eyeliner and blush, but he knew he might have gone a bit far. His motto is, "Any reaction is better than no reaction," and so when he set out to shock and annoy Black John, he was just too excited and pleased with his plan to think it through. Until he found that circle of power in which he could safely stand, he had taken a lot of abuse. As a child he had kept it a secret. He didn't know that a word to Aunt Minnie would have bought him peace in the Bend, and I think he was ashamed of being bullied. He repaid them all; it warped him even more. Now he talks a lot about forgiveness and how important it is not to hold resentments. He talks a good talk. But really now, he did push that wretched, uni-eyebrowed, adenoidal child down into a pit full of methane and fire, went home and baked one of those scrumptious butterscotch pineapple upside-down cakes — for which I would walk barefoot through a pit of rattlesnakes — gave himself an avocado-lemon-juice facial, and then went shopping.

Go figure.

So there he was, deep in a snow-flecked cedar grove in north

Alabama, with a gang of hostile rednecks, a fully loaded .30-06 Remmington deer rifle and a face full of Esteé Lauder. He probably felt threatened, probably felt backed in a corner. So when Bob Pierson, the uncle of dear little Jimmy, let his face slip for a second, and Jackie saw the disgust in his eyes, he decided that the best defense was offense.

Bob Pierson had a bright red four-by-four that he polished more lovingly than he had ever polished his wife's clitoris; it was his compensation for having a three-inch penis. (I gleaned this bit of grease from Ronnie at the Tender Tendrils Beauty Emporium, and he heard it whispered directly from Louise Pierson's mouth into the ear of Sue Lyn, the manicurist, and Jackie knew it too.)

Jackie waited till the coast was clear, and pumped over a hundred copper-clad hollow points into the vehicle. When the men returned to camp and Bob discovered his shredded four wheeler, Jackie gazed sadly at him through Khol-rimmed eyelids and said it: "I thought it was a deer."

Black John wrote a check on the spot. Jackie sleezed into his Seville and glided away before the drinking began. Jackie never went deer hunting again, but he single-handedly kept Esteé Lauder in business in Birmingham, Alabama.

Beebus paid Bob a private visit and the whole incident was pushed, gasping and delirious, under the surface of the tar pit that is the secret life of the Bend.

Neva Jean

I have slept with exactly three men in my life. The fact that I tell most people to piss off has shadowed my real self. Around here, if a woman goes her own way, and is lucky enough to be rich enough to get away with it, they either call her a whore or a bitch. Fuck 'em.

When Jackie ran off to the Amazon, I nearly lost it. I missed that man like I would have missed my right arm. Since we were kids, we kept the Bend at a simmer. Even if he had of done something to that Pierson kid, and even if I had seen him do it, I would never have turned him in. And Jackie knew it.

As for Beebus chasing him to the Amazon? The day Jackie and Thomas Blaylock roared out of the Bend, trailing Obsession and curses, the sheriff was on his way to Quarter Pine. Beebus was going to tell Jackie to relax, that he had, as usual, fixed everything. And Jackie knew this.

Even if a body had been found in the sinkhole, there would have been absolutely no way to link Jackie with a murder. He couldn't have been touched. And Jackie knew this, too.

So why did he flame off to South America leaving me to molder and Junior to grieve himself right back into Clarion? Because he didn't give a damn for anybody but that dog. Because he was bored. Because he loves drama more than life. Because he loves to travel. Because Beebus was making demands that had nothing to do with the law. (Jackie had driven the sheriff just about crazy and promptly gotten sick of him.) He had screwed Junior out of a relationship with Ronnie, from the Tender Tendrils, and may have felt remorse. He had gone too far with James Randal Grant, a minor, and might have been afraid that it was about to become public knowledge.

But mostly, he was bored. He reached out and arranged a few facts to meet his needs and—presto!—he had an excuse to get out of the Bend and out from under the ever-present thumb of Aunt Minnie.

Why not just take off? Travel takes money, and at that time, he was completely dependent on his mother. Yes, she'd give him anything he wanted. Anything but his freedom.

When Cemetery Golf became such a success, he had his first taste of true autonomy. And then Jerry came along. Everything good seemed to fall into place for him. I'm surprised he handled it so well.

It was at this point that he got into a rift of what he called "self definition." He said a woman had once stated that unless we define ourselves, other people would define us to our detriment. Jackie had been off dope for about five years when he made his trip to the jungle, and it had taken him that long to really get his head clear.

I'll tell you something most people don't know. There are two Jackson K. Ludens, two distinct personalities. I don't know how much control, if any, he has over who is driving the boat. I can tell who is "out" and I act accordingly.

Or maybe he's just the devil.

Devil or not, Junior and I both love him. We three were about all we had when we were young. He's closer than a brother, but not quite a lover. What he was, was the spark plug that kept our engine firing. Even when it looked like we were gunning for each other, it was always a game. We love games. There's not much else to do.

When his "baby girl" died it was like the sun had gone out for him. Jackie's gotten over it for the most part, but he's not the same. Junior sees it too.

Junior was scrambling eggs this morning. He had his big, felt bathrobe wrapped around him, and his sloppy, comfortable house shoes on his size six feet. I was hunched over the table, my nose nearly lost in my coffee cup — I am NOT a morning person— trying to come to, when he turned to me and asked, "Did that really happen? The seeing-eye dog?" Every now and then we have to do a quick reality check. What my brother was talking about was how Jackie had attempted to disguise Honey as a seeing-eye dog so she could accompany him on planes and stay in nice hotels with him. It seemed like a brilliant plan. Jackie bribed

Doctor Gideon into giving him a paper saying that he was legally blind. He then cajoled Beebus into rigging some official-looking guide dog license for Honey.

Cleatus at the garage welded a bunch of Black John's old golf clubs into what, oddly enough, looked pretty much like a guide dog's harness.

At the time, Jackie was going on a trip to Arizona. He had met a woman at an NA convention who taped the people who spoke there. After the meetings, addicts would buy the tapes to listen to for reinforcement. The woman's name was Margaret, and they took a shine to each other at once. Jackie, though queer as a donkey with a bow tie, loves to be around beautiful women. To hear Jackie tell it, Margaret was a combination Garbo, Cleopatra, and the Mother of Jesus. Margaret probably liked Jackie because she didn't really know him. He was wearing his Indian regalia and toodling on about sweats and Grandfather Bear and The Moose Who Walks At Night and God knows what all. That sort of stuff has become very chic in recovery. Most of the true natives barely tolerate white people who are attempting to do the cross-cultural thing. Jackie just liked the beads and feathers. Junior said that during his Indian period Jackie resembled Bette Davis dressed as Geronimo. The upshot of all this was, Margaret invited him to Phoenix for a while. I don't know if she meant it, but Jackie took it at face value, and laid plans accordingly, including the guide dog ruse.

He had just gotten out of a really bizarre relationship with a supposed medicine man in the wilds of Canada, and was at loose ends. He had been recovering from this affair at his friend Stephanie's and her husband Bill's house in Kentucky. Jackie claimed that the chief (and just between us, there was a lot of doubt in Bill's mind that there was any native blood in John Bigbow's veins) had stalked him all the way from Canada to Alabama. If I know Jackie, John Bigbow was probably jumping for joy, or doing some equivalent native dance, in celebration that Bette Geronimo was gone! As usual, Jackie turned a simple breakup into the Crimean War.

It's true that Bill had to smuggle him off the reserve on his Harley, but that, I believe, had more to do with gambling debts than unrequited love. It's also very likely that Jackie spoke the truth when he said his lover was a total nut. Those were the kind of guys he went for. That was the kind of relationship on which he thrived.

You know, the blind act truly should have worked. Honey looked like a guide dog. Jackie looked like a blind man. He had the paperwork. Junior and I loaded this circus act into Jackie's Caddy and headed for the airport. Jackie strapped Honey into her harness, and grabbed his cane and his shades. Junior and I struggled with eight pieces of Vuitton, and we made our entrance into the Birmingham airport. The problem was, Honey didn't know she was a guide dog. She had never even been trained to walk on a leash. She weighed about a hundred pounds and was the strongest, most stubborn animal I had ever seen.

They actually made it onto the plane! Junior and I walked on either side of the dream team, carefully shepherding the Shepherd. The stewardess let us help Jackie settle into his seat, Honey curled happily in a large, furry ball at his side. Her long nose was tucked under her big, saber-shaped tail, her golden eyes glowed almost orange. Junior was sweating bullets and I was about to pass out from tension.

I thought that once we got those two onto the plane, we could head for home. Junior looked at me, giggled, and told me that he thought it would be a good idea to wait until the plane was actually off the ground.

That dog sometimes obeyed Jackie, but for the most part, didn't. The rather disjointed story, that I was later able to piece together, was that things on the plane were fine until the stewardess began to give her lecture on what to do in an emergency. She was waving an orange oxygen mask around, about six inches over Honey's head, and the dog wanted it. Honey leaped over the helpless Jackie, took off in hot pursuit of the terrified stewardess, and chased her right into the cockpit. If the plane had been airborne, it could have been a terrible disaster. As it was, the plane merely left the runway and became mired in the dirt of the airfield.

They didn't arrest him. He had his paperwork and Beebus lickety-splitted to the airport to rescue him.

He drove to Arizona, but he enjoyed the blind act so much that every now and then over the next few years, he would put on his shades, strap

Honey into her harness, and go for a walk. He said it gave Honey a sense of purpose.

She was a dog. She was just a dog. But besides a childhood friend who died badly, she was the only living thing for which Jackie ever really cared.

Besandra Wulmothe

As the oldest living human in Ludens Bend, it would seem that I would have a great deal to say to you.

I don't. Words are a waste of time. People hear what they want to hear, no matter what one is trying to say. You see, people listen but most of them don't really hear. People watch but seldom truly see.

My forte has always been action. When I saw Black John withering away to nothing, living on morphine and black coffee, and wincing every time he moved, it was I who took Jackie aside and told him what had to be done.

Jackie will give you the impression that he's cold and hard. He's as soft as custard. But the years of abuse and neglect built walls and masks around him. I am the only one who really knows just how good a man he is. And Amy Grant. Jackie would not have survived the childhood he endured if not for Amanda Grant. Minnie knows it. How do you think Amanda lives in that fine ranch house, drives that pretty Buick, and buys anything she wants at Wal-Mart. She just about lives at Wal-Mart. She has no income but a small Social Security check. Her children aren't able to help her.

Minnie takes care of her, the same way Minnie takes care of everybody in the Bend—one way or another.

Just in case somebody is paying attention for once, and I doubt anybody is, I will clear up a couple of points that, as usual, Jackie rearranged to suit his purposes.

The Goats. I didn't particularly like or dislike the goats. We had two, and before we knew it, we had fifty-three. They just sort of sneaked up on us. And nobody wants goats. I had a choice of keeping them or shooting them. Keeping them was easier. I was a lot easier in my mind when they fell into that big hole down back of the house. As for goat

Down from the Dog Star

cheese, that's one tall tale that even I can't figure out. I never milked a goat in my life, and even when this was a working farm, it was easier to buy cheese at the store. That Jackie.

Yes, I most certainly did, with Neva's help, send Beebus McCloud down to the swamps in search of a Canecutter. And I knew for a fact that if he took a gun into that swamp he'd come back on a stretcher. Beebus McCloud had been playing Neva, Jackie, and Junior against each other for years. Even when they were children, before they discovered the ultimate tool for manipulation and pleasure, Beebus toyed with my babies. He had a certain deliciously low quality about him that was irresistible to them. Some would call this quality street smarts (I hear that on television a lot) but I just call it craftiness.

Beebus was a lout. If he had been a bumpkin, I might not have sent him hunting. A bumpkin can't help being stupid and mean. A lout is both of those things by choice and design.

Minnie sent me one of her pecan maple nut pies the last day Beebus came to the house. The day before, she and I had sat on the front terrace of the Farm and talked about this and that. She simply said that Beebus hadn't been all that effective a sheriff lately and that it might be time for a change. And I knew exactly what she meant. When the pie came it was a certainty that Jackie's Cemetery Golf range was about to get a new customer.

Now this is the thing: Beebus knew as well as I did that he was walking to his death. He could have said no. In the past, he would just have smiled and changed the subject. It wasn't to please me, and it wasn't to impress Neva or Jackie. Beebus committed suicide and we'll never know why.

Minnie's gotten her way all her life and that is as it should be. Absolute power does not always corrupt absolutely. Just look around this valley and you'll see what I mean.

The one thing she hasn't gotten that she needs, as well as wants, is a grandchild out of Jackie. That's one thing she'll never get.

Thomas Blaylock

It's best to keep them guessing. Oh my, yes! Never show anybody your cards. Oh my, yes! That's what my mama taught me and that's what I'm teaching you.

They all wanted a piece of my fine, black ass and nobody ever got any at all. Junior was crazy in love with me. Miss Neva Jean looked me up and down like I was one of her horses. Mr. Jackie did, too, till he found out I was as much a lady as he was.

I knew good and well that no Ku Klux were coming to get me just because I was in some church play. I went to the Amazon with Mr. Jackie because I knew he needed me to look after him.

When my brother got in all that bad trouble with the law over that crack cocaine, it was Mr. Jackie who got him out of jail, sent him to treatment, and turned his life around. When I didn't have no shoes to wear to school and not a decent pair of pants, it was Miss Minnie Luden who took me to Sears and Roebuck and bought me a whole new school wardrobe. It was Mr. Black John who sent my two sisters to nursing school. Not LPN school either. He sent Hondette and Peruvia to the University of Alabama where they got RN degrees.

I don't care what anybody says, and I don't mean no disrespect, but Mr. Jackie couldn't find his ass with both hands if he had all day to search for it. I knew he wouldn't make it in the Amazon without somebody with sense to ease his way. Helen got me aside and told me flat out that she was worried about her baby. What was important to her was to keep him safe but never to let him know he was being looked after.

He didn't even catch on to the airstrip or the Friends or that Dr. Wulmothe was all mixed up in it, till he was strapped down on that flying saucer about to be experimented on.

Wulliam Wulmothe. If there is such a thing as evil in the flesh it is him! Who was it that started Mr. Jackie on drugs in the first place? Who was it that kept him doped up on Tussionex and Dexedrine for nigh on twenty years? Who was it that reported his every move to Miss Minnie? Who was it that planted the seed in my boss's mind that his little dog had been poisoned? That's right. The doctor.

He's an old man now. He can't live much longer, especially since he brought that French girl home to the Manor. Aunt Estelle, Miss Besandra's cook, says that those two yowl like alley cats, snort like hogs, and generally rattle the roof every night.

I'm pretty patient and I would like to see that old devil brought low by age and sickness. That would be a fit end for him. I can wait. But if he ever looks like he's even thinking about getting his hooks into Mr. Jackie again, he'll end up just like Beebus McCloud. I still have that big old butcher knife from The Eternal Life Cafe and Souvenir Shop For Jesus.

But I do run on. I declare, sometimes I can be SO flighty!

Oh my, yes.

HONEY

I saw everything. Everywhere he went, I went. People don't pay much attention to dogs. They'll say and do anything in front of one of us. I watched him seduce and destroy that big fat sheriff and I watched him when he ran a pipe from the manifold of his car to a hole in the floor board.

Does it surprise you that a dog knows what a manifold is? Well, we know anything that you know. You say it, we remember it. And that's not all I know. My mother told me everything she had seen, and what her mother had told her, and what her mother's mother had told her mother. We've lived a long time in the valley and we haven't forgotten a single thing. And we have the courage, since we had no part in it, to tell the truth.

Oh, how I loved him. And oh, how he loved me. My earliest memories of my life after they took me from my mother, was the smell of his neck when I'd snuggle with him at night. He wore a perfume called Angel. He could do that. He could do anything. The perfume tickled my nose and made me sneeze. When I got to be a big dog (though not a wise dog), I decided that I wanted the bed all to myself. I learned how to nudge him gently onto the floor. First I would pile up a lot of pillows and blankets on the spot on which he'd land. Sometimes he wouldn't wake up. It never occurred to me that I would be the one to leave the bed. I didn't argue, afraid that I might then end up on the back porch.

He had a funny look on his face the day the old man died. I never saw that look very often. It was a sad look. When I was a baby, there were these hickory smoke-flavored chew sticks that I was crazy about. Black John always seemed to have one in his pocket for me. I was supposed to sniff about his pockets and try to act as if I didn't know exactly where it was. With MY nose! I knew where it was the second he got within ten feet

Down from the Dog Star

of me, but he enjoyed the search and it displayed my superior sense of smell to perfection.

Jackie hated it when anybody touched me, especially his father, but Black John was always kind to me and that's the only way we have of judging a person's goodness or badness. There's this beautiful Shepherd called Gretchen here who used to live with Adolf Hitler, a man most humans don't care for very much, and Gretchen says he gave the best ear scratchings and belly rubs that she ever had. Gretchen didn't care for his girlfriend; something about pillows and Shepherd fur. Now that I am up here with Mama and Grandma I understand a lot of things better.

There is way too much confusion about how I died. It had nothing to do with that ice cream. It is NOT what killed me. And I was NOT poisoned. I'm glad he pushed Jimmy down the sinkhole, though. Jimmy threw a rock at me once and hit me on the head. It hurt. But I was not poisoned. I could have smelled poison. The ice cream did make me really sick. I threw it up all over the kitchen floor. He put me to bed with a cold washrag on my head.

My heart stopped. Simple as that. I had a bad heart. According to a Schnauzer here, who used to live with a cardiac surgeon, the electrical conduction system of my heart was faulty. I went to sleep the night I lifted that fabulous Frantically Fudgey ice cream that Jackie had ordered all the way from Atlanta (it was good!) and woke up here, here on the Dog Star. I have a choice. I can stay here for a while or go back now. The pup he now has used to be an Afghan; poetic justice for Helen, but he'd be pissed!

Helen never once said the Freedom Bus was full of attack-trained Afghans. She said the biggest comfort she had on the freedom bus was a hand-knitted Afghan BLANKET. Jackie takes liberties now and then. Can you blame him? Why settle for dry dog food, when with just a little dramatizing, you can get steak Diane?

Cemetery Golf was MY idea. We were visiting the old man's grave one spring day. Jackie had brought a golf ball for me to chase and when I got tired of chasing it, I buried the white egg at the head of Black John's grave. The rest is history.

You know, LZ and I are the only ones close to my friend that are really happy that he's off the pills. I don't think anybody else wanted him to find himself.

He said, once, that envy was the fear that I wasn't going to get what you had and that jealousy was the fear that you were going to get what I had. He was always dropping these little stones into the pools of people's minds and most people don't like ripples.

It's not all that hard being dead. Dead isn't a really good name for what this is. I have a lot of fun. I rollerblade the rings of Saturn, piss on Martian fungus, and terrify those aliens by my close relationship with my old buddy Peanut.

That's one part of the story Jackie had right. If it weren't for Peanut, the Friends would have made hamburger of the planet. They were getting ready to when Peanut growled them down.

You see, the planet has nothing to do with evolution. It was not created in a few days by some mumbo-jumbo God. It was no accident. It was designed and created and carefully nurtured and tended by the Friends. It was supposed to be a farm and the crop was to be human souls. What were the Friends going to do with human souls? Ever hear of Naugahyde? The Friends have an equivalent.

The mistake they made was letting us dogs get a foothold. They've been cruising the universe for aeons, taking anything they wanted, with no regard for anybody. Well the future is here and it is us.

Haven't you ever noticed that dog spelled backwards is God?

Dog Town was no accident. It was put in Jackie's mind by The Big Poodle In the Sky. I won't talk about The Big Poodle In The Sky. Some things are too sacred to talk about.

I *will* say that the Gabor sisters did a great deal to advance our cause by directly raising Poodle Consciousness and they have great rewards in store.

How we adore Zsa Zsa! It is no accident that she has had such great success. All orchestrated by The Big Poodle In the Sky.

The Friends' (and that is one heck of a deceptive name) plan to harvest the Earth faltered and ground to a stop the night Peanut bit the alien that was trying to kidnap Sister Grant. They had always been invincible. More than the shock of Peanut's powerful jaws, it was the very DOGNESS of his psyche, that finished the whole lot of them.

As for Peanut's bowtie, he was just copying me. Jackie had two hundred and twelve different bandannas for me and there's no way to count the collars. He made a lot of the collars himself. Embroidered, beaded, knitted, crocheted, leather-worked, silver chased, one was studded with genuine rubies, one woven from horse hair, plaited from wire.... they went on and on. One of the best parts of the day for me was when my friend would get up in the morning and, before he even had his first cup of coffee or peed, he would help me choose my costume for the morning. We usually changed at noon unless the outfit truly had that look of grace for which we strove. I had considered getting my ears pierced but decided against it. How could I have scratched my ears if I was wearing earrings? And besides that, my hearing is very important to me. Would earrings have hindered my hearing?

People talk a lot about morality. They talk about what is good and what is bad. They wonder what is evil and what is holy. They create formulas: If a bitch eats her puppies, then she's truly evil. If the father eats his puppies, he's following his natural instincts. But what about survival? What if it's a really bad winter and there's no food for the mother? What if the only way the mother can survive the winter is to eat her pups? What if she spares her pups and they die and then she starves? Who wins? Nobody.

One thing that we canines know — and more importantly, accept — is that stuff just happens. Who cares? Stuff happens, and either you go on and deal with the stuff that follows, or you get stuck and are unable to deal effectively with any stuff at all.

Jackie was the ultimate predator. He was the only human I ever knew who understood that stuff just happens and sometimes you have to eat your pups to live.

I never bit anybody. If I had bitten somebody it would have been Jackie because he wouldn't have cared. A dog can get put to sleep for biting. "Put to sleep." Ha! Call it anything you like, it's still murder.

My luck was great. For me, there was more food, shelter and love than I could possibly use. The sad dogs are the ones who have to put up with children. Parents who put us into the hands of those little hellions should be bitten. They pull our ears, try to ride us and, when nobody is looking, they kick us and hit us with their toy machine guns. I don't like children. Jackie absolutely hated them. He always said all that children did was suck you dry, wear you out, and then grow up and railroad you into a nursing home. Children are like puppies in that they need to be bitten and bitten hard often. But nobody bites them. That's why the human race is so darned bad.

Sometimes it seems we should let the Friends go ahead with their plan and let them harvest the Earth. If we had hands, we probably would.

There was something fishy about Beebus and the Canecutter. Very often I would trot down to the swamp to gnaw a bone or two with my friend Harry. Harry was the alpha Canecutter in the bottom-land. We talked and talked. The Canecutters feel just like I did about biting people. They knew that if they caused too much trouble, the people would eventually destroy them.

On several occasions Harry had told me that the only thing they really wanted was to be left alone. Harry and his people could easily have avoided Beebus that day. The swamp is big and the cutters move quickly and quietly.

Why would Beebus go down there? He knew they'd get him. I have a theory. What if Beebus wasn't killed in the swamp?

What if he were killed somewhere else and dragged there? What could give the appearance of an animal kill and who or what could have a reason to exsanguinate the sheriff?

Just about everybody in the Bend would have a motive, but very few people would have the method.

A dog or a wolf would have the snout and teeth, but not the strength to rip a man's guts open that fast and that clean. A human with a scalpel and a knowledge of human anatomy could do it. Who was really angry at Beebus and who knows anatomy?

Dr. Wulmothe is too old. Neva Jean is too weak. Junior? Junior is fat

Down from the Dog Star

but very strong. Junior knows anatomy because he grew up at a surgeon's knee. Junior could have gotten close to Beebus without arousing his suspicion. Motive? I don't know.

Maybe it *was* a Canecutter. Eventually somebody will show up here who knows the truth.

In the meantime, Mama and I have made plans to go stay at Grandma's for a few days. Mama is hoping to pry Granny out for a trip. We were thinking about going down to the ground to visit Jackie. Perhaps I'll go see Harry and his friends.

I can't talk to them, of course, but if I sit quietly and just listen, maybe, in the evening when they have their story circle, I'll hear the truth.

I like it here. My chipped tooth grew back. I don't have that bald spot on my tail and there are no fleas. The best thing of all is the food! More beef and pork and chicken than you could ever hold, and you never throw up anything!

It's a good place. I just miss my buddy.

We can come and go as we please. We can choose to stay here as long as we like, but most of us return to the planet fairly quickly. This is a place of regeneration, a place of synthesis, a place of sharing knowledge. Most of us are anxious to get back down to the ground where we can play with people and other animals.

Gretchen is an exception. We are influenced greatly by the people with whom we live. Our spirits can be wounded or enhanced by our owners. Gretchen was hurt pretty badly by some things her master did. She says she may never go back down to the ground.

Sorbet is the bitch from hell! The only dog I know who even comes close to being as snotty as Sorbet is that weird Cocker Spaniel who used to live with Maria Callas. That dog is one Diva!

But Sorbet is who I started to talk about, Sorbet is a Gaze Hound who belonged to King Arthur the Pendragon. (Jackie would LOVE this! He had a vicious crush on Franco Nero when Franco played in "Camelot," the movie. Poor Jackie. Those shadows in the glass box were much more real to him than the surrounding world in which he lived.) Sorbet says that not only did she run the whole court, for in those days dogs could talk, but she was an accomplished chef. Some sort of ice cream-like desert that she invented was named after her.

Sorbet has her own retinue and Truffles, Maria Callas's Cocker Spaniel, has hers, and they're always trying to outdo one another. When Sorbet threw her "Spring Fling Gala" and had those cheesy Cat Dancers from cat heaven dance—a wild sort of Isadora-Duncanesque-round-house—with chartreuse chiffon scarves and old hula-hoop-looking props, Truffles topped her by singing the whole score of Tosca. She sounded darned good, too.

Sorbet decided to throw a dinner party, an intellectual dinner party no less, and invited, as the guest of honor, Winston Churchill's dog, a mongrel, but a mongrel of impeccable taste, great dignity, and dinner conversation to die for.

Of course Truffles had to go further but made the mistake of inviting both Gertrude Stein's Maltese and Hemingway's big gruff Wolf Hound. Talk about fur flying!

Truffles has an unfair advantage over Sorbet. She's Greek, after all, and lived with one of the most fascinating women ever to grace the stage. We tend to pick up a reflection of our master's characteristics. Sorbet belonged to a king who was betrayed by his wife and his best friend. Arthur and Lancelot were definitely lovers, and the truth is Guinivere was a boy in drag. An interesting nugget of knowledge, yes? If Arthur had been hung heavier and Guinivere, whose real name was George, hadn't had a butt shaped like a butterbean, the whole mess would never have taken place.

Gretchen and I hang out together. She says Jackie sounds to her a lot like her old master, and that Eva Braun would have made soap of them all, especially Guinivere.

I don't make the news, I just report it.

A few of us were lying around in the cantaloupe patch the other day, talking things over. It was one of those wonderful fall days that can often be confused with a spring day, warm and cool, moist and dry, all at the same time. Gretchen was lying on her back, her legs splayed flat to the

Down from the Dog Star

ground east and west, her nose and tail in a compass line north and south. She looked like one of those cartoon dogs run over by a steam roller. Gretchen is a big black and tan Shepherd, the tan almost red. She weighs about a hundred and fifty pounds and was bred to be a killer. Grandma, Mama, and I are black-and-cream saddle backs and were bred to be genteel. We each weigh less than a hundred pounds. Mama says any more than that would be ostentatious.

Gretchen was sleeping sweetly, with not a whimper or a twitch. Her tail looked so inviting, tempting me hugely to nip the end and then scoot away for a race. Not many other dogs here would do that. The smell of dry steel and cold flint hovers about her. Nobody fights here, but Gretchen has unspoken, though understood, boundaries.

I was distracted from my attack on my best girlfriend by something I heard Grandma say to Mama. Grandma was sniffing the cantaloupes, rolling the crazed-skinned mellow globes about with one of her front paws. It's interesting: younger dogs will roll things about, lift pieces of wood and rocks to see what's underneath, in general use their noses as a tool. Older dogs usually use their paws because, as Grandma told me once, "You've got four paws but only one nose!"

Cantaloupe is my favorite sweet. I'm glad it grows here, though most other folks here don't care for it. I inherited my love of various melons from Mama, and she hers from Grandma.

Granny batted a fine, musky smelling little fellow over to Sorbet for carving. Sorbet can really be a pain sometimes, but she has the longest canine teeth up here, and she takes great pride in sectioning the melons for us into near perfect quarters.

After she dissected it, she very kindly (and rather uncharacteristically, I thought), brought a piece to Grandma, one to Mama, and one to me. Granny gave her a nice lick on the side of her jaw, turned to Mama and said, "Little Bo Peep and the motorcycle cop? That's an old one. Why, Neva Jean used to put Beebus through that at least once a week, until Beebus woke up with a sheep's head in bed with him one morning."

Mama glanced at me from her left eye and glared at Granny from her right, "The girl!" she hissed past a chunk of cantaloupe that she had neatly snicked from her wedge. "Don't talk such trash in front of the girl!"

"She's no baby anymore, Lucy." Granny said. "You have to let her grow up someday. What if I had guarded you the way you coddle your daughter?"

"You did, and still do." growled Mama, and flicked her right ear three, quick snaps.

"Don't flip your ears at me, young lady!" Granny yammered. "I could nip you when you were a pup and I can nip you now!"

I pretended to be intimately involved with my lunch. I knew good and well that if I acted the least bit interested in this seedy sounding adventure of Neva's and Beebus, I'd never hear any of it.

"And anyway," said Mama, calmly crossing her front paws, "it was a goat's head, and not a particularly large one..."

This is the story I heard: Every now and then, Neva would go on a fantasy toot and warp Beebus into being an actor in her passion play. Her favorite was "Little Bo Peep and the Motor Cycle Cop." Neva Jean would thunder along a dark back road in the big white van Uncle Wooley used as an ambulance. She would be wearing a frothy white frock with a blue sweater, on her head a curly blonde wig, in the back of the van, a few nervous sheep. Suddenly a siren! A blue light pierces the night! The Motor Cycle Cop (aka Sheriff Beebus on Cleatus McCloud's old Harley) dressed in black leather and mirrored sunglasses, roars up beside LBP and waves her over. He leaps lightly off his Harley, (no mean feat for a man with such a big belly), swaggers up to the side of the van and says:

MCC: "Little Bo Peep! You got gin on yore breath, girl!"

LBP: "Oh, officer, I'm a good girl! I'll do ANYTHING (here a suggestive look at MCC's crotch) not to get a police record!"

MCC: "Little Bo Peep! What's those sheep doing back there, woman?!"

LBP: "Oh, Officer! Please don't hurt my sheep! I'll do anything to protect my sheep! Please don't send them to prison!"

MCC: "Those prisoners are bad, Little Bo Peep. Those old boys will surely fuck the fur offen yore sheep!"

LBP bats her eyes at MCC, he drags her from the van and throws her to her knees. He unsnaps his black, leather chaps, crushes LBP's face into his throbbing groin and . . . Here it gets too predictable and too full of sloppy ethnocentric dialogue to continue.

One night, with Neva bent over the greasy old Harley, and Beebus panting like a Labrador Retriever at a water trial, Jackie slid by in the T-Bird he had gotten the week before for his birthday,

Jackie just eased on by and acted like he didn't see a thing. This was long before I was born, long before even Mama had come down from the Dog Star. But Grandma was there! She was riding in the back seat of the Bird and saw everything.

Jackie went to Wulmothe Manor, rustled a goat, and late that night, after Beebus passed out in his bed from too much bad gin, Jackie neatly slipped the yellow eyed, horned cadaver's head onto the pillow next to his betrayer.

The big black Harley was never again seen chasing a gin-soaked Mother Goose character across the midnight landscape.

I suddenly realized Mama was staring intently at me. I was so engrossed in Granny's story that I had forgotten to pay attention to my food and lay there with my mouth wide open, my tongue dragging the ground.

Mother harumphed, got up, stretched, and trotted off over the hill.

Granny belly-scooted over to my side of the patch, smiled at me and kindly said, "Don't pay any mind to your Mama, Honey. She just wants you to be a lady. Things were a lot rougher in those days, before Jackie cleaned up from all those drugs, and the things he did colored everything that happened around him. You weren't born then, you came down about a week after he got off the dope. He may do a few things every now and then that are questionable, but as they say, "It's progress, not perfection!"

I noticed that Gretchen had one eye open and wondered how long she had been listening. I must have looked embarrassed at my family's weird behavior, because Gretchen flipped over onto her stomach, yawned, grinned and said, "Remind me to tell you about Adolf's and Eva's big fantasy, some day. It involved the whole world, and you know what? They came close to acting it all out."

I thought about it for a while. It's funny: What seems horrendous to one person is only mildly amusing to another. It's sort of like Jackie's theory on the acceptability of spit. He said once that if somebody spit on you, you'd be forced to kick the shit out of them, but if that same person had his tongue down your throat and his fist jammed down the front of your jockey shorts, then spit was just fine and dandy.

Oh, well.

Helen

One

Helen sits at the table in the warm, quiet kitchen. This kitchen combines the past and the present. It is the heart of Quarter Pine. The table is a worn affair, built over a hundred years ago from the wood of a lightning-struck popular tree which had grown near the creek in the bottom lands of Quarter Pine.

Helen is in her middle seventies, the same age as Minnie Luden, but appears to be a woman of forty. She is the color of a fine piece of polished, walnut furniture, her hair auburn, a sharp widow's peak in front, combed very high, a slight curl down the back. For her only jewelry, she wears a pair of canary yellow earrings in the shape of small stars, a present from Miss Minnie and Jackie on her seventieth birthday, and a tiny gold watch. She draws a small, blue book close to her from the center of the table and begins to speak, thoughtfully and with care, her voice rich and lovely:

Now why would Beebus write such things as this? Nobody around here tells the whole story. Mr. Jackie may have helped Black John out of this world, but what nobody but us three knows is, he was terribly sick. He had bone cancer and the pain medicine wasn't holding at all. I wasn't here the day he took my baby's car to town. Minnie and I were in town looking for cloth to cover a love seat.

But I know for a fact that Mr. Jackie and Black John spent the morning together in the library with the doors closed and the implicit order in the air that they were not to be disturbed. If Mr. Jackie did do something to the Seville, I think it would have had to have been at Black John's request. My baby couldn't stand the sight of his daddy, but in her own way, Minnie loved him, and Mr. Jackie worships his mama. He would never do anything to hurt her.

I knew something was up when I saw Minnie getting her pie pans out and had me start shelling pecans. She'll use store bought pecans for ordinary baking, but for her pecan maple fruit pie, they have to be Quarter Pine Pecans, Pawpaws from the grove in the bottom, and real maple syrup. That's about all I know for sure she puts in that pie. It's the one recipe she won't share. But I did see her grinding some nightshade seeds once, before she baked it.

Mr. Jackie treats his mama like a queen. At the funeral he stayed right by her side. He thinks she's fragile as a moth, but the truth is, she's strong as a lion and twice as dangerous, where her people are concerned. I'm proud to say that I'm one of her people.

We grew up together. In the order of love, Minnie loves herself, her son, and then me. I have to keep Mr. Jackie at a short distance. The one secret I've never told him is just how much I love him. He can use love like a twelve-gauge shotgun. Just look what he's done to Junior.

I remember those two boys when they were growing up. Jackie was always beautiful as the sun. Junior was dark. Black hair and fine hazel eyes. He followed Jackie like a puppy. But he loved him too much and let him know it. Mr. Jackie seems to lose respect for those who care too much for him. Over the years, he broke Junior's heart and sucked the spirit right out of him. Junior learned that as long as he had something in his mouth, he didn't hurt quite so badly. He went from a slim, beautiful boy to a big sloppy man with a fifty-inch waistline. I don't think Mr. Jackie set out to wound Junior. He just has some piece missing, some little piece of compassion that most other humans are born with.

But not when it comes to dogs. Jackie will just as soon spit on any human that crosses him, but I once saw him cry like a baby when Honey caught a rabbit and broke its back. I believe it was quite a shock to discover that his dog had the killer instinct inside her.

When she died, I was pretty sure Mr. Jackie would, too. His friend, LZ, came out to the farm and helped dig the grave. He even carved a nice tombstone.

Mr. Jackie was hurting bad, but he's so crazy. There was a bunch of Alabama Power men on the road right across from where Mr. Jackie and LZ were burying the poor dog. Mr. Jackie was squalling like he was like to die. One of the power men saw the grave and the tombstone and made the mistake of asking what had died. Mr. Jackie looked at him, as serious as could be, and told them that his feeble, old mother had passed in the night and they couldn't afford a funeral, so they were burying her in the front yard, wrapped in a blanket. This statement with this mansion house right behind him, two Lincolns and a Cadillac sitting in the drive.

Mr. Jackie was sure somebody poisoned the dog. That's when the real trouble began.

Helen rises from the table, places the book on a high shelf behind some pots. She stares at this hiding place for a moment, chuckles and shifts the book to nestle, in plain sight, among her cook books.

TWO

Helen paces quietly through the rooms of Quarter Pine. It is twilight and time to close the house for the evening. On tables and mantelpieces, on shelves and on what-nots throughout the house, sit small glass candle holders with translucent shades in whimsical shapes and colors. She carries a small basket of votive candles. As she lights the fairy lamps, she replaces those candles that look as if they will not last the night. She murmurs her thoughts, hums a gentle song, and enjoys the order of the house that she has tended for sixty years.

Sixty years. And not a one of them broken. I remember my first job here was to light these candles. This one, in the shape of a rosebud, was given to Minnie's mother by Besandra Wulmothe. This one here that looks like a frog, Mr. Jackie brought from New Orleans one time when he went to Mardi Gras. Here's a pretty one. Looks like a bunny. Me and Minnie put it in our Easter Basket one Sunday . . . how many thousands of days ago? And this funny looking thing, this one Miss Neva Jean made with her own two hands, out of pieces of an old broken, stained-glass window that came from the First Baptist Church when they went modern and remodeled it. This ugly thing! A snake! A cottonmouth with the light shining from its eyes! What could have possessed Big Mama Luden to bring this terrible object home to Quarter Pine?

Minnie's mama was an odd one. They say she was the strangest of all the Luden women. I know for a fact that it was she who settled on Mr. Black John to be Minnie's husband. And it was Big Mama who predicted the sinkhole would open. I heard the premonition happened at a picnic when Big Mama was just a child. They were all gathered in a park behind Wulmothe Manor one Sunday evening, about to head for home, when Big Mama (her name was Clarissa but Jackie called her Big Mama from the first time he could talk and the name stuck) stood stock still and started shaking. She said that on the place where she was standing, fire would come forth, and hell would follow. Nobody knew what she was talking about. But right on that spot is where the sinkhole opened up into the old coal mines. Big Mama Luden foretold the future all her long life. It would have been nice if she could have controlled what she saw, but mostly it was just useless information about common-day things: how many eggs a certain hen would lay; when a certain person would go on a trip; what the weather would be next day. One time she predicted when a town person was going to die and it happened just like she said, just when she said.

I remember she predicted the day and manner of her own death. The night she was suppose to pass over, she had Minnie fix her hair real pretty, put on her best lace nightgown, and laid herself down prim and proper between brand new cotton sheets. The next morning she woke up, looked around, laughed and ordered a big breakfast. She lived twenty more years.

Down from the Dog Star

It was Big Mamma's mother who started collecting these fairy lamps. Way back then, before the pharmaceutical business took hold, life was pretty hard here. I just imagine what they dealt with most was trying to keep enough food on the table. There was definitely a lack of pretties to please a woman, just hard, grinding work.

Look here—this is supposed to be the first fairy lamp to come to Quarter Pine, in the shape of a happy blue dog with red glass eyes. Brought by a peddler and paid for by a hot meal and a bed for the night.

Minnie knows the story behind each and every one of these lights. She doesn't preach a lot and she never bothers our baby much, but I know for a fact that she's drilled the history of these lamps into his head.

Now, with all the electricity around and with all the different night lights we could buy, why do you reckon we keep burning these candles night after night after night?

No, they aren't used here to keep away burglars — which was the original reason why Victorian people burned fairy lamps. No, it's not so we can see our way around at night. And no, it's not some kind of superstition. We use them because they are just so darned pretty, we use them because we have always used them, we use them because they connect us to the past, to our ancestors, and they light the way into our futures."

Helen moves sedately and surely through the house she has loved and tended for sixty years. She murmurs quietly and occasionally hums a bit of a song. Clocks tick. In its basket, a puppy sighs sweetly in its sleep, perhaps dreaming of gentle hands stroking its fat round belly, and the fairy lamps twinkle, twinkle, twinkle, sending beams of pastel serendipity into the darkest corners and crannies of the ageless, sleeping house.

THREE

Helen walks down the path beside the drive to the front gates. At one in the afternoon, she goes for the mail. The day is still and hot, the sky hard and blue. The quality of light gives objects far and near sharp clear edges. Everywhere the smell of pine, the smell of cedar.

Pine straw is thick under her feet, cicadas sing high in the poplar trees lining the long curving drive. She reaches the mailbox, opens the flap of a door, and peers into the dark hole where a bundle of letters rests.

I remember when Mr. Black John bought this mailbox. A red horse painted on one side, the house number on the other. It was one of the few things his daddy ever did that Mr. Jackie approved of.

Some folks can't understand why the boy took such a firm disliking to his daddy. Mr. Black John never raised a hand to the child. He never spoke a harsh word to Jackie. But then again I can't remember him ever holding the child or giving him a word of praise. Mr. Jackie would, when he was a tiny thing just learning how to walk, grab his dad's pants leg and try to hold on to him. You could tell he wanted to be picked up and cuddled. Black John would gently push him away or hand him to his mama or to me. Maybe that's why our boy learned to think of his father as the enemy.

There was never any open hostility there, but it was easy to see, after a while, that Minnie loved her son more than her husband. If she had had to choose, Mr. Jackie would have come out on top every time. Maybe that's why his daddy had hard feelings for his son.

Always pushing Jackie to do this and do that. Tried to make him play sports. Well, Jackie really surprised us at Little League! He wouldn't play football (way too messy) he was too short for basketball, but the first time he held a bat in his hand he knocked the ball clean out of the park, right over the fence. And run! Lord, he ran like fire on a dry sage field. He could throw the ball far and fast, and it always went right where he wanted it to go.

He surprised himself more than any of us. Black John was proud but he never told Jackie. He would always find some niggling fault with Mr. Jackie's performance.

When he was about twelve years old, he decided to learn the piano. The boy picked it up fast and it was about the only thing I ever saw him work truly hard at. He'd practice three or four hours a day. He got to be good at it, too. But when he played for Black John it seemed that he'd always miss maybe one note. And of course the man would pounce right on that one wrong note and ignore the hundreds of notes Mr. Jackie played perfectly.

When Mr. Black John caught Junior and Jackie in the corn crib doing what most young boys do, you'd have thought the world had come to an end. It was at that point that Mr. Jackie embraced his feminine ways with a vengeance. If there was one thing with which he could castrate his father, it was that.

He started wearing eyeliner and blush. Combed his yellow hair up into what was just short of being a beehive hairdo. And priss! Even Miss Neva Jean couldn't swing her hips the way my lamb could.

Minnie bought him a brand new gold Thunderbird automobile when he turned sixteen. He always had a pocket full of spending money and ran wild as a buck through the county. That sorry sheriff let him get away with anything, short of murder, and I can trace the beginnings of his drug problem back to Beebus McCloud. It's true that Doc Wulmothe wrote the prescriptions, but it was Beebus who made the DEA agent skip those particular prescriptions when he audited the drug store books each month.

A twisted tree, a tree with sweet smelling blossoms and bitter, bitter fruit.

I think it's possible to love the sickest child best of all. They're the ones who need it the most.

Helen trudges up the drive to the waiting house cresting the hill. In a downstairs window stands her mistress, impatient for letters and bills. Upstairs, leaning from a balcony, leaning into the breathless air, the airless

Autumn, her lamb and his big, smiling dog greet her with kisses in their eyes. The cicadas sing their shrill, high song in the tops of the yellowing poplars. The dry, resinous smell of pine blankets the day, wraps them all together in a parcel that has always been, will always be, and the day swings from afternoon towards evening, towards the lightening of the burdens, the lighting of the lamps.

FOUR

Helen is in the kitchen garden. The day is humid. A grumble of thunder behind the clouds promises rain. She leans into a tomato bush, then lithely and lightly, turns sharply at some inconsequential sound behind her. The orange-red, opalescent fruit reflects the pearly afternoon light into the curve of her throat. In the act of her turning, she carries us fifty years into the past. Of all the mysteries of the Bend this is one of the most illusive, the quintessential experience of the valley. How can this woman be in her seventh decade? How has she side-stepped time and the etching of years? She picks the Beefsteak tomatoes and drops them into her basket.

Green onions. I'll make a salad with these tomatoes, a few of those green onions and some capers. I do love capers. Boil some of this fresh corn and make a little mess of these field peas. Bake some pork chops. Maybe Minnie can make some of her biscuits. Got to cook a lot today. Junior and Miss Neva Jean coming up for supper. Dessert? Strawberry pie.

We've never lacked good food. Good food and a lot of it. My mama taught me how to cook and I taught Minnie. We grew up here. I was her best friend. Still am. If Minnie got a new dress I got one, too, and not no hand-me-down. Minnie's mama, Big Mama, took us both to town and we shopped at the same store. Of course to look at us you would have

Down from the Dog Star

thought it was normal for the time. Rich white woman, spoiled little girl, and maid servant. We knew it wasn't like that. But it had to have that appearance, otherwise I couldn't have set foot in those cool smelling, white-only stores. Water fountains labeled "White Only." Stores had entrances marked "Colored enter in back."

If you were dying you sure couldn't go to the white hospital. You had to get to Atlanta, somehow, or see the vet. We were lucky, me and my family. There was never much of that nonsense in the Bend. It was Minnie and Miss Besandra that put me on the Freedom Bus. Minnie set a big box of food onto my lap and put one hundred dollars in ten dollar bills into my pocket. Besandra Wulmothe wrapped the most beautiful Afghan I have ever seen around my shoulders. She crocheted it herself. She spent a whole winter making that blanket, shades of rose and peach and pale mint green. I still have it in my trunk at the foot of my bed.

George Wallace surely knew the tide was turning and the sand castles of segregation were dissolving in the ebb and flow of the mighty waters. He knew it. He also knew that if he didn't show some token resistance, he would never hold office in Alabama again. A short man, a man who knew his world was changing, a man who played his game secret and close.

When the federal marshals appeared, he gave in with surprising dignity. Mr. Wallace did less damage than good for the state.

When that low-life shot him, I felt sad. They say he loved Lurleen more than anything on Earth. Named bridges after her. Named schools after her.

Have you ever stopped to think about how fleeting it all is, how somebody can be famous and toasted with champagne one day, and just a short time later be dust and forgotten? Then, when the last person who knew them passes, it is truly like they never were at all.

I heard Miss Besandra ask Minnie what it was like, now that Mr. Black John was gone. Minnie thought for a second and then said, "Was he really ever here?"

Helen passes through the gate from the garden to the gravel walk leading to the kitchen door. Her basket overflows with the colors of fall, the rewards of a well tended garden. On her upturned face, the first light drops of rain.

FIVE

Helen is walking along a narrow path beside a barbwire fence. The land is rough, the path almost closed by blackberry brambles and saw briar. She wears a large straw hat tied to her head with a pale blue scarf. In her hand, a plastic bag containing almost a gallon of muscadines. They were given to her, fresh picked from the woods by Thomas Blaylock, with whom she has passed a quiet morning on the side porch of his house.

Don't see these very often anymore. I remember when I was a girl you couldn't walk a foot in the fall without something good to eat slapping you in the face! Persimmons, pawpaws, possum grapes, hickory nuts . . . You could have lived off what came to your hand way back then. The woods are still here, my eyes are still sharp, but the wild edibles seem to have vanished.

Take blackberries. Back then, we could pick ten gallons in a morning with no sweat at all. Tote them home, clean them a little, boil them with sugar and pectin and then we had blackberry jam. Seems like blackberry winter gets them every time now. In the spring the blackberries look around, decide it's time to put out blossoms. They bloom like crazy and that night a short, killer frost falls. No blackberries that spring!

Frost doesn't fall, either. It rises from the ground, and it flows like a river, like many tiny streams through the land. Just watch, and you'll see every year that some places are devastated by cold, and not twenty feet away it's as green as can be.

Blackberry Winter came right inside our homes. The frost rose up around Mr. Jackie, around Junior, around Miss Neva Jean. Didn't touch me or Minnie or old Besandra. Frost hurts the young, tender shoots, the

Down from the Dog Star

fine, pale green leaves and the white, scalloped blackberry blossoms. Frost destroys the promise of the future; it cannot touch the past.

Helen stops on a slight rise of ground, the path at her feet opening onto a view of the land most people never see. She takes a fine, white handkerchief from her skirt pocket and blots a bit of moisture from her brow. Below her, the pastures of Quarter Pine spread far to the west, boiling like sea surf into the distance, to where the dark ocean of pine begins. The house, white and shining, waits on the hill, waits for Helen, waits for them all that come and go.

In a corner of the well-tended front yard, a small mound of soil, now covered with grass, at its head a white marble tombstone, some name etched into its surface.

Grateful Acknowledgments

There are so many people to thank for the love and support that made this little book pop out into the world. First, my mother, who did not live to see it published but who believed that I could do anything. Thank you, Mama. My buddy LZ, Lawrence Rives, who made me write this book, and who makes me be happy — I love you, friend of a quarter century. My lovely Charlotte Hagood, who taught me how to ask for a cup of coffee, thereby teaching me how to ask for the world. Sylvia Bradley, my first teacher. I would sit at your feet and worship, if you'd let me, my dear. Laura Martin gave me the dream for Pentecostal Catfishing and the poem "Down from the Dog Star." Kisses from both me and Booful. Penny Williams. Oh, Penny, you've given me so much of your heart. I'll see you in Phoenix in the fall! Lynda Verbance, tamer of flame! Remember the campout, Lynda? Remember how big and red the moon was? Remember your charming night with Penny in the back of my '72 Volvo? Mispah Clay, my present spiritual teacher. My brilliant, bull-headed, patient editor, Grady Clarkson. Remember the first manuscript, Grady? You used all the red ink in Birmingham, you sweet man. The enigmatic and glamorous Gloria Robinson. You told me I had talent. You helped me believe life could be good again. Hang an ornament on the tree for me, Gloria, and give your hubby a squeeze for me. And of course Randall Williams, my publisher, my mentor and my friend. Give 'em hell, boy! I specially would like to recognize the countless bastards who have made my life a living hell. Without you I would not have been driven crazy enough to write this book.

D.G.